MAX BRAND

TIGER MAN

Author Of Millions Of Books In Print!

"Brand is a topnotcher!" —*New York Times*

A writer of legendary genius, Max Brand has brought to his Westerns the raw frontier action and historical authenticity that have earned him the title of the world's most celebrated Western writer.

In *Tiger Man,* Blas is ready to blow away any six-shooting scoundrel who crosses his path. The townfolks don't know whether to figure him for a straight-shootin' hero or a trigger-happy swindler. But one thing's certain: His aim is flawless and his instincts are ruthless.

MAX BRAND

TIGER MAN

LEISURE BOOKS   NEW YORK CITY

A LEISURE BOOK®

May 1996

Published by special arrangement with Golden West
Literary Agency.

Dorchester Publishing Co., Inc.
276 Fifth Avenue
New York, NY 10001

Printed in the United States of America.

Max Brand is the best-known pen name of Frederick Faust, creator of Dr. Kildare, Destry, and many other fictional characters popular with readers and viewers worldwide. Faust wrote for a variety of audiences in many genres. His enormous output, totaling approximately thirty million words or the equivalent of 530 ordinary books, covered nearly every field: crime, fantasy, historical romance, espionage, Westerns, science fiction, adventure, animal stories, love, war, and fashionable society, big business and big medicine. Eighty motion pictures have been based on his work along with many radio and television programs. For good measure he also published four volumes of poetry. Perhaps no other author has reached more people in more different ways.

Born in Seattle in 1892, orphaned early, Faust grew up in the rural San Joaquin Valley of California. At Berkeley he became a student rebel and one-man literary movement, contributing prodigiously to all campus publications. Denied a degree because of unconventional conduct, he embarked on a series of adventures culminating in New York City where, after a period of near starvation, he received simultaneous recognition as a serious poet and successful popular-prose writer. Later, he traveled widely, making his home in New York, then in Florence, and finally in Los Angeles.

Once the United States entered the Second World War, Faust abandoned his lucrative writing career and his work as a screenwriter to serve as a war correspondent with the infantry in Italy, despite his fifty-one years and a bad heart. He was killed during a night attack on a hilltop village held by the German army. New books based on magazine serials or unpublished manuscripts continue to appear. Alive and dead he has averaged a new one every four months for seventy-five years. In the U.S. alone nine publishers issue his work, plus many more in foreign countries. Yet, only recently have the full dimensions of this extraordinarily versatile and prolific writer come to be recognized and his stature as a protean literary figure in the 20th Century acknowledged. His popularity continues to grow throughout the world.

Chapter One

Sheriff Stefan Gregory came over the hills so fast that the wind up the San Pablo valley parted his mustache as with a comb. He looked at the green fields strewn over the plain in neat squares as though they were an eyesore to him; and he scowled black at the great cypresses which stood near the river, and which arose a mighty height above San Pablo itself.

The sheriff, as he saw this pretty picture, swore in a strange language. Men said that "Gregory" was a corruption of quite another name, worn by peoples living somewhere far off—Serbia, Lithuania, Russia itself—no one knew quite where. But they did know that Stefan Gregory was as honest as the day was long, and that he was a fighting man of the first caliber. He had come into the office of sheriff by acclaim, and he still was returned at every election, as a matter of course, one might say; for, in keeping the mixed population of that southwestern county in order, he had done a much better job than any other. He could talk enough Spanish to make himself understood. He could talk English, of course. And he could even chatter in their own tongue to the Polacks who were working in increasing numbers in the mountain mines.

He swore, then, in strange tongues—in corrupt Spanish and in English, too; and he came down upon San Pablo like a storm. More than one hand stole toward knife or gun as the big sheriff swept through the narrow, winding streets of the little town.

But nothing was done. He had come among them before, more than once, like a whirlwind, and he had gone out again leaving the memory of some stinging deed behind him. But, though they shrank and snarled under the lash, they could not quite rouse themselves to strike back. Tradition was in favor of it; but experience was against it. And those who had tried their hands against Stefan Gregory were many; but those who had lived to tell of the deed were few.

So he came down through the quiet streets, and the women in their doorways, patting out tortillas, shrieked at their children and their pigs and their chickens, to get them out of the way of the flying horse. He seemed to give them not so much as a look, but he missed not a detail. And when he entered the street of San Salvador, there was hardly an item that missed him. For instance, in the third house from the right, as he turned into the little crooked lane, there was a sound of merriment and drunken rejoicing, and he guessed shrewdly by this that old Onate had managed to come back from Old Mexico.

Old Onate was wanted by the law, but not by Stefan Gregory. He did not go by rule. He laid down laws of his own. He had no wedded wife except his office; and he had no children except all the people of the county—especially the ill-doers. The good men knew him not, and he knew not them, except on election day. But the criminals came constantly into his ken.

Now, old Onate, it was said, had committed more than one crime in the past. But the present was a little more than the past, surely, and for the present the hardy ruffian was maintaining the wife and the children of his dead son. He was maintaining them well, and accomplishing it by honest labor. Therefore, the hand of Stefan Gregory would never fall upon his head.

Just opposite to the Onates, the house of Pedrillo da Vaca bloomed with new whitewash all over it, and a brand new door to replace the one which he, Stefan Gregory, twice had battered down with gun butt and foot. This was very well. Prosperity was not to be condemned. But the prosperity of da Vaca was not apt to be rooted in hard, honest labor. He had certain ways with a pack of cards. With a knife, also, he was a known expert. And though he had promised to reform after his last hard lesson, the sheriff felt that there would probably be a necessity of paying another call here in the near future.

Only a little farther on, and he swept past an old

man who sat in his doorway with his white hair falling over his shoulders, and his eyes fixed straight before him. He gave no heed to the sheriff. And the sheriff gave no heed to him, but each knew the mind of the other. That was old Gonzales. His boy had been found dead at the edge of the river only the month before. And the sheriff had been working, ever since, steadily upon the case. He had a hope that he was on the trail at last. But he could not be sure.

He was easing his horse from its hard gallop, now. Then he swung straight across the street and dismounted before the dust cloud had finished boiling up from around the forefeet of his pony.

The man in the doorway took off his sombrero with a gesture; and it was difficult to know whether he was saluting the sheriff or brushing the dust fog away.

"And here we are, Enrique," said the sheriff.

"We are here, senor. Thanks to the mercy of God!"

"And you are all well?"

"We are all well, I thank God. And you, senor?"

"I'm never sick, old son. You ought to know that. How's the senora?"

"She is honored to have you ask after her."

"That's a cheap honor. And Eugenio?"

"He is of good health, senor. May you have a son as strong and well before many years!"

"Thanks. There's Felipe, too?"

"He is a strong young bull."

"Then you are all here, together?"

"All here, senor."

"Blas, too. I almost forgot him."

"He is well."

"All right," said the sheriff, with a sudden change in his voice. "Then let me see where he is!"

Senor Lavera spread his hand in an attitude of charming helplessness.

"I would to God that I myself knew!"

"You've just told me that he was well!"

"I can speak no more than I knew when I last saw him, and no more than I hope. What man can do less, Senor Sheriff Gregory?"

The sheriff cast a sidelong glance of some penetration at the other. Then he strode across the threshold and stood in the big room in which the Lavera family did the greater part of its living. The senora came forward, bowing and smiling. She was not more fat than most of her age and nation. Her black eyes still could look young and beautiful, on occasion. But the sheriff gave only a grunt in return for her greetings. He stepped on, through the back door, and looked out into the little enclosure where the cow stood, and where a goat or two worked patiently at the remains of the vegetation, near the bottom of the mud wall that served as a fence, separating it from the neighboring yard.

There was no human occupant.

So, the sheriff came back and paused again in the doorway.

"No, Enrique," said he in his bad Spanish, shaking his head at the proffered cigarette. "I am glad to smoke with any man that keeps the law. But not with bad men, Enrique."

"Ah, ah," said a voice softer than melted honey, "is poor Enrique Lavera become a bad man?"

"He keeps bad sons!" said the sheriff. "And

how's a father to be judged better than by his sons?"

"God be my better witness," said the other, raising his face with an air of the utmost solemnity.

"You got a lot of God in your talk today," said the sheriff.

"Witness, then," said the Mexican, "if my boys Felipe and Eugenio are not quietly and earnestly at work at this very moment in the field of—"

"Never mind them," said the sheriff. "They ain't the meat that I'm after. But I'd give the price of a gun to have my hands on that Blas Lavera. Where's Blas? That's what I want to know?"

The other raised his two hands. One could see, as he made the gesture, that they were curiously deformed, the thumbs doubling in, and the wrists appearing to have been broken under a heavy wheel.

"Where is the wind, senor?" said Lavera. "Now it blows out of the north. In a moment, it carries along the dust from the south. Then it stands in the east."

"Fancy talk and smooth talk," admitted the sheriff. "But you know and I know that he was the root of the trouble down yonder on the edge of the Dorando."

"Senor, you speak from a cloud and I cannot understand!"

"You old scoundrel!" grinned the sheriff.

Senor Lavera bowed. And with this bow he concealed a grimace of the most savage disgust and contempt.

"What is it that I know, then?" said he.

"That your boy was down at the Dorando, I say.

That it was he who rode the bay horse into the fight. That it was he who killed the one man and shot up the two others. That it was he who left his dead horse behind him, but had the nerve to take time to unsaddle it under the bullets of the rest. That it was he, too, who got into the boat and lay down while it floated him off along the river, with the rest of them pelting lead at him."

"Alas!" said Lavera. "You tell me strange news!"

"Humph!" said the sheriff.

"But why should my poor boy do these things?"

"For a lot of reasons," said the sheriff. "But the main one was probably because that gang didn't talk polite to him. Behind that there's other reasons, too. One of 'em is that he's never been taught to work, Lavera, as you very well know. And the other is that you've allowed him to keep guns and knives in his hands since he was a baby."

"Senor! Senor! One must shoot straight to kill an antelope or a deer."

"That's right, and one must keep a sharp knife for cutting it up after it's dropped. But the kind of deer and antelope that Blas is beginning to practice on ain't the kind that runs on four feet. Come here, Lavera."

"I listen, senor."

"I'm speaking of friendship."

"The kindness of the senor is a treasure to poor old Lavera."

"Humph!" said the sheriff. "Tell me what you got in mind for that boy? Is he to be an expert gunfighter and make his living that way? If that's what you have in your mind, you're wrong. This ain't the century for that sort of thing. The telegraph and the fast mail have made it hard lines for the gun fighters, Lavera."

"I cannot guess who has been slandering us to you," said Lavera.

"Can't you?" grinned the sheriff. "Well, I can't make you talk if you don't want to. And I'm not going to wait here to catch your boy, because I know that he won't show up. But I came over here fast to let you know that I've got this information about him. It was he that done the work with Vega's lot."

"Is Vega a man that the senor treasures as a friend?" asked Lavera politely.

"Vega is a crook and a bad one," said the sheriff. "We both know that. If your boy had just shot *him* up, it wouldn't have been so bad. But the ones that he *did* salt away are fellows that the law ain't got a thing on. So I'm looking for Blas. Not hard, mind you. I know that the boys with Vega are pretty apt to be as bad as Vega himself. But Blas ain't got the right to take the law into his own hands. I'm going to let this slide. I'm not going to bust myself to get your Blas. But the next time that he makes a slip, I'm going after him. The next time that he pulls a gun, I'm coming for him. You write that down in red. Now I got to get on my way, because I've still got a long ride ahead of me. I just stopped off on the way to warn you."

"Senor may be sure that we shall never forget."

"That's right. Adios!"

He was in the saddle again, and swinging the head of his horse around.

Then he said, "Tell Blas for me I admire the way that he handled things over there on the Dorando.

I like a cool fighter, and he's that. I like a straight shooter. And he's that! But tell him that the way he's riding winds up in a cell and a free suit of stripes. Adios again!"

And he was gone.

Chapter Two

The dust cloud which he left behind him had hardly settled before Senora Lavera called softly, and a door at the end of the room opened. There walked in a tall youth built after the fashion of a whipstalk—the handle, his shoulders, and the taper point, his heels. He had the same grace, the same supple strength. He was dressed after the fashion of any young Mexican dandy, and he came in with the eternal cigarette fuming between his fingers.

"God have mercy!" said the senora, folding her hands. "Is it true, Blas?"

Blas looked at her with the utmost indifference in his brown-black eyes, and he walked into the doorway. The senora followed him in great anxiety.

"It is why you have kept in hiding ever since you

came home. Is that the reason, Blas? Oh, child!"

Blas turned his head to Lavera.

"Father," said he, "tell her that I am tired of talking."

"Tired of talking!" shrilled she. "Has he spoken a word?"

"I have listened to the sheriff," said Blas, "until my tongue ached. Now I shall sleep, I think."

He looked casually up and down the street, while Lavera watched him with shining eyes.

Then Blas turned back to a corner of the room and stretched himself upon a bed of goatskins laid over a straw pallet.

"Enrique, Enrique!" moaned Senora Lavera at the door, clutching the shoulder of her husband. "Do you see? He has lain down. As though there were no trouble! As though the sheriff might not come back for him at any moment! As though the friends of Vega do not fill San Pablo! Oh, God protect him, because there is no wisdom in him to protect himself!"

A voice spoke from the interior of the house above the sound of her murmuring.

"The flies! They trouble me!"

"Do you hear?" asked Lavera sharply.

"I hear. But am I to sit there all the day and fan the flies from him in order that he may sleep? And then shall my sons come home and find there is no food prepared for them?"

"Do as I tell you!" commanded Lavera. "Be quick! What! Do I need to argue and explain?"

He spoke with such a sudden flash of the eye that his wife shrank from him and went sullenly to perform the task. She squatted on her heels beside the bed of Blas and waved slowly, back and forth, above him a fan made of the joined wings of a great turkey. Her face was black with rebellion when she began. But presently, as the cooling current of air closed the eyes of the boy, she herself began to smile.

She whispered, "Enrique!"

He came, stepping softly.

"No noise!" he whispered.

"Tush!" said the woman. "He sleeps like a baby. See!"

She took the arm which he had folded under his head and straightened it; and though her practiced grasp was firm and strong, his eyelids did not so much as flutter.

"If I were his own mother!" said she, "could I move him more freely?"

"Fool! Fool!" cautioned her husband, in a snarling murmur.

"He is sleeping. He cannot hear!"

"A sleeping wolf can always hear!" said Lavera. "And if he guessed, he would tear the secret out of my heart, blood hot! Never whisper it near him again. Never dream it while you look at him, or he will read it in your eyes! Here, I will take the fan. Get on with your work. The boys will be hungry when they return!"

She resigned her place to her husband almost unwillingly, and she hung for a moment over the sleeper, drinking in the beauty of face and body, the beauty of those slender, swift, strong hands.

So Enrique Lavera crouched beside the boy and fanned the flies from him, fanned him cool, while the cookery went gently on at the farther end of the room.

The afternoon cooled towards evening. Then two wide-shouldered young fellows returned and strode through the doorway. They had the look of their mother. They were very handsome, but not in the manner of Blas. The senora met them with a hushing finger laid on her lips.

"He is sleeping!" she cautioned them.

"Blas?" said Eugenio.

"Yes—"

"I wondered if he would be here!"

"He came after you went away to work."

"Where had be been?"

"We don't know. In trouble, we fear. The sheriff has been here. And God protect us!"

"The sheriff!" whispered the two, in one breath. And they turned in mute excitement towards the sleeper. "What has he done?"

"We don't know. He is like a stone. He will not speak—"

"Until the right time comes," said Blas suddenly, in the full, clear tones of someone wide awake.

"Ha! The scoundrel!" cried the senora. "He has heard every word. And how long have you been letting me go about on tiptoe, while your father wagged the fan over you until his arm ached?"

The youth closed his eyes in quiet thought.

"Since the dog of Onate took the dog of Diaz by the throat and they snarled in the street."

"An hour ago!" cried the poor woman. "Oh, what a devil is in you, Blas, to give us so much trouble!"

"It will make the arm of my father strong," yawned Blas, "to move the fan over me. Besides, it kept me cool, and that was good. What have you brought me, Eugenio?"

"I? Nothing today."

"You are a pig. But you, Felipe?"

"I found a rabbit at the corner of the fence and knocked him over. I brought back his skin. It is a very fine one, you see. But the meat was too old and tough and dry for eating. I threw it to the dogs as we came in."

Lazy Blas raised himself upon one elbow and stroked the fur.

"This is a very good one," said he. "When I have half-a-dozen more, there will be enough for a blanket of them. You must hurry to get them for me, Felipe. Then, when I have the blanket made, I shall let you use it sometimes, when the nights are cold."

"Oh, that is a grand reward, eh?" growled Eugenio.

"Eugenio," said Blas, "you are bigger than Felipe?"

"You can see! Twenty pounds!"

"Then I shall teach Felipe to roll you on the ground as easily as I can roll you!"

"It is not true," said Eugenio sullenly, but retreating a little. "You cannot do it. Besides, he is too slow to learn your tricks!"

"No, no!" cried Felipe, in an ecstasy. "I shall work like a dog to learn them, Blas."

"Ah, well," said Blas, with the air of a king dispensing favors. "We shall see about all of this in time. But I need six more rabbit skins. Do not forget, Felipe."

"I shall not. Hah! With a little luck—tomorrow night—"

"Hey, Blas!" cried Lavera suddenly.

"Ay?" said Blas.

"You spoke of the dogs. How did you know that Onate's dog took Diaz's yellow brute by the throat? Do you see around corners and through walls?"

"I could tell by the sound," said Blas, yawning again. "That white dog of Onate's snarls high, like a woman crying. And the harder he is fighting, the higher he squeals. But Diaz's dog speaks from his belly—thus: woof! woof! And when I heard his voice half choked, I knew that the white dog had him by the throat. It was perfectly simple."

Senor Lavera half closed his eyes and nodded back and forth with the air of one who knows more than he cares to admit.

"Oh, yes, yes!" said he. "Very simple. Why not?"

"Where were you, Blas, last night?" asked Eugenio in a wheedling tone.

"That is what I know," said Blas, still sleepy-eyed. And he pillowed his shoulders against the wall, with the goatskins heaped comfortably under him. "That is what I know, and what you wish that you knew!"

"Ah, Blas!" said Senora Lavera sadly. "Was it true, what the sheriff said? Were you not fighting Vega's men at the Dorando?"

"Vega's men! It was you! It was you!" cried Felipe. "We have been hearing nothing else all day long. Oh, God, Blas, how much trouble you have brought on yourself, now! All of the men of Vega in the town will be after you! What will you do?"

"I know nothing of the Dorando," said Blas.

"Give me some tobacco, Eugenio."

"If you will tell me where you were last night."

"All night?"

"Yes."

"I shall tell you what I was doing most of the night."

"Here is the tobacco, then!"

"Thank you. But not yet. You cannot make such a cheap bargain. My boots need to be cleaned and polished. You see that they are filthy. Polished until their toes shine like diamonds. Do you hear?"

"Well, what has that to do with me?"

"Only this. If you polish the boots, also, I shall tell you what I was doing most of the night."

"Well—it's worth it, then. Give me the boots!"

He was off with them. From outside the door they could hear his excited voice:

"Everyone is talking! Why, Blas, if it was you, you'll be famous. There was one man that attacked the seven as they were coming in with their boat. He killed one. That was a man named Garcia."

"No!" broke in Felipe. "His name was Gatas! I heard it twice!"

"He wounded two others. The rest from the bushes started firing at him, but he got into their own boat and floated away. Ah, Blas! Have you done such a thing? Will you confess it, after I have shined these boots?"

"You shall see," said Blas.

"Very well. Here they are."

He carried them in.

"That heel is still dim."

"You are a devil, Blas. So—on my own sleeve! Now does it suit you?"

"That is better!"

"Now whisper what it was that you did last night."

"Most of last night," corrected Blas.

"Yes, yes."

"I don't need to whisper. I only need to say that I was riding a horse."

There was a yell from Eugenio.

"Do you call that an answer? I shall make your boots as dirty as when I found them!"

Blas raised himself gently upon his elbow again. "Don't touch them, Eugenio!"

"It is only fair! Is it not, Felipe?"

"Yes," admitted honest Felipe. "It is only fair."

"Will you stand by me?"

"Yes, in this."

"Then, I'll do it—"

"Children, are you going to smash the house?" screamed the senora.

For, as Eugenio reached for the boots, Blas raised himself and, like a cat, leaped from all fours. Eugenio pitched heavily over him. Felipe, attempting to aid, was gripped from below, and fell in a heap before he knew what had seized him. They had fallen one upon another. And when they attempted to rise, they howled with pain, for Blas had gripped them by the arms.

The senora screamed with fear and excitement and rage, but Enrique Lavera merely stood by the door with his head back and with his nostrils spread in savage exultation.

"That is the way of it!" he said softly to himself. "That is the way of it!"

"Enrique! He is breaking the arms of Felipe and

Eugenio! Do you stand there and only watch and smile? You cruel devil!"

"He will not hurt them—more than they need," said this strange father.

"Do you hear me?" Blas was saying quietly. "I let you both up if you swear that you will not attempt to attack me."

"Ever?" growled Eugenio. "Do you mean that?"

"Bah! No, indeed. What would there be to do around this house if I could not fight with you now and then? But I shall let you up if you will promise to be very quiet—until tomorrow night, say!"

"Very well!"

"And besides that, I want you to go to the end of the town and buy that grey mare which belongs to Guadalupe Pissano."

Here the senora ran in and shook Blas by the shoulder.

"*Madre de Dios!* That wild devil of a mare! She kills men! Besides, that fool Pissano asks five hundred dollars for her! Do you mean that you have that money?"

"Stop pulling my arm, mother. Eugenio, will you go ask for the horse? You could get it for four hundred. It would cost me six!"

"Why?"

"Because you act like a poor man—and I, like a fool! Do you promise?"

"Ah, but where could you dream of getting even four hundred?"

And here, suddenly, a voice spoke from the doorway, "Ask me, because I can tell you!"

Chapter Three

They turned in all haste.

For in the doorway they could see a handsome, black-mustached man in dapper clothes of the Mexican style, with a magnificent crimson sash all worked with delicate golden brocade. On a day, that sash had done duty as an altar cloth in a great church. But now it was suited to the person of this elegant gentleman of Mexican fashion.

"You can tell us, Senor Vega?" said Senora Lavera in a rather whining tone. "But that is only a little jest of his. He talks of hundreds of dollars. I have heard him talk of thousands, too. That is his way. It means nothing."

At this, Vega showed his fine, even white teeth in a smile that flashed doubly bright beneath the shadow of his curving mustache.

"On this day it means a great deal more than

nothing. And, senora, shall I tell you that one day he *can* speak of thousands? Unless, like a wise man, he gives them back to the hand from which he took them!"

And he stepped just into the shadow at the doorway, and paused there, with his hands upon his hips.

Young Blas had risen to face the other. And Felipe and Eugenio, unbidden, but by the force of a dangerous instinct, began to creep forward a little, keeping close to the edge of the wall on either side of the room.

Only Senor Lavera, himself, with his crippled hands did not choose to make himself a threat. But he stood back, looking on as though he had no real desire to join in any brawl, even if God had given to him, again, hands perfectly sound and perfectly strong once more, as they had been in the olden days.

Said Blas: "Go back and keep away from him, brothers. I do not wish to have you come into any danger from him. I shall talk with him all by myself!"

At this, they paused; but they would not actually retreat. So he lashed at them again with his tongue:

"Do you hear me? I don't want any help against him. Go back and stay behind me, and keep your hands away from weapons. He has not come to do any of us a harm."

"Good!" purred Porfirio Vega. "Now, there is a young man who knows my mind very perfectly. I do not come to make trouble, no matter what some fools have said of me. I am a man loving peace—"

"Peace and your own way," said Blas coldly. "You love to have absolute serenity, and your own full wishes in everything. And I, senor, am a man of the very same mind as yours!"

The other bit his lip.

"Do you say this?" he asked. "Do you say it by way of provoking me, Blas?"

"No, Porfirio," answered young Lavera. "I speak to you as a matter of truth, but not as a matter of insult. You are now standing in my house!"

"So," said Blas, and the eyes of Enrique Lavera burned like the eyes of a hungry lion, so great was his joy.

"I like this way you have with you," said Vega, though it was plain that the calmness of the youth had surprised and irritated him. "And I have simply come to talk to you, hoping that I would find you, as you are, a gentleman of much intelligence, and capable of seeing that it would be well to step outside your door with me, and talk for a moment alone."

"Willingly," said Blas, and was starting for the door when Senora Lavera threw herself before him, clinging to his arms.

"You shall not go, Blas!" she wept. "Enrique! Enrique! You will not let him go with Vega—"

"Peace, peace!" said Lavera. "Let him do as he himself thinks best. He is no longer a child. He knows his own mind. By all means go if you wish, my son!"

And he brushed his wife aside, so that Blas

could step freely through the door with the out-law.

They stood so that their shadows fell across the threshold, talking softly.

And, inside the house, Felipe and Eugenio stole as close to the door as they dared, revolvers in their hands, and cruel, cold looks of waiting mischief in their eyes. It would be well for Vega if he attempted no quarrel, considering who these two were and how steady their hands, as they held the guns!

But he, on the outside, was saying calmly, "Now you see, Blas, that I have not come here to make you any trouble. My only wish is that you will do justice to yourself and to me. To yourself by not making me your enemy. To me, by returning the property which is mine!"

"To make you my enemy," said Blas, "I have no desire. We know you, Senor Vega. All men know that you are brave and a great fighter, and that you have other great fighters with you. But what is the property I have which really belongs to you?"

"Do you wish me to tell you?" said the older man, with that flash of white teeth in a mirthless smile, again.

"I wish it, of course."

"Four thousand and five hundred dollars, taken from the pocket of poor Estrada, as he lay dead."

"Estrada, then, had money of yours?"

"You admit that you shot him down, Blas?"

"I shall not argue about such small things," said the youth. "But that is not the point."

"Not the point?"

"No, what we must talk of is this: How am I to

know that the money was yours?"

"Might I not ask how the money comes to be yours?"

"I shall tell you," said Blas. "I meet gentlemen on the shore of a stream, as I ride down it. They come in a boat, and as they land, I speak to them, kindly. But when I speak, they draw guns and they begin to shoot. I feel my good horse drop beneath me. From behind his body I begin shooting in turn—"

"No, my son," said the outlaw, "but you began shooting while his body was still falling through the air and before it had touched the ground. I watched and I have eyes to see, even by the cursed starlight! I had eyes to see. And when my gun jammed, seeing was all that I could do!"

A little spasm of fury crossed his face, and drew the light in his eyes to burning, penetrating points, but he banished it at once and made himself as calm as before.

"I saw, Blas. You fought very well, and when Estrada tried to rush you, and you shot him down, he fell beside you, and you took the wallet from his pocket."

"It tumbled out on the ground."

"That is not the question."

"No, the question is, how can the thing that belonged to Estrada now belong to you?"

"You know, Blas, that what my men take is mine until we have made a division of it."

"I have heard that. But what your men take— does it really belong to you?"

"Why not?"

"By right of what, Senor Vega?"

The other stiffened a little.

"Are we to talk of law, Blas Lavera?"

Then Blas, hesitating, shrugged his broad shoulders.

"No," said he, "I think that it would be better that we should not talk of the law. We admit, in the first place, that the money was stolen."

Said Vega coldly and slowly, "Perhaps, speaking here, together, we might admit that. And I might say, my son, that forty-five hundred dollars is a great deal of money, and yet such a share frequently comes to the brave men who follow me. I might say, my son, that the loss of Estrada filled me with grief, because he was much loved and trusted in our band. He was a brave and a steady man. But if we could change him for one who is even better—why, Blas, you understand me! You are the man! You are not meant to follow a plough or to work where others can say, 'Go!' or 'Come!' You are meant to be free, like the rest of us. And if you will join, I say, keep from the money enough to buy that horse. Five hundred for that. Even another five hundred to buy presents for your family and such clothes and other trinkets as you wish for yourself. But then, by all means, give me back the rest of the money."

Blas Lavera raised his head and pointed:

"Look, senor. What do you see?"

"An eagle soaring, Blas."

"When the eagle strikes down a prey, does he share it afterwards? Or does he ask the owls or the hawks to hunt with him and help him?"

"By the mortal God!" snarled the outlaw. "Do you say this to me?"

And Blas smiled full in his face.

Chapter Four

They had their dinner in gloomy silence. Senora Lavera could not look at the handsome, careless face of Blas without having tears spring into her eyes. And every now and again, Eugenio or Felipe whispered to each other, struck with awe at the thought of the thing that had been, and the thing which might be.

For Vega ruled the town. There was no doubt of that in the mind of any sane and reasonable man. From the top to the bottom, San Pablo was thronged with his admirers. All of his work did not show on the surface. It was only now and again that he was detected, in person, at his nefarious labors. But it was surmised that here and there his hand was in all sorts of business which is supposed to be quite outside the sphere of a gunman and a safe-cracker and a highway bandit. He was no fool, that Vega. He did not have to drink and bluster when his pocket was filled with money. Indeed, it was said that his pocket never remained actually filled, very long. The gold which he took in was shrewdly invested, here and there. It was sometimes whispered that the coin of the great Vega was responsible for the working of more than one mine among the mountains. It was said that he had money invested in banks, yonder where the gringos herded their cattle by millions, over the great plains. And most certain was it that he owned a little of everything, in the San Pablo valley.

He had many and many a rich acre of the alfalfa land. He owned fields of beans, too. Yonder where the pepper fields extended, the great Vega had his share. And where the irrigated and flooded lands ended, and the cattle country began, he had a cattle ranch here, and a horse ranch there. His own herds of sheep wandered slowly through the mountain valleys. And his own goats grazed along the upper heights, where they bore hair of the longest and the most silken texture. He had other interests, too. It was said that he had invested heavily in the ownership of the boats which piled up and down the San Pablo river, carrying all sorts of provisions in, and bearing hides and hay and all manner of agricultural produce away again. This gave the great Vega further connections in distant gringo cities. And always there was money and yet more money rolling in for his purse.

It was only wonderful that he should have cared to take the road, for his adventurous expeditions, when he could have built for himself a great house after the Mexican manner, and settled down in it, surrounded by more or less industrious mozos and with all the comforts which man can yearn after. But still the lure of the road held him, though it was very creditably reported that, beyond the long, yellow waters of the Rio Grande, in that southern country where men breathe more at ease, where the roads are not paved with macadam and unrest, and where law is a sleepy goddess, Vega had in fact broken ground and erected a great, sprawling habitation. The lure of the road kept him from that place of idle residence, though broad fields surrounded it and his peace might have been unbroken by any dread of the sheriff. Or was it, as some said, that if he settled down, he would be unable to dispose of his friends suitably?

That, generally, was considered the true explanation. Because he had gathered to his interests so many gallant men, young and old, hard riders, straight shooters, reckless livers, and he loved so much to control them and their destinies, it was felt Vega could not surrender this pleasure for any other, and that he did not continue his career of crime for the sake of the pelf that it brought in to him, but because he dared not, or would not, surrender the reins by which he guided so many lives.

It was most understandable! For what could be more delightful than to be able to stamp upon the ground and, like a Scottish chieftain, surround oneself at once with a horde of trained and ardent fighters, devoted to one's interest? What more delightful than to be obeyed by men who asked not what was right or what was wrong, but simply, what was the will of their leader?

At any rate, such was the position of Vega.

He rode into San Pablo and out of it at his pleasure. There was only one shadow to embarrass him, and that was the active vigilance of the sheriff. But what could the sheriff do? There were sufficient hundreds of people in San Pablo to make a shifting screen for the outlaw when Stefan Gregory plunged down upon the town like a hawk from the center of the sky. There was hardly a family in the town which had not received the charity of Vega at one time or another. And there were very, very many who had contributed one or more recruits to his bands. Therefore, all were bound to him. And the very fact that the bond was illegal made it the more gripping. Vega, in San Pablo, was in the position of one who can do as he wills. He was a tyrant, and that was the reason that the Lavera family sat in silence through their meal.

A shadow crossed their threshold. All, save Enrique and Blas, jumped. For Blas appeared not to notice; and as for Enrique, his flaring eyes were too continually fixed upon the face of Blas to give heed to any other thing in the world. For, he seemed to be reading, with a deep intentness, the soul of the youngster.

The shadow was a tattered fellow, with a guitar tucked under his arm. He took off his rag of hat and so exposed a shaggy mane of hair which was at once tossed into greater disorder by the wind.

"Walk on, Juan Capote!" said the senora sternly. "We have nothing to spare."

"That is well, senora!" said Juan. "To talk with

honest friends is as much to me as food in the belly!"

"That is a lie!" yawned Blas.

The beggar started, and then his frown disappeared and a grin came.

"It is Blas!" said he.

"It is I."

"Do not be angry, Blas. A little lying makes the world spin around."

"That is true," answered Blas, judicially. "But there are lies and lies, and this last was a foolish one. Are you really hungry?"

"Food? Ah, Blas, I am so hungry that even the smell of rich victuals—such as the senora cooks in this house—is a repast to me."

"Come here," said Blas.

"Oh, the dirty feet!" complained the senora, but she dared not more than murmur. For as great a tyrant as Vega was in the rest of San Pablo, Blas was in this little house.

"Look at this great liar!" said Blas, taking sudden hold on the belt of the beggar. "You have eaten within the hour. The food is scarcely wiped from your lips! Now, tell me the truth!"

"It *is* true," said Juan Capote. "But I am like the beast that goes long marches over the desert and must keep a little fat upon the ribs. When may the starving time come? So I get what I can get. But you, Don Blas, are stripping away all of my little deceits."

"You see," said Blas, speaking to his family, but eyeing the beggar, "that he is brave enough and he will speak the truth. Therefore, he must have another plate of beans, if he can eat them."

"The blessing of God—" began the beggar.

"You will pay for it, and not with blessings. Tell me everything that has happened in San Pablo today, and everything that will happen before tomorrow morning."

"There is only one great thing," said the beggar, taking the basin of beans which the senora had grudgingly spooned out for him. "And that is, that poor Juan Capote has fallen into a shadow because he dared to stop at the house of his friend, Blas Lavera!"

"That is a pleasant riddle. Explain it, then!" commanded Blas.

"I shall explain it, gladly. Has not Porfirio Vega frowned on your house?"

There was a moan from the mother of the family. But Blas checked the noise with a side glance, like the blow of a whip.

"Juan!"

"Senor?"

"Aside from the cutting of my throat, what does Vega do in San Pablo tonight?"

"He has almost forgotten even your throat, Don Blas. He has found something more important to him."

"And that?"

"A woman!"

There was a murmur from all saving Blas.

"Then it is true, what we have heard about his house in old Mexico?"

"Perhaps."

"And now he is getting a wife! But where is there one for Vega in this town? He has an eye! And is there anything in San Pablo?"

"He found one. Liseta Juarez," said the beggar, his mouth filled with beans.

Senora Lavera cried out, "That little bundle of rags! That thieving little brat! Pah! You are mad, Juan Capote!"

"Peace!" commanded Blas, and looked again askance at the senora. She subsided at once.

"You have said that Don Porfirio has an eye. It is true that he has. But a few weeks ago, he rode down the street with a roll of cloth under his arm. He saw Liseta fighting with a boy and beating him. He threw her the cloth.

" 'Make a dress of this,' said Vega. 'Go home and be a woman!' She went home. The dress was cut out and sewed up. She took a twist in her hair. Suddenly, people remembered that she was eighteen. She was a woman! Have you heard nothing of this?"

"Yes, yes! Something. But we did not believe. Liseta lives on the far side of the town, by the river, you see!"

"Ah? Well, it is all as I have told you. And there is a ball tonight, where Liseta will go, and there, if you wish, you may send Eugenio or Felipe, and see Don Porfirio dance with the girl! They will be married in the week, or I am a fool and not Juan Capote."

"Why should I not go myself, Juan?"

"Because you do not wish a knife in the hollow of your back. That is the reason."

"You have said enough. And you have finished your beans. Here is a bit of silver. Do not tell too many lies about me. Only little lies. Not great ones, Juan Capote. Adios!"

Juan Capote went, laughing, through the door, and Blas turned to his brothers.

"Hurry, Felipe! Hurry, Eugenio! Help me to dress in my best clothes. There is not much time. I must go to see the woman that Vega saw in the bundle of rags!"

Chapter Five

There was a frantic protest from the senora, while Eugenio and Felipe sat aghast. But Enrique Lavera, his face pale and his eyes blazing, merely said, "You have considered then, Blas? You know that there will be a hundred of his men nearby. They will kill you with a smile, if he so much as lifts a finger!"

"I have thought of that," said Blas. "I have made up my mind. I shall not be persuaded. Madre mia, do not be a fool, but give me my white silk shirt! Now, father, while I am dressing, tell me more of the story."

"I shall lose all my poor wits!" screamed the senora. "You will sit there like a great block, Enrique, and let your eldest son go to be stuck like a pig?"

However, her husband regarded her not. And she went weeping to execute the mission of her son.

"I am dressing his corpse, not his body!" said she.

"What did I tell you last?" said Enrique.

"You told how the dam was built," said Blas, yawning again. "The devil take these flies. Tell me what comes next."

"It is almost the end of the story, Blas."

"Ha? No, I have listened to it for ten years, and now you say that it really has an end?"

"It has an end!"

"Very well! Then tell me the end, or as much of the end, as you can, while I dress."

"Well, let me see. The dam was built. When Guido Forseno saw that the dam was finished and that the canals were dug, he closed the sluice gates and waited while the water raised. He was very happy!"

"Yes," said Blas. "He was a peon. Work always pleased him a great deal, did it not?"

"A peon? Yes! He was a peon! That is very true. But still, even a peon has a soul, Blas. Eh?"

And his eyes, under their shaggy brows, gleamed at the young man.

"I suppose that a peon has a soul," said Blas calmly.

"And are they not people," shrilled the senora, looking up from her work, "who would say that *you*, Blas, are a peon, too—and that Eugenio and Felipe are, also?"

"Are there people who would say that of Eugenio and Felipe?" answered Blas calmly. "However, they would never say it of me!"

And he leaned back from his stool against the chair and smiled in indolent and proud self-content, while he began to pull off his boots. The senora would have answered, but the glance of her husband checked the bitter word that was on her lips. As for Eugenio and Felipe, they did not even lift their heads to notice the slight. They were too accustomed to the overbearing ways of their elder brother.

Said Enrique, "However, this thing would have pleased more than the soul of a peasant, for as the water raised, it filled the entire canon. It covered all the fields. It covered the old houses. It flooded the dens of the snakes. You remember the snake den where Guido Forseno had been—"

"I remember everything," said the boy, "as clearly as if I myself had been Guido."

"Though you are not a peon?" murmured Enrique through his teeth.

"That is not a thing to laugh at," said Blas. "Continue the story!"

"However, the water raised and raised. Finally, it made a great lake reaching back into the mountains like a great arm of silver. Except that it was more precious than silver."

"And how could it have been?" asked Blas, yawning.

"You will see! One day, Guido went to Don Teofilo. He said, 'Senor Dial, the thing is done. I am about to carry water to all of that dead desert!'

" 'Good,' said Don Teofilo. 'That I shall believe when I see it with my own eyes!'

"Poor Guido began to tremble.

"He said: 'Ah, senor, if you will come today, before the sunset, you will see the thing which I have promised to do!'

" 'Well,' replied Don Teofilo, 'I shall come!' "

"But," interrupted Blas, "do you mean that he did not know that your Guido had been building the dam?"

"He knew, but he did not stop to think what it meant. He never stopped to think. He had his fine house. He had his servants. He had his stables filled with beautiful horses. He had his lovely daughter growing each day more wonderful, and therefore, why should he consider the actions of this Guido?"

"Aye," said Blas carefully, "but then the building of the dam, as you said the last time you told of it, cost a great deal of money!"

"That is true," nodded the other. "It cost tens of thousands. And still, what was that to Teofilo Dial? What did money mean to him? Why should he care what Guido did? He knew that Guido was wise and would do no wrong!"

"It is true," nodded Blas. "Because this Dial was really as poor as a beggar, except for his great noble name, until he gave his affairs into the hands of Guido Forseno!"

"As poor as a mouse in winter!" said Enrique. "He had had nothing except that great tract of land, and nothing on it except a few starving cattle. And now all had been changed in the years during which Guido Forseno had been the ruler of that place. For as I have told you, he had turned the little herd of starved cattle into great swarms of tens of thousands. And all of the other things which he had done, you know about—They had made that Teofilo Dial a very great and rich man!"

"Yes," said Blas with a sigh. "Someday perhaps

I shall find someone who will work for me in that manner. But continue! Why do you not listen, Eugenio and Felipe?"

"We have other things to think about. Besides, it is only to you that our father wishes to tell the story. Does he want to have us with him, also?"

"No," remarked Blas. "And why is that, senor?"

"Let them be! Let them be!" said Enrique, frowning with a sudden violence. "What do they care for this Guido? Whereas, you are fond of him, are you not, my son?"

Blas nodded with eyes half closed. "Yes," said he, "I have heard you tell me so many stories about him that I really feel that I know him almost as well as though I had seen him in the flesh. What a great friend you must have been to him, father! You seem to know, always, the very inside of his mind! But continue!"

"Very well. Don Teofilo was pleased to hear what Guido had to say, and he said that he would be there before the sun set in order to see the thing accomplished."

" 'And yet, Guido,' said he, 'this thing cannot be. It would be a miracle! To bring waters out on the desert?'

"However, Guido did not answer that remark except to say: 'I had a great hope, senor, which has made me wish to perform a miracle for you!'

" 'What hope, Guido?' said Don Teofilo.

" 'The senor has forgotten,' said Guido. 'But long ago—was it not seven—eight years?—You told me that if I were to bring the waters onto that desert, and so many of them rich with green acres, you would give me anything in the world that I might ask from you. Does the senor remember?'

" 'Why, yes, Guido,' said Don Teofilo. 'I remember. I have not forgotten. A Dial does not forget such things, you must know. And what do you ask of me, then, when the great moment comes, and you send the waters out on the desert? And how are the waters to go, will you whip them before you, like a herd of galloping horses?'

"By this you see, my son, that Don Teofilo was a child in many ways. He did not know how that water could be sent out onto the plain!"

"Nor do I!" said Blas, frowning.

"Ah, my boy, you have only to remember that the waters behind the lake had been piled into a great lake which filled the huge ravine and backed into the mountains. Do you not remember that?"

"Yes."

"Then what remained except to level the desert into checks, and lead the water from the lake, through canals into the desert?"

"Well, now I remember that you have told me how Guido made the canals! Go on!"

"Now, this was to be the greatest day in the life of Guido, as you can imagine. And, before the setting of the sun, there came the great and rich Don Teofilo to see the miracle performed. And with him came that beautiful Maruja—"

"Who was so kind to Guido," nodded Blas. "But I do not think that if *I* had a daughter, I would want her to smile on such a man!"

"Do you not smile, yourself, on Juan Capote, on the thief, the beggar, and the liar?"

"Things are permitted to men that are not permitted to women. But continue with this story, if you please. I wish to know what happened when they were both on the dam. Were they surprised at the great lake of water that they saw?"

"Yes, they were amazed, and then while they were still wondering—because they had heard only vague reports of the things which he had been doing with the building of that dam, since the sluice gates were closed in it. While they were wondering at this, he gave a signal, and the gates were opened again and, with a sound of roaring like a thousand bulls foaming and trampling and bellowing, the water rushed out, all white and shining, until the sunset light struck it red. And all red it ran through the bare bones of the desert— red and gold, my son, a beautiful thing to see!"

"Aye," murmured Blas. "I should have liked to see that. And Don Teofilo?"

"He threw up his arms. He was so rejoiced that the tears started into his eyes.

"Then he said: 'It *is* a miracle. See the desert drinking deep for the first time in ten million years! Oh, Guido, you are a great and worthy man! Now tell me the great thing that you are to ask of me. Have you reflected? Have you made it great enough?'

"Guido stared at Maruja. She was as beautiful as the sunset itself, and she was a little flushed, too, because I think she guessed what Guido was about to say, and perhaps it was not altogether displeasing to her.

"'Ah, senor,' said Guido suddenly in a loud voice, 'I ask for the hand of your daughter!'"

Chapter Six

There had been enough in the story to arrest the attention of everyone in the room, at this time, and each one responded differently. The senora cried out: "Aha! There was a heart of gold! Oh, poor Guido! God bless him and give him good fortune! I hope that there is good fortune waiting for him. My Enrique, tell me now, what happened. And how many children did they have?"

So chattered she, unmarked by her husband, while Eugenio grinned with a broad delight, and young Felipe fell into a deep daydream, forgetting all else that was around him.

But it was not upon these that the narrator looked. It was the face of Blas that he watched with a hawklike intensity, as though life and death itself might turn upon the manner in which the boy accepted this point in the story.

But Blas merely shrugged his shoulders.

"I had begun to guess," said he, "that there would be some such foolishness!"

The older man turned pale.

"Foolishness?" said he. "Is that all that you can say for it, Blas?"

"Well, consider this yourself," said Blas. "You married my mother. I suppose that you loved her, then, even if you forget now that she is yours. But in those days—"

"You scandalous scoundrel!" screamed the senora. "I'll have you—I'll—"

"I cannot think when there is such a noise!" said Blas, laying his slender hands over his ears.

"Peace!" said Enrique to his wife, and his voice was so gruff, so brutally stern, that she shrank from before him, cripple that he was.

"Ah, but it is a shame to hear such talk in one's own house, from one's own flesh and blood—" She whimpered.

But Blas was saying, "As for this love—why, it is always interesting, as long as it bites some other man, and some other man's dog. I don't want it near me."

Said Enrique softly: "And why, my lad?"

"It spoils all of a man's sensible plans. That's the best reason that I can give against it. It is always in the way. It keeps a man from being brave and free and happy. A man is like a mountain lion, but much finer. But a man who is married cannot hunt where he pleases. He must leave off hot blood and raw meat. He must eat beans, and sweat, all day. Why? So that a lot of howling brats may screech at him, and when they grow up, damn him because he did not give them more. And in the meantime, what has become of the pretty girl that he married? Well, if marriage is a fire that covers a man with soot, it burns the woman herself to a cinder! God help the married men. And God pity the married women. For my part, I shall remain free!"

"You will never marry?" said the father, with an ironical smile. And he watched him like a cat.

"Yes," said the youth. "I shall marry—a woman with much money. I shall spend her money for her. I shall see her now and then. And I shall take care of all of you."

He waved a generous hand at the group.

"You will marry a rich girl, then, my lad?"

"Yes. It is the lazy way to do. If I were not lazy, I should be willing to work for money, and then I should not have to marry. Because no matter what I can do for you and mother, I can never repay you for the miseries that I have caused you! I know that! Money cannot be paid for such pain—"

"Such joy—such love—dear—foolish—"

"There she begins again," broke in Blas, and closed his eyes, wearily. "Begin again with the story. The important thing is not what we think, but what is going to happen!"

"Yes, and that is very true, lad. I shall tell you, then, that when Guido spoke to Senor Dial in this manner, Don Teofilo threw back his head and blinked both his eyes, as though a shaft of lightning had blared before him—"

He paused, squinting his eyes and shaking his head a little. He had grown paler than ever.

"Well?" said Blas.

"Well, after a moment, it seemed that Don Teofilo could speak again, and in the meantime, poor Guido had been looking at his master and at his mistress, also—"

"Do not say that!" snapped the youth.

"Do not say what?"

"Do not refer to them as master and mistress, because it makes me angry! It makes me wish that I had been there to throw them all three into the lake! But I suppose that that was what Senor Dial, himself, did to this Guido?"

"Ha?" cried the father. "Do you think that that would have been the right thing, my son?"

"Why not?"

"After Guido had done so much for Senor Dial?"

"Guido was honest. I like honest men. But also, Guido was a good deal of a fool. I know that there is trouble coming to Guido, however, and I suppose that that will make me hate Don Teofilo again. Continue, father!"

"At last," said the father, "Don Teofilo was able to open his eyes and to see clearly and to know what had happened, and worst of all, he managed to espy a rather shy, kind glance that young Maruja cast at Guido. When he saw this, it threw him into a flame. He gritted his teeth and he leaped at Guido and was about to take him by the throat—"

"But Guido knocked him down?"

"Knocked him down! No, no! Guido would as soon have thought of stabbing himself, as of touching the master!"

"There is that filthy word again. He did not, then, touch this master, as you call him?"

"Certainly not. But Don Teofilo did not touch him, either; for, he suddenly seemed to remember that to touch this Guido would be to touch a peon!"

Here Enrique made a quick pause breathing very hard.

Young Blas leaped up and strode to him. He placed his hand upon the shoulder of his father.

"Father," said he, "when I see you like this, it makes me love you. For sympathy with that Guido, your heart is burning. What a good man you are! What a kind and true man! God bless you! Now tell me the rest!"

The father reached up his crippled hands and caught at the young, supple fingers of the boy.

"Well," said he, "Don Teofilo called out. Remember that he was like a king in that place. He called out, and when men came running to him, he commanded that they should seize that Guido and tie him hand and foot!"

"But Guido broke through them!" shouted Blas suddenly. "And he caught up the girl, and he leaped onto a horse that was standing there, and as he rode away, he turned in the saddle, and he fired at them, so that they dared not to follow him—Ha, father! Was not that the way of it with your friend Guido?"

"Do you think that it was that way?" said Enrique.

"No!" said, Blas, and dropped his head. Because I know that that Guido was not a lion. He was a fool and a lamb. He let them tie him, and he threw his sheep's glances at the girl, worshiping her and loving her, as that fat fool, Vega, will be doing with the girl that he picked up out of the streets—as

Vega will be doing this very night, and I shall be there to watch! Bah!"

He had fallen into a fury.

"You are right," said Enrique. "Because Guido could not resist. It did not come into his mind that he might resist, I tell you; for he felt that the will of the senor was the will of God, in a way. Then, besides, he knew that he had been given a promise by the senor, and he felt that that promise was a sacred thing, because the word of the house of Dial is a sacred thing. Do you understand? He remembered all of his services, and he did not see how his master could really do him any harm!"

"Go on!" gasped Blas.

"And so Guido was tied hand and foot and thrown over the back of a horse—"

Here a sudden scream broke from the lips of the boy.

"No, no, no, no! They did not dare to do that! Even if he was a peon. They wouldn't dare to throw him over the back of a horse like a sack of meal—"

"They did it, though," insisted Enrique Lavera, solemnly, "and then they carried him to the house—"

"Which the money he had made for Don Teofilo had built!" cried young Blas through his teeth.

"That is true," nodded the father. "And there he was carried down to the bottom of the house—do you remember how, when he had the foundations dug, they struck a moist cold rock, and there the lowest chamber—"

"They put him there!" said Blas fiercely.

"Yes!"

"*Madre de Dios*, had I been there!"

"What could that have done?"

"A death for that Don Teofilo. I could have done that!"

The eyes of Lavera, buried under the shadow of his brows glistened with a savage pleasure.

"Aye," said he, "they carried that poor Guido there, and—"

"No more!" broke in Blas. "I cannot hear any more. I will not hear how Guido was treated worse than I would treat a dog! I am through with the story for tonight. I never wish to hear another syllable of it. Eugenio, throw me that cloak—"

"Do not, Eugenio!" cried the senora bitterly. "He will go to throw his life away at the dance! The men of Vega—"

But the cloak was already in the hands of Blas. He turned to the door and paused there for an instant, while others, in an awed circle regarded him.

"I am going to the dance, thinking of Guido!" he cried to them. "I tell you that this Vega is like Don Teofilo—a beast and a brute, because he has too much power in his hands. But I shall laugh in his face—for the sake of Guido. For the sake of Guido, I shall dance with the girl that Vega found in the gutter—"

He was gone.

"Stop him!" cried the mother, wringing her hands.

"Eugenio and Felipe!" commanded their father, "stay where you are. Do not even stir to go with him and protect him. Either he is a snarling dog, and hardly worth the saving, or else he is a lion— and then he does not need your protection."

Chapter Seven

The entire family listened to this speech with astonishment, and the senora, at least, heard it with joy, also. For it was no secret that Blas always had been the favorite. In all things, he had come first with Lavera. The two other sons were sent out to labor in the heat and the dust of the fields, but toil was never exacted from Blas; and, as the sheriff had said of him, it was only expected that he should amuse himself with guns and horses. And this careless speech in which he seemed to say: "If Blas is worthy of his salt, he will be able to take care of himself!"—this speech made all the others stare.

They sat up for a long time, waiting to receive news of the adventurer. But finally the two sons went to sleep and left their father and mother sitting at the doorway.

She was murmuring to him, "What has it all meant, these years, my Enrique?"

"What are you talking about?" said Enrique.

"The thing that I am never done thinking of, as you well know! I am wondering what your purpose has been, Enrique, in watching Blas turn into a tiger!"

"A tiger?" snapped her husband.

"Oh, well, you may call it what you will. But you know that he *is* a tiger, my dear. Otherwise, would he dare to go out hunting among all the dogs of the Vega pack? But besides that, all these years you have had sparkling eyes when you watched him fighting! Even when he was a small boy and tussled in the street with other little ones, you laughed when he beat the others, and you have been sad when they beat him. Is not that true?"

"You have eyes in your head," said her husband sourly. "You may make up your own mind from what you have seen. What else do you know of Blas?"

"Not the chief thing!" said the senora bitterly. "If you are his father, still I don't know who his mother may have been."

"Am I to tell you?" asked the gloomy Enrique.

And so a heavy silence fell between them again. Each had private thoughts which the other could guess, but never surely knew. They waited, and the slow hours ran past them, with no sign of Blas.

Blas had forgotten his home and the people in it, for the time being.

Look in upon him as he whirls through a dance in a big low-ceilinged room, with twisted streamers of crimson, yellow, and green paper strung across it, sagging so low that the heads of the dancers almost touched these decorations. A sort of half-light illumined the hall. In brackets along the wall, smoking lamps threw dull hemispheres of light, showing the fog-white mist of tobacco smoke, mixed with the fumes from the lamps themselves. Near the walls, where the chairs were lined up, all was clear enough, but towards the center of the big apartment, all was an uncertain limbo. On a raised dais at one end, the musicians labored, with a wonderfully patient enthusiasm.

To one who did not know, it would have seemed much the same as any other Mexican dance. But one of the initiated could not fail to notice the difference.

There were two centers of attraction. One, was the form of Porfirio Vega; the other was Blas himself. A little whisper had originated no one knew where, and it had circulated through the entire hall and buzzed even to the street beyond, where little clusters walked, now and again, to enjoy the freer, fresher air.

That whisper said definitely that Vega and young Blas were at outs, and this was enough for the whisper to tell, since all the town knew Blas, and all the world, one might say, knew Porfirio Vega! His deeds someday would creep into song, as many of them were already in print. And as for Blas, who could tell what he would be?

That was the question that the crowd of whisperers asked one another, while the dance went on. That which, in the beginning, had been of the greatest interest, now became a secondary affair.

All had come with eyes on fire to see the great Vega and the girl who had been selected by him. This was his way of showing her to the world and making the world admire his choice. They came to see Liseta Juarez. But they remained to wonder what would happen when the power of Vega encountered the tigerish strength of Blas!

And the eyes of all trailed constantly in conflicting directions—from Liseta and Vega—towards Blas—and back again. What would happen?

They had had their moments of wonder at the beauty of the girl from the gutter. Now there was something more important. It was the great lull before a battle!

A sudden crisis came, most unbelievably. As a dance began Liseta for one instant was left without the presence of the great Vega. He had stepped away to speak to one of his lieutenants—one of those dark-eyed, sinister men of whom there were already half a dozen here and there, all keeping a sharp lookout on Blas. Their presence added an additional excitement. They seemed to promise that, no matter what happened when the crash came between Vega and the youth, Blas would never leave that hall alive!

But as Porfirio Vega stepped away from Liseta, Blas stood in front of her. She raised her head; but when she saw him, her smile went out and her face became as blank as the stare of any well-schooled dowager, putting an offender in place! It was not long since she had left her rags. Nevertheless, that time was a whole world distant from her. There was a greater space between her and the ragamuffin that was, than there could be between her and the greatest of queens!

Blas, however, was not chilled by those blank, black eyes. He bowed low before her. And when he stood erect again, he said, "They are beginning to play the music for that dance of which we know. Are you ready senorita?"

His effrontery startled her into a quick glinting of interest.

"There is no music," she said coldly.

"Pardon me," said he. "The music is beginning at this moment!"

He turned as he spoke and waved his hand towards the musicians, and they made instant answer with the crash of an opening strain.

She knew, suddenly, that he had arranged all this—the signal to the musicians—and the money beforehand to bribe them to do his pleasure! She knew these things, but she could guess at still more—and among the rest, she could imagine that the word which had called the Vega from the room, had been a message discreetly sent by this same Blas Lavera.

Such scheming was a direct tribute to her. Such cleverness and forethought, also, warmed her heart. She felt a fire ready to run from her heart into her eyes, and she had to control it with a greater effort than before.

"That man-killer, Diego," said Blas, "is coming up behind me. And his cousin, Horacio, is coming from the left. Do you wish me to be killed at your feet, senorita? Or, will you dance with me and let me escape them in that way for another moment or two?"

It was too much for Liseta.

She stood up. She threw back the brocaded scarf of blue and gold which had cost the great Vega so many thousands of pesos. She was revealed in crimson, with crimson stockings, and little crimson shoes, traced with gold. In her piled hair was a comb set with rubies. Truly, a queen would have been proud of the jewels which were set in it!

So, she stepped straight into the arms of Blas and away he whirled her under the very noses of Diego and Horacio.

This dance, coming so quickly on the heels of the last one, had taken everyone by surprise. There was a tangled stream of couples moving about on the floor but there were no dancers except this pair. They had their own way. All others gave them room, and the laughter, the murmurs, died as though by command.

Only a dreadful little whisper—and then heavy silence from all hands.

And the music sang and welled and thrilled and beat through the room, and the two dancers glided gracefully over the floor!

Oh, what grace! And well might they have it! Had she not danced since she was a little child, whirling in the streets, through most intricate reels and fandangos, while her worthless uncle strummed at his guitar? She had brought him a living and he had given her the crusts as he finished eating, as one might say. So now, she was a miracle of art on the polished dance floor. And what had that lazy Blas to do except learn how to handle weapons and ride horses, and do all the things which make a young man accomplished in the Mexican sense?

Dancing was one of them. He who groaned with weakness and weariness if poor Senora Lavera asked for more wood for her fire, had the ardor and the power to practice an intricate movement for hours.

So he was well mated with Liseta. They dipped and whirled and glided over that floor until the breath came into the throats of the watchers. For even in their expectant fear, they smiled.

What was Blas saying?

"He will have me murdered before I leave the hall. But what matters that? When I saw you, I knew that I must dance with you once."

"Wild Blas Lavera!" said she. "Do I not know you perfectly? You wish to dance with me only to madden Don Porfirio. That is true, and I know it!"

"Do you think so, really? When a man sees a hungry lion, does he walk into his den and then snap his fingers under the lion's nose?"

"*You* might do that," said she.

"Liseta," said he, "they are waiting to kill me. Look me in the face. Tell me if you do not see that I am glad to die—for you!"

Chapter Eight

She pushed herself a little back from him and looked up into his face.

Then she chuckled.

"You are a devil, Blas! You do not care for me any more than you do for the stone that you use to throw at another man—or the bullet. I am simply your way of insulting Vega!"

"Liseta! Liseta!"

"Oh, it is true! I know you—tiger! I have seen you fight in the street when we were both a lot younger. I have not forgotten. Now you want to drive Don Porfirio completely insane! You want to make me smile at you and blush and seem happy as a girl in love. That is want you want!"

What said Don Blas, then?

He tilted back his rascally head and laughed. And he laughed again. And then he whirled her through swiftly circling movements, while their feet moved swifter than the darting heads of sparrows when they pick eagerly at a patch of seeds. But always those flying feet were in a perfect rhythm.

Never had such dancing been seen in San Pablo, where all men and women danced.

"Is it not true?" she was gasping.

"Yes, it is true!" said Blas. "Oh, little hawk, is there anything that you do not see?"

"When one has learned how to beg, one develops sharp eyes. That is why I knew the truth about you!"

"Do you know," said Blas, "that you—why, when I came here, I thought that you were only a bright rascal. Now I see that you are a great deal more. I see, Liseta, that you are a treasure great enough to overflow the hands of a good man!"

"I don't think you mean what you say," murmured she, "but still it makes me happy to hear it. But tell me how you are to escape from this hall without being cut to pieces? Look at Don Porfirio. He is choking. His face is swollen!"

"I wish that his heart would burst!" chuckled Blas. "Do you not think that there is any way for me to run away?"

"No. Unless you sink through the floor! I think that he will step up, in another moment. He cannot stand it!"

"He *will* stand it, however! He must learn to stand a great deal more than this. I have barely begun with him. He has always been proud. I am going to teach him to be humble. Now listen to me, Liseta. The men of that Vega have surrounded this place. They are watching every window. They are watching every door. They wonder where I will try to run through. But I shall not run. I shall walk away. You will see! Not a shot will be fired, unless it is I who do the firing! And Don Porfirio may stand there and curse and choke!"

"He will never speak to me again except to curse me!" said Liseta. "I have thrown away a rich fortune for the sake of dancing with you."

"No," said Blas. "You have thrown away nothing. Why is he so furious now? Partly because I have dared to dance with you; partly because he is mad about you. He has been mad with love. Now he will be mad with jealousy, also. Is not that clear?"

"You and I are not fools, eh?" chuckled the girl. "If only that Porfirio does not go mad and choke me to death with his great hands!"

"You do not need to fear for that. Besides, put off the wedding day. Wait, Liseta. It may be, that before long, I shall have made so much money that you will be willing to marry me. And would not that be better than marrying that Vega?"

"A thousand times!" she answered frankly.

"And, in addition, it may be that I shall have to kill Vega. He has spoken very roughly to me."

"Is it true that you have taken some money from him?"

"Certainly. I killed one of his men and took the wallet of that man. Estrada was his name."

"*Madre de Dios*, do you tell me these things?"

"You have heard them already, or you will hear them hereafter. You might as well hear them from me. But this is the point. I was never born to be

killed by such a wild pig as that Vega. You believe
that, my dear. And consequently, he was probably
born to be killed by me. If you marry him, you will
very quickly be a widow."

"Look! There is a man in front of every window.
Poor Blas! You will never escape!"

"Do you think not? Only watch me, now, and do
not hold back, but dance where I guide you!"

He steered their course swiftly past the very spot
where the Vega stood, with a livid, puffed face and
staring eyes.

He swung on with the gliding girl and just as he
seemed about to dance past the doorway, he
whirled suddenly with her through it, and past the
startled faces of two stray men who were standing
there. One of them reached out his hand—but it
touched the bare shoulder of the girl and he
shrank as though he had handled a live coal.

There was a babel of voices from the interior of
the hall, at this moment, as the pair of dancers
disappeared through the doorway. And the voice
of Vega, like that of an angered king, was heard to
shout with terrible wrath.

Blas, at the head of the outer steps, leaned to
touch the forehead of the girl with his lips.

"You have saved me!" breathed Blas; and, a moment later, he was leaping to the ground below.

The two who had guarded the door were after
him in a flash, but he had plunged through a
thicket of brush growing in an empty lot. When
they emerged from the thicket, there was no Blas
in sight, and he himself was wandering slowly
back towards his home.

When he reached the house, he found that the

senora was asleep, leaning against the wall. But the cigarette of Lavera was still burning.

"And now?" whispered Lavera.

"I have pulled the lion's beard," whispered Blas in turn, "and I have danced with Liseta, and here I am safe again!"

"Safe?" murmured Lavera. "He will be here to find you in another moment! He will be here with twenty men!"

"No, he will ride to every other place. He will not dream that I dared to return to this house. So I shall rest here, while his men are searching. Afterwards, I shall ride away." Then indicating the senora, he said, "Send her to bed!"

The senora was too sleepy to protest. She gave Blas only one startled glance, thanked God in a murmur that he had come back alive, and went to her bed. Blas sat down with the father of the house.

"Now," said he, "since we have time to kill, tell me the rest of the story of Guido Forseno."

"Very well. If you think that you are safe here?"

"Safe until morning. Before the dawn, I must be away from this house. And now what happened to Guido?"

"I told you that he had been taken to a place like a dungeon, in the bottom of the Dial house."

"Yes, you told me that."

"After he had lain there in the damp for two days, Don Teofilo came down to him. He held a lantern close to the face of Guido.

" 'Now,' said he, 'have you changed your mind about the marriage with Maruja?'

"Guido looked up to him and did not speak."

Said Blas, "This Guido really loved her, then?"

"You can guess that he did when I tell you that he was not a very brave man, and yet he had dared to ask her hand from her father!"

"Yes, that is true. And still he would not take back his request?"

"Don Teofilo said: 'I have given you my word. You may have whatever you ask for—unless I can induce you to change your mind!'

"And as he said that, he smiled like a devil.

"He went on: 'But I advise you to be wise, Guido. Tell me that you have changed your mind. You wish to ask me for a great sum of money, but not for Maruja. You have seen that that is very wrong!'

"Still, Guido did not answer.

"So Don Teofilo called out, and two men came in behind him. They took Guido and they hung him by the fingers from the ceiling of that cellar room. Then they went out, and Don Teofilo sat down to wait.

"Understand that Guido was very strong in his hands and for a time the strong tendons and the muscles withstood the weight of his body, but after that, they began to fail him. He felt a dreadful agony. The fingers seemed to be pulled from their sockets; he could feel the tendons stretching and stretching. But he decided that he would die before he would give up Maruja.

"But there was no pity in the heart of Don Teofilo. He sat and waited and watched, while he smoked a cigarette. Before the cigarette was finished, Guido moaned in his suffering.

" 'Have you changed your mind?' asked Don Teofilo.

" 'Yes,' said Guido."

"No!" broke in Blas through his gritted teeth. "He did not say that! He died, sooner than that!"

"He surrendered," insisted the father. "And Don Teofilo cut the ropes that suspended him. Guido fell to the floor and lay there insensible with the long agony which had worn him out. When he recovered his wits, he was lying in a bed, and there were bandages on his hands. And Don Teofilo was sitting beside him, saying: 'Now make your other request!'

"But Guido would not make one. And that next night, he slipped away from the house traveling out of the reach of Teofilo Dial."

"Tell me," said the trembling voice of Blas, "if his hands were ever completely healed?"

"No, never."

"By the mighty God—then *you* are Guido Forseno!"

"Hush, hush! Your mother will hear!"

"I have waited long enough," said Blas in a stifled voice. "For now I know where I must ride. Tell me where the house of Dial stands!"

Chapter Nine

They walked together into the darkness, for Blas
was bound for the house of Guadalupe Pissano, at
the end of the town. The wind was whispering in
the great cypresses, and their shadows sloped
away from the moon and stood across the surface
of the river, which here flowed so softly that it lay
like a lake with polished surface. And the white
walls of the houses seemed as if they, too, had
been built of squared blocks of the pallid moonshine.

Blas had no eye for the beauty of the night.

For Lavera was saying, "Now, my son, before
you go you must hear the end."

"Is there an end?" said Blas bitterly.

"An end of Guido Forseno, and a beginning of
Enrique Lavera!" said the older man.

"Very good. Let me hear, then. I may as well

have more reason for killing this Dial!"

"You will have them, my son! I tell you, that when Don Teofilo found that Guido Forseno—"

"Do you still talk of him as though he were not yourself?"

"Do not think that I am Guido!" said Lavera with a trembling voice. "I am the owner of a dirty little hovel. God has sent me three strong sons. And they are my only possession. But in those days I was a maker and a builder. I had taken Don Teofilo out of the dirt of poverty, and I had made him a great man. I had brought him such wealth as the whole mountains wondered at. That was the sort of a man that I was in those days, until Don Teofilo crushed my hands into these stiff claws—and crushed my heart and my soul, also!"

"I shall not kill him suddenly!" said Blas in a thoughtful voice. "I must be thinking all the while and devising the right sort of a death for him. He must die little by little, miserably, tasting death like wine, as it comes to him. That is what must be arranged!"

"I think, my son, that you will do it. I have watched you through these years, and I think that God sent an avenger to me in you. Ah, I think so!"

And he gripped the strong arm of the boy in his hand, like the hard talons of a bird. Then he continued.

"When Don Teofilo saw that Guido would not surrender completely and that though he had been forced to retract his first wish, he would not replace it with another, it made Don Teofilo very angry. He swore that he would be revenged on Guido."

"Revenged?" echoed Blas.

"Yes, because the creatures which we have wronged, we are always anxious to wrong still further. We cannot help loving those whom we assist; and we cannot help hating those whom we have trodden down by accident, or for no good reason! And Don Teofilo suddenly became a devil—"

"Ah, he was always that!" snarled Blas.

"Do not think so!" said Lavera. "No, for if you go to him with that idea, you will be so surprised that you may be tempted to think that I have not told you the truth. Because Dial is gentle in his voice and mild and kind in his eyes. He has the look of a good man who has never done much wrong in this world. He has the look of one who could be easily imposed upon. Do you understand?"

"But a devil beneath!" interposed Blas.

"You may judge that for yourself, later on. I tell you, that when he found that Guido Forseno would not give in, he cast about to see how he could most torment him.

"Finally, he hit upon a scheme.

"You have heard me speak, before, of a young American who lived on a ranch nearby and who often came to see Maruja?"

"Yes."

"Why, Don Teofilo knew that Maruja liked this fellow fairly well, and he determined that she should marry him."

"A gringo!" breathed Blas.

"Remember," said Lavera, "that Dial himself has little of the good blood in him. Was not his mother full gringo? Was not even his father half the gringo

69

blood? Yes, and it was easy for him to decide that the young Senor Enright should be the husband of his daughter. He sent for Senor Don Guy Enright. He opened his mind to him.

"The young gringo was delighted. It was not only the beauty of the girl. It was the thought of the broad acres, and the great dam with the waters piled behind it, to turn the desert green, and to bring in more and more wealth, through eternity! That was all in the mind of Don Guy. He accepted, of course. He was not the fool to refuse, even though it meant some forcing of the girl."

Here Blas broke in: "If she had loved you, father, she would never have looked—"

"Ah," said Lavera, "time is a great healer in these matters. And time took her in hand. It was a sad thing, to be sure, that Guido had disappeared so suddenly.

"But for six months, Guido lay rotting in the cellar of the great house and, at the end of that time, Don Teofilo began to talk of the other man to his daughter, and Maruja listened and began to nod her head. Six months is a dreadfully long time to a young girl. She had almost forgotten the look of the face of Guido Forseno, I suppose. But she had not forgotten his voice, as you shall learn!

"Now, on a day, Don Teofilo had Guido Forseno brought up from the dungeon to a little alcove through the cleft window of which he could look down into the private chapel which—you remember how Guido had brought down the rock for the building of that chapel, Blas?"

"Oh, I remember every word!"

"Now then, he was looking through, into the

chapel, and he heard the organ begin to sound—
You remember how he had had that organ built,
my son?"

"Yes, yes. I remember! And one of the pipes was
brought all the way from Italy, because there was
to be a note of a certain sort—"

"Yes, and that organ began to play, while the
fragrance of many flowers filled the church, and
passed thickly, through the narrow gap, to the
nostrils of Guido Forseno. Then Guido saw many
people entering, and finally he could see Maruja,
walking by the side of young Guy Enright. She was
dressed in white, and all that white was the finest
lace. In her clothes there was the cost of a great
fortune. Ten times the money that Dial had had
when Guido first knew him, was now laid freely
upon the back of that same child of his.

"And that was the added torment, that Don Teofilo had devised. A very clever one, eh, my son?"

Blas threw his hands to the stars, but uttered
not a word. Only, Lavera could hear him gasping
and choking with his passion.

"Guido Forseno kneeled on the floor while the
people in the church were praying for the happiness of the bride and the groom, Guido asked God
to punish such cruel wickedness as this!"

"And God will!" said Blas sternly. "Through my
hand!"

"But afterward, as the ceremony came to an
end, Guido went mad. All his scattered wits left
him. He stood up and screamed through the cleft
in the stone, 'I, Guido Forseno, pronounce a curse
on the bride and the groom, and on the children
that may spring from their marriage!'

"So said Guido and then he fainted.

"When he recovered, he was under the lash of a whip. They beat him back to consciousness and then they beat him out of it again.

"But when his wounds had healed a little after that thrashing, they turned Guido loose, and he went wandering across the desert—Do you remember how he had first come to the house of Dial?"

"Yes, very poor. With nothing but sandals on his feet!"

"And it was that way again. Guido Forseno went out with naked feet, and now even his hands were crippled!"

"Tell me!" exclaimed Blas. "You have been taught by the torture, and therefore you know. What should be done to a devil like that Dial?"

"What *can* be done? He is beyond the grasp of my hands—my crippled hands. I sank into a new level of life. I married a woman, hoping that she would bear me a son to revenge me. She gave me three boys. I watched them growing up. But there was only one of them of whom I had any hope. Then I taught that one all that I could. I made him learn guns and horses. I let him grow strong. I did not stiffen or dull his body with hard labor. I made life sweet for him, so that his spirit might be fresh when the great time of need came. And now—this is the end. I bring you the load of my hatred and my curse. Will you work it upon him, my child?"

"Shall I swear?" said Blas. "No, that is a childish thing to do. But I tell you that I am filled to the throat with this business! I shall never rest until it is finished! Here is the house of Pissano. I am going to buy La Blanca. Wait here!"

He struck at the door.

"Who is there?" called a voice, presently.

"One to buy La Blanca."

"You are drunk. She is not for a beggar!"

"Come down and open the door, Pissano. I have brought her price in cash. Five hundred dollars!"

There was a whistle. "Five hundred? To pay down in cash?"

"Yes."

"Very good, but her price is not that. It is a thousand!"

"Why, Pissano, you must not lie to me! I have heard you name her price, before!"

"Yes? A daytime price, but this is the night. A thousand dollars!"

"Well," said Blas suddenly, "bring her to me, saddled and bridled. That new saddle, with the silver mountings. Hurry! And a quirt also!"

There was a great scrambling and hurry. There was a noise beyond the house, in the corral, and then Pissano came, leading the mare.

"Light a match so that I may count your money, please. Ah, it is Blas Lavera! Blas, Blas, there is no wonder that you want La Blanca. But you will need four wings, and not merely her hoofs, to keep you away from the hand of Vega!"

Chapter Ten

They stood alone in the night—the glimmering mare, with the starlight quivering on her silken body, Lavera, and Blas.

"Before I go, here is something that will make life easier for you—whether I come back or not. Here is money. Two thousand dollars. You know where I got it, and you know what it leaves to me, father. For I may need money to do this work that lies ahead of me. Now, with this money—will you take my advice?"

"Tell me what you wish, my son."

"Use that money to buy the alfalfa field, up the valley. The one which Torre has planted and now wishes to sell again. Felipe and Eugenio can work the field. They understand such things, and it would be a greater profit if they work for you, rather than if they work for other people. Will you do that?"

"If we buy that land, people will ask from what place we could have gained so much money. And they will know that it came from you, and you got it from Vega. And will not the enmity of Vega cost me more than two thousand dollars?"

There was a little silence after this, and then Blas said bitterly: "I forget, Father, that Don Teofilo did not break your hands only! Well, take the money and spend it more slowly, then—or do as you please with it. I do not wish my mother to be beaten and whipped by poverty all her life!"

He swung into the saddle, and the mare danced sidewise, throwing her head and snorting.

"Can you handle her, Blas?"

"She will be like a pet dog, in a day or two. First, I must teach her to love me. After that, everything will be easy!"

"Unless she kills you, first—she is a tigress! A devil!"

"Only to fools who strive to master her with spurs and whips. You will see, before long!"

He reined her gently back towards Lavera.

"Will you tell me one truth, Father?"

"Ay, my son!"

"Then—is your wife truly my mother?"

The other started in the heart of the night.

"Is that a thing to ask me, Blas?"

"I have asked it, nevertheless!"

"Well, I must tell you the truth, then. She is not!"

"I knew it," said Blas. "But I wanted your word for it. I have known it for years. Your son—yes. But not hers! There is something lacking in her, and I knew that she could never have been my mother. Then tell me who, after all, my mother is!"

"I cannot, Blas."

The boy shook his head.

"I understand," said he. "I was born out of wed-
lock, of course. But there are worse things than
that. And after I was born, you took me—but you
let my mother go to the devil. Well, perhaps that
would be hard to forgive, but it would not be hard
to understand. Yet, I tell you, father, that I must
know the truth. There is a fire in my heart that
burns me up with a desire to know. I shall never
rest until I have her name. And I want to know the
town where she was born. I want to see the house
where she lived. I must know these things, Father.
And you will tell me?"

"I gave you my word that I would answer one
question, but not two. I have told you that my wife
is not your mother. And that must be enough."

"I tell you, that if you treated her badly, I shall
forgive it. For the sake of knowing the truth!"

"Why does it burn you so—to know about her?"

"Because until I know about her, I cannot tell
about myself. What am I? I am not Felipe and I
am not Eugenio. I do not grow from the same soil.
You are my father. Yes. But I was your eldest son,
while your heart was still the heart of Guido Forseno, a builder and a maker of things. Afterwards,
you shrank down to Enrique Lavera. I do not
mean to wound you, but I must tell you the truth.
And, in addition to this, I have to say that until I
know who my mother was, I am sick and dis-
gusted with this life. I have to know her, before I
know what I am fitted for!"

"Why do you have to know that, Blas?"

"Because I am either a gentleman, or a pirate!

Do you understand? But a slave to work in the dust of the fields—no, I am never that!"

"I understand. But someday I may tell you. The time has not come now. Believe me! If you were to know, you would forget the work which you have to do with Don Teofilo!"

"Do you think that? I tell you, Father, that after he has died in a torment, I shall come back to you, and then you will have to tell me everything. Now, good-bye. Give me your blessing, for I shall need it!"

A blessing he received, spoken in a trembling voice, and after that, the grey mare drifted him away through the night.

It had grown cloudy. The wind came wet and heavy to them, carrying from far off the scent of the alkali dust of the desert, which had been drenched by a recent rain.

As the Lavera started back for his house, arms of lightning began to reach above the edge of the southeastern sky, and the road was illumined by starts and flickers of crimson, angry light that worked snake-wise across the face of the windows on either hand.

Then the thunder began to roll up the heavens like a great cart over a bridge paved with cobblestones. Now and again it rumbled above the head of Lavera. He began to run, looking behind and above him in a guilty fashion, like one who knows that he deserves punishment of the most dreadful kind.

Behind him, he heard the rattle of the rain before he got to his house, and just as he reached his doorway, the curtain of rain was drawn past with a roar, and the fuming smell of the dust, now turning to liquid mud, rose against his nostrils.

He leaned in the opening, his nostrils expanded, his lips smiling, but still with his frightened eyes turning now and again towards the lightning, which split over the heart of the sky.

His wife came to him, muttering, and complaining in her weariness against the whole world.

"Where is Blas?"

"Blas? He is not here."

"Dear heavens, have you let the child ride out in this storm? It will kill him!"

"If this kills him, then he is no good for the work which I have in mind for him. Do not talk like a fool. This will not harm him. He is laughing at this rain, with his poncho swung over his shoulders. I myself would have smiled at such a storm when I was a boy. And what was I, ever, compared with him? What was I ever?"

"Aye," said his wife, "but why *should* you be compared with him? How much of your blood is there in him?"

He turned sharply around at her.

"Are you chattering like a fool again?" he demanded in a harsh voice. "Is he not my son?"

"How shall I tell? There is none of you in him that shows! Nothing! You might have raised a hawk, but never an eagle, my man. Well, you need not beat me for saying the truth!"

He had, in fact, raised his crippled hands as though he would strike her, but he recovered himself at once, and let his arms fall at his sides.

"But tell me where you have sent Blas?" she demanded persistently.

"What business is that of yours? Are you his mother?"

"By the pain and the care that I have given him—yes I *am* his mother. By the hours that I have watched over him—yes, I am his mother. So I ask you what you have done with him?"

"I shall tell you," said the cripple, looking up to the transfigured heavens. "I have stood up like the king of the sky. And I have taken the red-hot lightning in my naked hand. And I have thrown it at a mark!"

"You have sent Blas to do some devil's work!"

"Let Blas be. Talk to me no more. I am tired, and I have reason because I have just finished the hardest work of my life!"

So said Lavera, and turned slowly back into the house. There he lay down on his bed, and through the doorway, he saw the grey beginnings of the day, which made the pencil streaks of the rain faintly visible. He was contented. Into that day he had launched a great mischief. Time alone could tell what would come of it.

Chapter Eleven

There was no long ride this night for Blas Lavera. As soon as the volley of raindrops struck the mare, she put back her ears and began to pitch with a mulish viciousness. And he made no effort to ride her out. He sat through her outburst of fury, simply to show her that she could not master him. And that supple horsemanship which had been developed by sitting on the back of any mustang learned in the arts of bucking that came to San Pablo, now stood him in excellent good stead.

However, when La Blanca got over her ugly fit, he dismounted and led her into a wood, where he walked her up and down while the heaviest portion of the thunderstorm blew over their heads. And when the peals grew loudest and crowded most thickly together, she flattened her ears and pressed close against him, like a child against a parent. He soothed her with a soft voice and his hand.

The sun was well up, looking like a pale moon behind the rain clouds, before he started on with her. He travelled only to an old shack among the hills of the San Pablo valley. There he paused to make his first camp. And since he had not closed his eyes during the night, he hobbled the mare, rolled himself in his blanket, and was soon asleep.

When he wakened, the sky was filled with ragged piled-off clouds which a contrary wind had torn to pieces and flung over the heavens. While, in the south-eastern horizon, the steep, lead-colored bank of mist told of the course of the retreating storm.

Before he had saddled, even the scattered clouds were hurried away, sailing like awkward galleons southwards. The sun swept San Pablo valley with all of its accustomed power, and, looking down from the height, he could see in wonderful detail the distant white wall of the little town; he could mark the green heads of the cypresses; and, above all, he could distinguish the exact quarter where the house of Lavera stood.

Thinking of that, he remembered once more the strong gallant form of Guido Forseno, which during all of these years had figured through the continued stories of Lavera. He thought of Guido, and then he remembered the crippled hands and the crushed heart of Enrique Lavera, himself!

For he had gone all of this time, feeling that he had a father to be pitied and put up with. But now he felt that there was a sting of tragedy in the character of the older man. If only he could learn how to exact the proper vengeance for the wrong which had been done!

He mounted La Blanca again.

It was wonderful to see how well she knew him, after that one short ride through the rattling storm. The gentleness of hand and voice which he had lavished on her reaped its harvest of reward now as she pricked her ears and whinneyed to him. So he stood for a moment, with the weight of the saddle dragging down his strong arm—and he surveyed her contentedly.

She had everything that he wanted. There was grace and beauty and power and all the lines of speed. If only she had that other gift without which all of the rest were useless on the burning leagues of the desert! If only he could learn that she had endurance! He had a grave doubt. Had she been some lump-headed mustang, he would not have questioned that quality. But now her very beauty seemed a possible weakness.

However, there was no way of learning except by trying her. He saddled and rode her over the hills and through the gap which pointed into the long Lorenzo valley, beyond. And as he cleared the gap, he saw a sudden group of four horses sheltered among the rocks, with their riders seated around a fire where something was cooking. He had barely time to note the voice when a cry rang out. "It's Blas Lavera! Blas, throw up your hands—"

He had La Blanca instantly under way.

To escape the bullets, he had to drive her straight among the big, rough-sided boulders which were scattered down the Lorenzo valley. A single misstep meant broken bones for her and her rider also, but he noticed that she ran like a mountain goat, without fear of her footing, but pricking her short, sharp ears as she galloped.

She had barely swerved in behind the first huge rock when a torrent of lead crashed behind him. It seemed as though four guns must have begun chattering at the same instant, but though he heard the bullets whistling and singing around his head, he was in safety for an instant.

They had another glimpse of him among the stones, a moment later; and, two of them took advantage of it for pot shots—the others were busy mounting.

However, the bullets missed again, and now he dared to duck La Blanca back onto the trail where the footing was smooth and even.

She was always famous for speed, but rumor had never done justice to her, he felt, as she gathered head beneath him. With the wind tearing at his sombrero, he turned in the saddle and looked back, as she sloped into the broader part of the valley.

He could trust to her speed, or else he could try to hide in one of the side ravines. But most of those ravines were blind pockets, and he did not know them well enough to be sure. So he let range straight ahead, marveling at the oiled ease of her going.

He saw the others coming, now, two in the lead, and two more behind. They had paid that handicap for the sake of getting in an extra shot at him as he fled among the rocks.

It was no great advantage which the mare sustained. But it was enough to make rifle work absurd at a fast gallop. They would have to come closer before they could shoot him down. He gauged the distance between the mare and their leaders. They were gaining on her steadily but surely, so he shook out a bit of rein and she doubled his pace.

That held the pursuers firmly enough. They were running all out, it seemed to him, but still he could not be sure. He knew those horses, and he knew some of the men. It seemed that both of the best mounts had been in the rear at the start, for now they quickly ran ahead of the pair which had been cantering in the lead. These from the rear were Rafael, it seemed to Blas, on his chestnut gelding whose reaching neck and long legs Blas had admired so often in the past. He had eyewitness, now, of the significance of those same legs.

Under the shade of the sombrero, he could not be sure that those were really the dark, ugly features of Rafael, but he was confident that the shorter man on the shorter horse was Poco, the vagabond herdsman and vaquero who was usually out of a job, but never out of money. This was the reason for his affluence. He served the interests of the great Vega. And those who rode and fought for Vega were never without their spending money. The horse, too, he knew that he had seen. It was a powerful creature, built long and low, and yet with plenty of driving length from the hips to the low-set hocks. He had admired it, too, many and many a time, in San Pablo.

It was to be a real duel, then. For these were both famous riders, and yonder were two horses known for speed and stamina, combined. In addition, here was Blas handicapped by a lack of knowledge of his mount and her ways and her weaknesses. However, he was determined not to spend her strength foolishly. He kept her just at the safe distance from the straining horsemen, while they rattled down the Lorenzo valley after him.

The miles slid rapidly beneath her hoofs. She was dripping with sweat and it seemed to her rider that she plainly showed the lack of sufficient work. She was soft with idleness—well, she would not be soft when this ride ended!

So, husbanding her powers, he saw the Lorenzo river begin, and the walls of the valley step gradually back on either side. No matter how she sweated, there was no labor in her gallop, as yet. He came to a ditch and rode her down the near side and up the farther one. Then, looking back as she gathered way again, he saw the pursuers fly the ditch in stride and close so great a gap that Poco drew his revolver for a snapshot.

A flash of water showed before him. He rushed her at it, and she rewarded him by taking the runlet and its little ravine with a great bound. Glancing back, he had the infinite pleasure of seeing the two leaders ease their horses down the narrow gully, and when they came up on the near side, they were farther behind than ever. So far behind that they started whipping with active quirts. He watched the flash of their quirts, and jockeyed La Blanca to a still fresher pace, and still there seemed an ample store of untapped strength in her.

So, he counted her breathing in relation to the breathing of the runners behind, and he found that where she filled her lungs ten times, the cream was heaving its sides eleven, and the chestnut twelve. If she were tired, they must be more so, or that significant indication told a great lie.

At any rate, he determined to have the test over and done with at once. They were putting their nags to full speed now, straightening them out for the closing burst, and he leaned over the pommel of his saddle and gave La Blanca her head. It needed only a slap of his hand on her shoulder, and she was away with a bound, as though her effort before had been a mere pleasure gallop.

There was broken ground before Blas, but he put the mare at it with unabated pace, while her ears flattened against her neck and she stretched her neck straight in her labor. No blind running, either; for, she picked her way faultlessly through the handicap of broken stone.

For two long miles she gave her best, and then her head began to come up and her gallop, though unabated in swiftness, had a little strain and heaviness in it that told her rider she was badly spent.

Then he looked back again, and saw a sight that gladdened his very heart. Far behind him the cream and the chestnut had stopped, and Poco was dragging the saddle from his mount. Still farther to the rear, the distanced remainder of the party was coming up at a weary trot.

That moment, Blas stopped La Blanca. For a thin trickle of water ran down from a stream just before him. In that cold water, dismounting, he bathed her legs and shoulders and hips. He allowed her a swallow or two, and then rubbed her down carefully, still with an eye to the rear, now and again, to make sure that they were not leaping into the saddle once more to rush him.

The tremor in the legs of the good grey disappeared. Her head came up. And when he started on, leading her, she pressed up close to his shoulder, as though to tell him that there was still strength in her that waited only for his spending!

He continued at a walk, however, loosening the cinches to let her breathe more freely, and still from behind there was no sign that the pursuit would begin again.

Dusk was beginning when he mounted, and now he turned across Lorenzo valley and, topping a little hill, he paused and looked back. The sunset light still flooded the Lorenzo valley, and the river was a winding streak of crimson. And yonder, struggling slowly and painfully down the margin of the stream, went the four beaten riders.

Blas laughed through his set teeth. If the mare could stand off such horses on this day, what would she be when a season of steady campaigning across the desert land had tightened her muscles to ropes of hard rubber, and pinched the soft fat from rib and back? He felt as though he had the wings of an eagle to command, and so he dipped over the hill and sank among the intricate valleys of the upper mountains.

That night, he had a rabbit, shot in the dusk, for his supper. And, as he broiled it at the campfire, secure from all spying eyes, he watched the stars burning lower, and lower, down through the heavens. He breathed more deeply of the cold, pure night air, and he gave thanks to God that his boyhood had ended at last, and that his manhood had begun.

Chapter Twelve

It was perfectly clear to Blas that the insolence with which he had treated Vega had filled that worthy gentleman with an overmastering hatred. And it was old tradition in the valley of San Pablo that the hatreds of Vega were not idle passions. He had been known to spend months on a single trail, and therefore it behooved Blas to cover his trail if he could.

For that purpose, he worked his way well to the north, traveling steadily, but keeping inside the strength of the mare. He passed beyond the broad limits of the county over which the eagle eye of Stefan Gregory kept watch. And after three days in the hinterland of the mountains, he let himself be seen in a town. Not for long. He felt that he did not need to spend much time or to advertise his arrival. The thousand ears of Vega would be sure to learn of his coming, just as some of Vega's thousand arms were sure to reach after him again.

So he dismounted at the blacksmith shop and stood by while the smith fitted the mare with shoes. For that matter, he could have paused a dozen times at little crossroad shops to have had the same work done, just as well. But he preferred to stand here, or to pass restlessly from the overseeing of the work to the door, and looked down the road to the south, with an anxiously judicial eye, and then to return to the mare again.

That blacksmith was not one to waste words in idle questions. He was a little, wiry, hard-jawed fellow with eyes as bright as a ferret's and just as active. He cast a few keen glances at the boy and his actions, and then he seemed to have made up his mind.

So, Blas asked him about the northern trail, and in what condition the fords were for one who must press on and attempt the crossings even by the dark of night. The blacksmith told him in patient detail. Still he asked no questions about the destination of Blas.

He only said, as Blas mounted: "I suppose that you're riding for a doctor, eh?"

And Blas nodded gravely.

"In a way," said he, "that's just what I'm doing!"

He saw the twinkle of knowledge in the eyes of the other, and he knew that there would be much talk made before nightfall of that day. And the subject would be a young man in the plainest of travel-worn clothes, riding a horse that looked much too good for him!

As for Blas, he rode briskly out of the town and onto the northern trail.

But, when he had passed an hour along it, he doubled to the side and came back through the high hills, miles past the town. After that, he drifted in more leisurely fashion to the south. He was growing to know La Blanca, and she was hardening beautifully to the work which he demanded of her. It seemed to make no difference to her—mountains or plains. He felt half inclined to believe the tale which was current at San Pablo, that she had been captured from the band of an outlaw stallion which ranged through the high valleys of the desert far to the north. At least, altitude did not bother her, and she went up and down the steeps like a veritable mountain sheep.

They were close to each other before they came into the domain of Sheriff Stefan Gregory once more. There was no need of pegging her out at night, or of chafing her with hobbles. For he could be sure that she would not stray from him. In the morning, he could call her with his whistle, like a dog, and she would come in to him at a gallop and frisk about his camp for a moment. Then she would stand patiently for the expected saddle. And all the day, he could ride with a loose rein, watching the hills drift past him, and never giving heed to her footing. He could trust her for surety!

His days, as he traveled, were divided into regular proportions. He laid out certain hours for travel, mostly in the cool of the morning. And in midday, he let La Blanca graze in some spot where there would be shelter for her from the sun, when that was possible, while he devoted himself to his guns. He worked at them with a diligence which would have surprised those who knew him only as the careless lounger in the town of San Pablo. There was rifle work at distant targets. And then there was revolver play which was still more important—a studious effort to perfect himself in that fine art of whipping a revolver most smoothly from the holster and firing from the hip, or at the practice of whirling suddenly and planting a shot in a target which was directly behind him. Not that this was new work to him. He had done little of importance since his childhood except handle guns and horses. But there was a great difference, now. In those old days he had compared his work, complacently, with that of other youngsters of his own age, and what he could do was more than enough. But he had in his mind's eye, now, the cold, straight eyes and the swift and cunning hands of those hardy veterans who worked for Vega—or even Vega himself, with that list of dead men behind him.

So Blas worked as he had never worked before, with tensed nerves and with an anxious eye, and he found that he was improving by leaps and bounds. But after all, Vega was an enemy on the side. The main task was to get at Don Teofilo and repay him for the cruelty which had crippled Lavera.

So, in due time, he drifted La Blanca out of the upper mountains, and back into the domain of Sheriff Gregory.

Enough days had passed, he felt, to make Vega feel convinced that his prey had slipped away from him, at least for the time being. Therefore, he headed straight for that little town of which Lavera had so often told him.

In the old days, when Lavera wore the name of Guido Forseno and first rode into this country, he had found merely a crossroad's hotel with a black-smith shop and a General Merchandise Store under it. But his work in the up-building of the great Dial ranch had had its effect. The town of San Mauricio gradually came to life. There were houses erected on either side of the hotel. Another hotel arose to make competition. And other stores were built. For all the supplies for the big ranch and its laboring hundreds had to pass through the town, and it was the shipping point for the products of the Dial acres as well.

To San Mauricio, therefore, went young Blas, and he rode down a dusty street, watching the buildings with a sort of proprietary eye. Forseno was responsible for this spreading little city. Why it was larger now than that of San Pablo! It was far larger, and it was far richer, too! There was a network of streets. And here was the big station house of the railroad, and the railroad tracks, with long sidings, where lines of battered freight cars waited for their freight, or for the laboring engines which would haul them away to distant cities.

There was a bustle and a stir of life. Long teams of horses stood at the hitching racks in front of the hotels, with their big wagons behind them. On the window of one shack he saw the sign in great red letters, painted across the glass: "San Mauricio Trumpet!"

San Mauricio had a newspaper, then, among its other attractions.

And Blas felt as though a gun had been pointed suddenly at his head. He had done well enough, to be sure, in dodging the great Porfirio Vega. But now it was very likely that news of him would be quickly picked up again, and relayed to that genius, who lay like a spider, bunched in the center of a web, ready to be warned by the first tremor of the coming of prey.

So that young Blas shuddered again as he turned his back on the San Mauricio Trumpet and stopped his mare in front of the "Johnson Employment Agency."

There were half a dozen men of all ages in the office when he entered. And behind a desk, a busy fat man with a sweating face took down their qualifications.

He had an answer for each of them, too.

"The mills need you. You can feed a saw, I suppose? Can you swing a sledge hammer?—They still want miners. If you've had silver experience, you're the stuff—"

And so he went on, snapping out his sentences.

He came to Blas.

"Name?"

"Smith," said Blas in his gentle drawling voice.

The fat man looked sharply up over the rims of his spectacles.

"Smith? Well, Smith, what comes in front?"

"John."

"John Smith," said the fat man.

He looked up again, and his eye rested for a moment on the decorated sombrero, the dark and handsome face, the well-modeled head, and the neckerchief of crimson silk, spotted with gold.

"John Smith," Blas assured him.

"Well, you want work?"

"I do."

"Teaching school?" suggested the fat man.

Blas did not answer. But he leaned an elbow on the counter and waited until his silence had brought up the eyes of the other again. The agent winced.

"Don't take it too hard!" said he. "Well, what *is* your line?"

"I might do some hunting," said Blas.

"Might you?" grinned the other. "So might I. What for? Fun or money?"

"Or," said Blas, coloring a little, "I could try my hand with horses."

"That's better. Bronc buster, eh?"

"I could try that."

"Donaldson and Green both need some mustangs worked up for their saddle strings. Got any preferences?"

"I don't wish to work for either of them," said Blas.

"The hell you don't! What's wrong with them? There's nothing but Dial left. Mr. Enright wants a horse-breaker—but he likes gentle methods."

"I train them by kindness only," said Blas. And he smiled rather grimly. The fat man smiled back and nodded.

"You're too young, though," said he. "Enright never takes a man under thirty."

"A lucky chance, is it not?" smiled Blas again. "This is my thirtieth birthday!"

The fat man blinked, and then he broke into a roar of laughter.

"Smith," said he, "I'll send you out. If nerve will get you by, you'll win and stick. When can you start?"

Chapter Thirteen

What he got from the little fat man was a slip of paper stuffed into an envelope. The paper of the envelope was thin, and therefore, when Blas got outside, he held it up to the flare of the sun and read the shadowy letters without much difficulty:

"This fellow calls himself John Smith. Probably a half-breed. If you have some work with horses where no great responsibility comes his way, he might make you a good hand."

Blas smiled and was placing the envelope in his pocket when someone turned towards him on the veranda, and he saw that it was none other than Stefan Gregory, his brown face frowning as he nodded at the younger man.

He came up to Blas with the frown turning to a smile.

"I've been getting ready to demand you of Vega,"

grinned the sheriff. "How did you manage to turn yourself into air?"

"Did they kill somebody up north?" asked Blas curiously.

"They did just that, so far as I can make out, and I thought that it must be you. What deviltry have *you* been up to?"

"Sheriff," said the youth, "I have been keeping myself out of harm's way. I have been running away from Vega and hoping that he would never catch up with me! Do you think that I'll succeed?"

Mr. Gregory rubbed his hard knuckles across his square jaw.

"Kid," said he, "it don't make much difference whether you catch up with hell, or hell catches up with you. There's going to be an explosion when that happens."

"All right," said Blas. "But in the meantime, you haven't seen me here, if anybody should ask you!"

"Are you going to paint La Blanca a new color, son?" smiled the sheriff. "Because you've got to change horses before you can expect to get along without being noticed. They'll have word back to Vega in no time that you have been spotted up here."

"Well," said Blas, aloud, "I shall have to move on again, then."

But, in his heart, he knew that it meant his time was terribly limited, to do the work which he had planned.

He said: "Have you got news from San Pablo, sheriff?"

"Your father turned up with two thousand dollars in cash and bought some alfalfa land."

"Ah?" murmured Blas. He was glad that his advice had been taken in that matter, but he wondered what the result might have been.

"Some people said that Vega had a claim to that money. You know best, Blas!"

"I know nothing," said Blas. "What should I know about the money of Vega?"

The sheriff chuckled again.

"Let it go, then," said he. "At any rate, it was said that Vega paid a call on your father. And then *I* went for Vega and told him—"

"You got face-to-face with Vega!" cried Blas in great excitement.

"No," said the sheriff, "or else one of us would be pushing daisies up, just about now. But I went to his girl, Liseta."

"They haven't married?" asked Blas.

The sheriff scowled at him more darkly than before.

"That's something more that you ought to know about better than other folks, Son. I suppose that you got no idea why Liseta is keeping Vega off and postponing the wedding day?"

"Why should I have?"

"Why, lad, the talk is that after she danced with you that night, she changed her mind a little about Vega. His money didn't look so much to her."

"He has good teeth," said Blas with a yawn, "but otherwise he is not a handsome man, sheriff. Eh?"

"Well," said the sheriff, "all I know is that I talked to Liseta and told her that Vega would have to keep the fight between himself and you, Blas. He would have to keep his hands off of Enrique Lavera. And since then, he's let your father alone."

"Did you do that?" murmured Blas. "That was a very good thing and I shall not forget it. I *never* forget kindnesses which are done for me, Senor Sheriff."

"Kindness, hell!" replied the rough man of the law. "I got no kindness for you, Blas. It's only a question of how long you'll live, before you get yourself into trouble. That's all. Your father— why, that was just duty. Remember that, Blas! And remember, too, that when it comes along to be my duty to get you and bring you in, why I'll ride out and do it, Blas—or die trying!"

He tapped the youth lightly upon the arched breast as he spoke, and then he went slowly off down the veranda, limping in that leg through which Lefty Anson, five years before, had sent a bullet—that day when big Gregory found five of them and tackled them all single-handed. He left two dead. Two escaped, and Anson himself was brought bleeding back to the town, where he lived in jail long enough to dictate his famous confession, and then died, leaving the glory of a great deed to the sheriff. The whole story came swiftly back through the brain of Blas.

But he felt no fear or awe. Rather, there was a swelling of the heart and a sense of inward joy, and a fierce tingling through his blood, as though he were to engage in struggle with this mighty man on some future day and could hardly wait for that great day to come.

After all, Gregory was right about La Blanca. Her black stockinged legs and her flashing body of silver was enough to advertise him far and wide. He put her in the stable behind the hotel and went into the dining room, because he was very hungry. There was a swarm of noisy men eating there; but one corner chair was vacant, and Blas settled down with the wall at his back.

It was good to be among men again. He let the confused fragments of talk drift idly through his mind. The rush of noise, the clatter of dishes, the steam of food, threw him into a semi-torpor until something touched his heart like an electric finger, and he looked up with a start in time to see a man disappearing through the doorway. He had only the faintest glimpse of that figure but there was something familiar in the outline to Blas. He shoved a dollar bill into the hand of a Chinese waiter and left the room in haste.

There was no familiar face on the front veranda.

He went straight back to the stable, found La Blanca with her grain box eaten clean, and mounted at once. He had inquired beforehand of the trail to the Dial ranch, but now he chose to cut in that direction across the hills. For when one dealt with Vega for an enemy, it was folly to neglect even the shadow of a suspicion of danger.

A mile from San Mauricio, he rode out of a tangle of second-growth pine, and glancing down towards the road that streaked white among the hills, he saw a cream-colored horse on the near side of a thicket, at the edge of the road.

The eye of Blas flashed. Perhaps he was linking suspicion to suspicion too casually, but now, as he remembered the blocky outline of the man who had stepped into the door of the hotel dining room, and out again, he was more than reasonably sure that it was Poco who had found his trail so quickly. There were other cream-colored horses than that which Poco rode, and there were other short and bulky men, of course. But when he put the two together, he was assured that he could not be mistaken. Yonder was Poco, patiently waiting until Blas came up the trail from San Mauricio.

In that case, it meant that Poco had learned from the employment agent of the destination of Blas. And even if this ambush failed, another would be laid shortly, at the ranch itself. There seemed only one way of escaping the danger, and that was to destroy it on the spot.

La Blanca had been hastily reined back into the shadow of the lodge-pole pines, and there he tethered her. Then he started down the hollow, on foot.

He had not far to go and there was plenty of shrubbery to shelter him on the way. So, very quickly, he came close enough to spy out the cream, in detail. He needed only one glance to know that it was Poco's horse, indeed. These were the same powerful quarters, the same sloping, mighty shoulders, the same pretty head.

But where was Poco himself?

Blas slipped into the thicket as noiselessly as a snake, but as he passed her, the cream tossed her restless head and whinneyed softly; there was an instant answer, in the rustling of the brush, just ahead, and Blas, in time to see Poco himself coming quickly from the shadows, to the head of his horse, sank to his knees between a stump and a low-spreading bush.

There, gripping the bridle with nervous fingers, the Mexican scanned the hills with quick, searching eyes. He scanned them until he stopped and straightened his body with a soft exclamation. Blas looked in the same direction and saw reason enough for that start.

He had taught La Blanca her lessons only too well. Now she had pulled back on her reins to follow her master, like a dog at his heels. And here she came down the hillside, with the broken reins flying about her head, while she galloped, like a silver beauty, through the sunshine.

"Poco!" called Blas.

The Mexican wheeled with a leap. But, he left the gun undrawn from its holster, and he found himself looking into the muzzle of the Colt of Blas.

"*Madre de Dios*! *Madre de Dios*!" said Poco. "It is the end!"

"Put up your hands," said Blas. "We need to talk a bit before I send you west. Put up your hands, Poco!"

Poco drew one quick breath of agony—then his hands went up; still, when Blas stood close before him, taking knife and gun away, the eyes of the outlaw worked desperately against the eyes of Blas. But it was only for a moment. He saw his weapons thrown to the ground.

"Sit down," said Blas. "We'll have a little chat before the party!"

Chapter Fourteen

There was no one within sight or earshot. Beyond the thicket, the white road twisted in lazy curves, up and down the valley. All was silence, in the drenching waves of fierce sunshine. How easily the murderer could have butchered him and left his body in one of the neighboring narrow canons to be picked to the bone by wolves and buzzards, Blas could easily understand. No eye would have seen. No ear would have heard. And when the body was disposed of, how simple for the Mexican to mount La Blanca and ride across the mountains, with the cream attending!

If there were ever a stop and a question asked, why, he had bought La Blanca, of course!

Then, beyond the border, La Blanca could be sold for a handsome price. Now that she had been so thoroughly gentled, what would not many a man of uneasy conscience pay to have such a set of heels at his service?

All of this passed through the mind of Blas as he glanced over the valley and then brought his attention back to the other.

"I want to talk of the price," said Blas. "Tell me what I am worth, Poco."

The other shrugged his shoulders and reached towards a breast pocket.

"One minute!" snapped Blas. "Take my makings, and keep your hands away from your clothes. I haven't searched you for inside guns, Poco, but I know you have something of the kind. Now, the price, Poco!"

Poco, with a grunt, accepted papers and tobacco. And as he rolled the smoke, he lifted his eyes sharply, once or twice, and shot keen glances at his companion.

"Price?" said Poco. "For you, Don Blas?"

"For me," said the youth.

"That, I cannot understand."

"Clear your mind and get ready to talk sense to me, Poco. I mean, how much does Vega offer for me, dead or alive?"

"Nothing!" said Poco.

"Not a peso?"

"Not one!" grinned Poco.

"Only the love of Vega, eh?"

"That is all."

"And would you ride like this and work like this to cut my throat, Poco, all for the sake of the kindness of Vega?"

"Why not?" said Poco.

And he shrugged his shoulders again.

"Did you know that you were risking your own neck when you came for mine, then?"

"Ah, we all know you, Blas! But after all, a man can only die once. It might as well be while he's trying to do one great thing."

"Go on," said Blas. "I am trying to understand."

"Why," said the other, "now I am only Poco. Who is Poco? A short man with a fat belly—and a fast horse. He is good for little jobs, now and then. This horse will run far; and Poco can shoot fairly straight. People guess at those things. Even that Vega is not so sure. But suppose that I kill Don Blas—"

"From behind a bush?" corrected Blas.

Poco shrugged his thick, strong shoulders again.

"What difference does that make?" he asked. "Who will there be to ask how you were killed? I shall tell whatever story I please, if I ever have the good luck to send a bullet through your head. And people will have to believe me, when they see me riding La Blanca back. That was what I promised myself when I started out."

"And that Rafael, too, with his chestnut?"

"Of course."

"But you get nothing else?"

"That is enough. Vega would know the man who killed Don Blas!"

"So? And what does that mean?"

"That the lucky hunter would never have to worry again. He could live as he pleased. He could go to Vega and say: 'I am tired of this life. I wish for quiet.' I would have a little rancherio south of the Rio Grande. A little house, some good fast horses, and a few cattle, and plenty of goats. And enough cash to begin with."

Blas whistled.

"Vega would do all of that."

"Yes, you are worth that to him, I suppose. He does not count pesos when it comes to rewarding a great service, you know."

"I am filled with interest, Poco. Suppose that I should go to Vega and say: 'Let us be friends!' Would he treat me in that way?"

"You have killed nobody but Estrada," said Poco thoughtfully. "And Estrada was nothing but a fool. Besides, it was Estrada's fault. Oh, yes, Vega would do a great deal for you, I think."

"However, he might take it into his mind to cut my throat when I rode in to see him?"

"That is very likely, also," admitted Poco with perfect frankness.

"I have learned enough," said Blas. "Now Poco, you are about to die."

"Well," said Poco, "I am ready."

"If you have messages to any of your friends, you might tell them to me now. I may be able to pass them on!"

"No—no messages. Except, let me see! Yes, there is one for Rafael! You might give him a message for me, Senor Lavera!"

"Good," said Blas. "I shall do it, by all means, particularly since I have a feeling that I shall be meeting that same Rafael before very many days have passed. What is it that you wish me to say to him?"

"Tell him that I have remembered that it was only twenty-two pesos I owed him, when I paid him twenty-five. I borrowed that money from him when I was very drunk with mezcal, senor, and neither of us could remember exactly how much it was. You will tell him that?"

"Yes," said Blas slowly. "Is that all that you have to send as a message?"

"Yes," said Poco. "Tell him to use the three dollars in having his chestnut shod again. He is a fool to keep his horse on broken, naked hoofs!"

Blas stared at him as though a new sort of human being had been revealed to his wondering eyes.

"I shall forget nothing," said he. "Is that all?"

"Yes, that is all."

"Then you are ready to die, Poco?"

"Yes, I am ready."

"Will you close your eyes?"

"No, I'll watch it come. You have a steady hand, Blas. There is no shaking of the gun! You will become a great man, and perhaps you will even kill Vega, himself, but that I doubt—"

So he spoke, with perfectly calm eyes watching the tilting of the gun in the hand of Blas.

The sentence was not completed; the gun exploded and the hat leaped from the head of Poco.

But still his eyes did not waver and his color did not change.

"At the last minute," said Poco, "you squeezed the butts too hard. You were very angry. You thought of all the evil that I had wished to do to you. You thought of me sitting on the back of La Blanca. And so, in your anger, you pulled the trigger in a passion."

"Is that very wrong, Poco?"

"Wrong, of course. You should kill a man as if you loved him. You should do it with a kind heart and a smiling pair of lips. That makes the hands much surer—"

That sentence was shorn away, also, by the crash of the revolver, and the cigarette was clipped off close to the lips of Poco.

He did not start or shrink. Only, when understanding came to him, his eyes grew wider, and he gasped a little.

"That is it, then! Why, very good shooting, Blas! Very good shooting from the hip. It would hardly be believed, I know, if I should have a chance to tell Vega. He doesn't believe in fast work. Slow shooting and straight shooting is what he wants. But I wish that he could have been by to see this!"

"By heavens, Poco!" said Blas, "You are a brave devil!"

"Yes," said Poco, "there is not much fear in me."

"There are two things for me to do," said Blas. "One is to give you back a gun and let you have a fair chance to fight with me. Or, you can have a knife, if you'd rather. What do you say, Poco?"

The eye of Poco lighted, but it grew dark again, almost at once.

"Ah well," said Poco. "I don't know that that would be much good. I'm not as fast as you are, Blas. Not half so fast, and not as straight either, I suppose. I like time, and a rest, if I can get it, you see. No, if you want to finish me, do it now. There's no one standing by to call it murder, eh?"

"No," said Blas, "I could do it as securely as step. But I'll tell you a stranger thing, Poco. There is a disagreeable fool inside of me. My heart, I suppose. It won't let me do such a thing as this. Suppose that I were to say, now, that you go free, what would you do? Go straight back to Vega and tell where you've found me? Or try again to ambush me?"

"There is no use talking about such things," said Poco, with a frown. "I am tired of it. So shoot and be finished."

"Fat fool!" said Blas in anger. "I wish that I could. But I cannot. Go climb into the saddle and get away from me. Go quickly, Poco, before I change my mind!"

But Poco looked at him like a man who has been stunned by a dreadful blow. His color changed. His face grew leaden and his eyes wandered.

"Blas Lavera!" he cried at last, in a choked voice.

"Well, Poco?"

"I would have put a bullet through the back of your head! And you know that!"

"The luck was with me, Poco. What is wrong? Are you asleep? Adios, then!"

He, himself, leaped onto the back of La Blanca who had stood by snorting and sniffing at the air, tainted with powder smoke.

Chapter Fifteen

It was easy to get the mare safely away. She leaped sidewise, under the pressure of the knee of Blas. The shrubbery and the trees crowded between them and Poco; and, the next moment, they were scudding down the road, with Blas running the mare in zigzags, to avoid any chance bullet from the rear.

But after a moment, when the road climbed to a little eminence, he turned in the saddle and looked curiously behind him.

There stood Poco beside the cream, his hand on the shoulder of the horse, but his head bent, and his sombrero still on the ground, where it had been knocked by the bullet from the gun of Blas. One would have thought that his wits had left him, or that the sun had given him a stroke.

Blas, staring back at the other, shook his head,

a little puzzled, and then he went on again in a black discontent. He felt that he had turned loose a grim peril on his trail. But still, it had not been in the limits of his nature to butcher the fellow, after Poco had sat out two bullets with such unwinking nervelessness.

For his own part, he was already entering the confines of the great Dial ranch, and now he had other things to occupy his mind.

Coming over the southern hills from this direction, he could sweep the entire domain with a glance, and he saw that vision which had obsessed the mind of Guido Forseno alias Lavera. It was a huge circular valley. These low hills on the south were one boundary, and they stretched away on either hand, sometimes sinking low, almost merging with the white level of the alkali desert. And again, they swelled higher as they receded farther and farther away from him. Until at last they merged on each side with the foothills of the northern mountains.

That vast amphitheater had been the scene of the exploits of the Guido Forseno whom time and cruelty had transformed into the Enrique Lavera that San Pablo knew.

There were numbers of sharp-sided ravines that split the mountains and opened into the valley from the north; and, across the face of one of these, the afternoon sun glinted along a vast wall of masonry. That was the famous dam which Guido Forseno had erected at such cost of labor and thought. That was the dam into the building of which the money of Dial had been poured by his overseer.

Now it was still doing its work stoutly. In front of that wall of hewn rock, there began gleaming fields of green which spread far on either side and stretched without break long miles across the palings:

There was little agricultural knowledge in the careless head of Blas; but he knew that the entire population of San Pablo lived upon a far, far smaller acreage of green fields than these which were now under his eyes. He regarded them with a smile of satisfaction; for, after all, it was something to be the son of the man who had done these things!

He started down the road into the valley itself. He passed through the hills where the cattle spotted the sun-dried hillsides everywhere. He journeyed down into the hollow and found himself with magnificent orange groves upon either side of the way. And as he jogged La Blanca softly along, he saw a team of stout horses, sleek-sided with strength and good fare, drawing a deep-bladed plough between a row of trees, while the rich soil flashed as the furrow turned.

The orange groves stretched on and on, one even rank of trees succeeding the other. Now and again, the road beneath sounded hollow under the hoofs of the mare, as she crossed a culvert made to bridge the sluggish waters of an irrigation or drainage canal. And everywhere, he saw men at work; and everywhere, there were the glorious trees with the fruit beginning to turn from the green towards the colored stage of ripening. It did one good to rest one's eye upon such wealth. For what is more delightful than the riches of deep-rooted trees?

Now here were great trees, far loftier, with a fine open foliage and glistening trunks. These were walnuts, and a mighty host of them, too! Walnut trees in such profusion he had never expected to see gathered together. And how long did one have to wait before the frail trees passed into a strong maturity? And then, how long was it before they produced paying crops? He thought that it was some seven or eight years, but he could not be sure. But he remembered how Guido Forseno, in the planting of these lands, had determined to use the resources of Dial to establish slow-growing hosts of trees which would come most gradually into production, but which would last long, long after he who had put them into the earth!

The walnut trees ended, and here were the figs—the low, huge-limbed monsters spreading over a great stretch of ground individually; but how the mouth of Blas watered as he looked upon them! Black figs and white—and every tree loaded with treasure! They would go onto great drying trays. Then they would be carefully packed. People would eat these figs, one by one, out of oiled paper wrappers, and wonder at the richness of their taste. But who would be thinking of Guido Forseno?

No, but it was his work, it was all his work! Would the thing ever have been tried, if he had not first seen and ventured? No, the desert would have remained uninvaded by this delightful strip of greenery! Yes, and who but that same Guido Forseno would have known how to select the right spot? For there were other attempts. Up and down the face of the mountains, many and many a million had been squandered in the erection of dams which did not pay, because the water supply was uncertain, or the cost of building would not repay the investor. But Guido Forseno's work had paid. Ah, yes! One had only to look to either side, upon these grand orchards.

Here were apple trees, too, growing stately, as though they had lived a long life already. And beyond them spread a sudden acreage of grapes with their soft green arms trembling and stirring in the wind, and their tender yellow-green flashing softly through the dust which had settled upon the leaves.

Young Blas, with a critical eye, inspected the giant clusters which weighed down the stout arms of those low trunks. Each plant seemed to promise enough of a harvest to load down a single man. And how many thousand of vines there were, sweeping far and far away—!

It enlarged his heart even to think of them. He felt as though his personal wealth had been increased a millionfold.

He looked back from greater vistas to what was immediately at hand.

Besides those big groves of priceless trees, there were long ranges of mere shade trees, here and there—some on eminences, where not sufficient water could be brought for fruit bearers, but where good shade trees would grow in an abundance. And one field would be fenced from another with magnificent elms, perhaps, and along the roads and the lane grew lofty poplars, or the huge horse-chestnut, or a dozen other varieties of tree all in a handsome maturity.

Then Blas shook his head and wondered. For the story which had been told him was only yesterday, but now he remembered that the work of Guido Forseno had all been finished twenty years, or more, ago. Yes, twenty-five years before, he had ended his toils; he had left this valley green; he had transformed it from desert to paradise.

And now he lived in his hut in San Pablo while that proud and wicked Don Teofilo—

Blas drew a long breath. There was no great development of a religious nature in his heart, but he felt blindly that God would help him to use a heavy hand and to punish these transgressions.

He turned past the face of the dam. It rose to a staggering height above him. And as he examined the size of the single stones, he wondered how human power could ever have hewed them from the rocks and heaved them into their places, course by course.

No, human labor was not used for that work by wise Guido Forseno, but great steam cranes groaned and swayed and lifted the stone monsters to their ordered places, and they were cemented into their niches, one by one.

There, at the base of the big dam, were a series of stoutly built, squat-shaped structures. Men hurried here and there, about them. And as he rode closer down the road, he heard a great humming, as though ten million bees were singing together in a deep voice, far down the wind.

Those were the dynamos which had been installed by that same Guido Forseno. That humming voice proclaimed electric current, which was being created and slid along the big buried cables of copper, all wrapped in thick insulation, and pointed here and there, about the valley. Then it had been brought into the house, where lights were needed, and into the big dairy, where separators had to be whirled, and into the ice-house, where ice was to be made, and to the rails which drove from the ranch itself to the town of San Mauricio, bearing, over the private tracks, the loads of fruitage from Dial ranch, to the main steamline.

Oh, a thousand other uses for that electric power, also! It turned the huge pumps which, here and there, flooded high places in the valley, or which drained the lowlands. And in the shops, it whirled how many lathes and set how many machines groaning with effort! But for all that could be used on the ranch, there was still a handsome surplus, Guido Forseno had said, and if San Mauricio ever grew into enough of a place to attempt manufacturing, the electric giant could be rented there at a vast profit!

Well, San Mauricio had grown to the necessary size. And what was the income of Dial from this point alone? To say nothing of the tens of thousands of acres among the hills where his beef cattle roamed, or the fine pastures where his blooded horses wandered, or the rich levels where the alfalfa fields drank of the waters from the dam and gave back seven crops of alfalfa a year—or the patches of grain, rich past belief, sowed when the alfalfa was ploughed up—or the thousand other

features from which Dial could draw his reve-
nue—oh, what a king the man was who owned
this beautiful domain! And what had become of
the king-maker, himself?

Chapter Sixteen

He had not gone far up the valley when he heard a rattling of hoofs behind him, and looking back, he saw a man on a magnificent bay horse riding towards him. The riders who appeared on such fine horseflesh were beginning to excite his suspicions. But it seemed that this was a fellow with no danger of a connection with Vega, at least. He was a handsome youngster of twenty, perhaps, with a sturdy pair of shoulders and the brim of his hat furled away from pale brown hair and a pair of blue eyes that had mischief enough in them, but which appeared as honest as the day was long.

He drew beside Blas with a careless wave of the hand in greeting. Blas, running a critical eye over him, decided that here was a boy of wealth. There was nothing flashy in his clothes. They were of the sober pattern which "gringos" were most apt to wear. But everything was of the best. His saddle was of the most exquisite workmanship. And best of all, the horse which he rode proclaimed from every line: "Thoroughbred!"

Looking at the springing step of the bay and its length of leg, something told Blas that this was a speedster in very deed.

"I thought that was a fine horse, when I saw it at a distance," said the youngster. "That's why I came after you! But now—"

He waved an apologetic hand and fell back with a smile.

A few days before, Blas would have let it pass. Particularly since he had come into this place where it behooved him to appear at his best and most peaceable. But La Blanca was something more than a mere horse to him now. She was a companion, and the cut at her, casual though it might have been, was like a whip falling on the naked flesh of Blas.

He turned, on his part, with the politest of smiles.

"Some are born blind," said Blas, "except to things that are far away!"

He would have let it pass at that, but the stranger brought the long-legged bay instantly alongside.

"Did I understand you?" he asked, looking straight into the eyes of Blas.

That was the gringo fashion. No finesse—no grace—no gentle indirectness, even in insult, but a blatant stare and a challenging voice, as much as to say directly: "I am ready to make a fighting matter of anything!"

But Blas smiled again. Battle was the breath in his nostrils. But he had no intention of falling into trouble now.

"An old proverb," said Blas. "You must have heard it before."

"Humph!" said the boy, and he shrugged back his shoulders while he stared at Blas—shrugged them back as though to feel the rippling might of the muscles which clothed his frame. "I'm not very much up on proverbs—Mexican ones, particularly!"

There was another lash in the last part of that speech, and Blas looked down, unwilling that the flare in his eyes should betray him.

When he looked up again, he could smile straight into the hostile blue eyes of the other.

"There is much to learn in Mexico," said he softly. "Even her proverbs are a wisdom all in themselves."

"Mexico for Mexicans!" said the other curtly. "We get on without their—proverbs, in this part of the world!"

He hesitated just long enough before his speech to make it all-inclusive. Blas was beginning to breathe with distended nostrils.

"Each country to its own ways," said Blas. "You Americans forget your elders and their wisdom, senor. With us, it is otherwise!"

There were many people in San Pablo who would have smiled at that speech, coming from the lips of Blas Lavera. But this young "gringo" did not smile. He was the sort of flint from which sparks were struck quickly.

"As you say," he answered, "each country has its

own ways. An American, for instance, will fight with his hands. You prefer knives on the other side of the river, eh?"

Blas half closed his eyes. He was looking back, down a crowded list of battles which had thronged his days from the moment when he was able to stutter insults at the other boys in the town. He saw himself rolling in the dust with two or three biting, scratching, pommeling antagonists. He saw himself, in later days, standing toe to toe with grown men. Mexican or gringo styles of combat were equally familiar to him. He would never forget the day when he had first encountered a real boxer. His flesh still ached in memory of that occasion. But the lesson had been worth the pain.

And now he smiled again on the other.

"We," said he, "know that hands are safer, of course."

A flare of red passed over the face of the American.

"Now what do you mean by that?" he snapped.

And the last small cord which sustained Blas snapped somewhere in his soul.

"Even without proverbs, you should be able to understand me, senor!"

The other reined his bay horse to a stand and jumped to the ground.

"Do you dare to come down?" said he. "Will you stand in front of me and say that?"

Blas was standing, in the dust, in a flash. A pair of heavy Colts flashed from his holsters and were thrown carelessly into the grass. A long knife followed them.

"Now," said he, "what is it that you want me to say?"

"That hands are safer!" said the youngster.

"I say it!" said Blas.

A convulsive start ran through the body of his enemy, but still something held the latter back.

"I don't want to take any advantage of you," said he. "You're smaller than I!"

It was true. There was not much difference in their height, but if Blas was as supple and swift as a tiger, there was the burly strength of a bear in the American.

"Am I smaller?" said Blas. "However, this will make us equal!"

He stepped lightly in, as he spoke, and struck the other lightly across the face with his open hand. The answer was lightning fast—a straight-driven blow that shot full at the jaw of Blas. He dodged it by a fraction of an inch and an arm like a huge piston shot across his shoulder.

"This," said Blas—and he smote with either hand—"will teach you what proverbs are worth."

He saw his enemy reel back, staggered and astonished.

"Good!" said the youngster. "I'm glad that you know how to box. That will make an evener thing of it. Now watch yourself!"

With this fair warning, he came gliding in with his left arm extended, and his right fist poised. It was the way of one who knew this sort of business. As he closed, he feinted with the left, but Blas let that hand go unregarded. It was the right that meant mischief; and, when it came, he ducked beneath it and sank his own fist in the body of the foe.

Then he fell into a clinch.

He knew instantly that he had made a mistake. The extra twenty pounds in his foeman were all hardened muscles. The fellow seemed, truly, as strong as a bear. With one arm he crushed Blas to him. The strong right rose like a hammer and crunched against the jaw of Blas.

He felt as though his knees had been tapped from behind. They sagged under his weight, and a spinning darkness curled before his eyes.

He had barely strength to twist out of the grip of the other. And here came a bull-like charge.

Only instinct could have saved Blas, and instinct was with him, together with the practice of a thousand battles. He managed to side-step. And when the stranger whirled to get at him, he found that the legs of Blas were no longer shaking. Coldly bright black eyes stared into furious blue ones. The American lunged with all his might; Blas slipped aside from that ponderous stroke and put his own power in his good right hand. Famous was that hand in San Pablo. Men had gone down before it like standing straw when the fire touches it. Now he drove it true to the mark—the broad point of the American's jaw. It landed with cruel force. The whole arm of Blas went numb, and he stepped back to let the big fellow drop face downwards in the dust.

But there was no fall.

He saw the other reel and stagger. He saw his face convulsed with pain and his eyes dim with darkness, but still there was fight in him. He met the charge of Blas with a half-power blow that had weight enough to stop Blas in his tracks. Somewhere down the road hoof beats were rattling. But Blas barely heard them. He was too intent upon his unfinished work.

Already the eyes of the big chap were beginning to clear. His guard was again high and true, and perhaps he would have staved off defeat against any other man, but he had a relentless tiger before him, now.

A driving blow to the body jerked the hands of the American down, and as he leaned with a grunt of pain, that accurate right fist of Blas flashed across to the temple of his enemy.

Down went the "gringo." But in his lunging fall Blas himself was involved. Thick, nerveless arms grappled him. He was dragged into the dust.

"Fair play!" snarled Blas. "Is this a fistfight or a wrestling match?"

"Damn you, I'll break your neck!" groaned the other, and reached for a wrestling hold as they twisted in the dust of the road.

He had no chance. The arm of Blas was already a bar of steel across the throat of the youngster.

"Have you got enough?" demanded Blas.

"No—damn you!" gasped the other.

It needed only that to increase the pressure. Under that leverage, the American gasped, and his mouth gaped open. But still he strove to fight it out.

Then a roar of hoofs sounded around them. A stinging dust cloud struck the eyes of Blas; and powerful hands took him by the shoulder and tore him back from his prey.

Chapter Seventeen

When he struggled to free himself, a blue-barreled gun was thrust under his chin.

"Just calm yourself, my Son," remarked the bearer of the weapon. "If it's excitement that you want, you'll have your share of it coming to you, later on! You might give a turn of that rope around his wrist, Alec! How's Christopher?"

They were pouring water over the half-blackened face of the youth. They were brushing the dust from his clothes, and they were raising him tenderly. But his wits were still far at sea, and he was gasping through stiffened lips: "I'll break you in two—" as he struggled futilely against the hands of these friends.

A rope was drawn tight around the wrists of Blas.

"We'll take him on to see what the boss wants

to do with him," said the wielder of the gun. "Help him on to his own hoss, Alec. Stand by, boys!"

Into the saddle of La Blanca they lifted him.

"A fine and peaceable gent he is," said he who still exposed the naked Colt. "You can see by the cut of his hoss that he's a peacemaker. Are you Mex or white, kid?"

"By birth," said Blas in Spanish, "I am American."

"Birth being a sort of an accident, eh?" grinned the other.

And they started down the road, with the leader of the party calling back to the others to bring on Christopher as soon as possible.

"What made you try it right there in the road?" said the chief of these men of Dial. "If you wanted to murder him, why didn't you pick a better and easier chance? Didn't you know that somebody might happen along?"

He had made his voice gentle enough, but there was a world of hard meaning in his face.

Blas made no answer. He had discovered in times past that when the tempers of men are up, the best way, is to let them cool off. He looked calmly upon the other and then turned his eyes straight down the road.

Guido Forseno, as he remembered his father telling, had planned this road, which swung along at the base of the hills, climbing by easy grades among them. It had cost a pretty penny to cut it, often through the rocks, but when the work was done, the son of Guido Forseno could be ridden smoothly along it to be strung up at a tree, perhaps, when the ride was finished!

So thought Blas, but said nothing as they hurried along that road.

He took note, from the corner of his eyes, of these guards of his. They were a hardy lot, he could tell at a glance. Well-found in horses and saddles, armed every man with revolvers, and some with rifles as well, they looked exactly the part of fellows who could use the weapons with which they were outfitted. And, in the meantime, they stared back at him with hostile, unwinking eyes.

"I'd like to know one thing," said Blas, "who is that Christopher?"

There was a loud laugh.

"You didn't know?" they mocked. "You picked him out by chance, most likely?"

He returned no answer to this talk, for he saw that he could gain nothing from them. They believed, apparently, that he had decided to assassinate this Christopher, who was either of importance, or the son of some rich man. So, he shrugged his shoulders, and did not speak again until they came in view of a great house set off among its surrounding trees on a sort of plateau. The big mountains were at its back. Before its face spread out the broad plains of the valley where the water which Guido Forseno had conjured out of the mountains, was performing its work of magic.

To the big house itself they did not proceed. In the hollow beneath it there was a cluster of buildings which made a veritable town, with neat-faced cottages, surrounded each with the green of a pleasant garden, and shops, and small offices.

Not one street, but several had been planned to

accommodate the workers on the ranch. And that, again, he recognized as one of the schemes of Guido Forseno. He had heard his father go into the thing in enthusiastic detail—how Guido had planned the place, and how he had laid out the streets, and how he had apportioned to each cottage a certain plot of ground, so that every man could have his flower garden in front, his vegetable patch behind, and a little pasture room for a cow, a horse, and some sheep, perhaps, if they were so inclined. It made the village swell to a considerable space, even in the plans of Guido Forseno, but in the imagination of Blas, it had never been such a handsome reality as this.

And as they dipped down the hill towards the town, he saw the crowning stroke of the fancy of his father—a glistening stream of water which ran down the center of the main street. Tall trees grew on either hand of the little brook and green grass—the accomplishment of a prophecy.

For, those many years before, Blas remembered how Guido Forseno, sitting at the side of his employer, Dial, had pointed down the hill from the veranda of the big house—pointed down into the hollow, where the wind raised the blow-sand in swirling columns and where even the cactus would not find a rooting.

"Down there," said Forseno, "I shall make the trees grow and the water run!"

Well, it had been done, though the whole fact was accomplished after his time. But the intention and the plan had been his, and his had been the genius which had transported the water from the mountains, to this spot.

They passed down this broad avenue under the cool shade of the trees, and they paused before a structure somewhat bigger than the others, a simple, dignified building, set back behind a surface of smooth, green lawn.

They took Blas from his horse and led him down the path and through the big open double doors into a great hall, and on either side of the hall he saw doors with brass labels upon them—"Employment"—"Fences and Saddlery"—"Machinery"—"Irrigation"—

There was the brain of Forseno leaving its visible print upon the world, again. So many times had he heard of these things which his father had done or hoped to do, that it was like being carried bodily into the middle of a dream.

Every great department of this monster ranch had been organized and a central head was here in this building. Here the controller of the organization could press a button and call to his side every bit of information that he wanted. Here he could sit and issue his orders—

They came to a door with the legend "Manager" written across it. They passed into a reception room—

"We found this gent choking Christopher to death, down the road, near the dam. We thought that maybe the boss would like to have a look at him and say what's to do—"

It was enough to open the inner door as though by magic. And so Blas found himself in a quiet little room, furnished, he thought, not nearly so well as that of the second-rate lawyer in San Pablo whom he had had occasion to consult so often in his troubled life. Behind a desk sat a wide-shouldered man with a great expanse of brow above a lean, haughty face. He wore a mustache clipped close away from the upper lip, and though time had sprinkled that mustache with gray, Blas knew the man.

He had heard his father describe him too often, not to know. How he had come to the ranch first; how his influence over Dial had grown; how his will and wits had become of more importance in the affairs of the rich rancher than the wit and the will of Guido Forseno himself, even while Guido was building up the greatness of the Dial estate.

And here, finally, was the man on whose behalf poor Forseno had been crushed and cast away. Here was the man who had married that woman beloved of poor Guido. This was that Guy Enright the description of whom had filled so many hours of the narrative of his father.

He was not greatly changed from the man whom Guido had known. Except for that greyness of the mustache, and a little greyness in the hair, too, at the temples of the man, Blas felt that he would have known him as by a photograph.

There was only one respect in which his father had failed in the description. He had not done full justice to the cold and quiet strength of the other.

And yet, he had always added: "No matter what I say of Guy Enright, still there was more to him. There was a great deal more!"

"A sneaking scoundrel," Blas had cried out once. "He wanted to steal your place and your influence. He wanted Maruja when he knew that she should have been yours. And then—he wanted the money of Don Teofilo!"

"Do you think so?" Enrique Lavera had said. "No, that was not his way. He was a just man. He was *too* just. His heart was too quiet!"

And Blas could feel this, even now. A steel-grey quietness, such as comes in the morning just with the cold of the dawn, that was the thing which he felt most keenly—a sort of chill, emanating from the other.

"Is this the man?" said Guy Enright.

And Blas closed his eyes a little and drew a breath. For it was the voice which his father was never done describing—steady, level, monotonous, except for a sort of clink of metal in it.

"This is him."

"Farman, I'll talk to you. The rest of you boys may go back to your business. Thank you! I'll not forget!"

No, it was very plain that he would not forget. His steady, deliberate eyes checked over their faces, one by one, as they filed through the doorway. And then those eyes turned back to the face of Blas and rested upon him, not with hostility—but with something worse than hostility—a bloodless, fleshless, inhuman searching after facts.

Chapter Eighteen

"Now Farman," said Mr. Enright.

"What we seen," began the leader of the party that had taken Blas in, "what we seen was Christopher lying flat on his back on the road, with the dust boiling around him, and this gent on the top of him. He was like a ferret with its teeth set in the brains of a chicken, Mr. Enright. He was so busy with his work, that when we come up he didn't notice us. He didn't pay us no attention. He had a regular stranglehold clamped down on the throat of Christopher. Christopher's mouth was open and his face was turning black. He was so far gone, that he hadn't quite come back to his wits when I started on with this gent, because I thought that you'd want to see him."

"Thank you," said Mr. Enright, whose facial expression had not altered a particle during this narration. "Have you left anything out?"

"Not a thing."

"You didn't see the start of the thing?"

"Mr. Enright," said the other, "if I'd seen the start of it, and seen him go at Christopher, from behind, most like, maybe we wouldn't of had this gent riding in with us. Maybe we would just of had to tie his body on the back of his hoss! I still shoot reasonable straight."

"I am glad," said Enright, "that it did not come to that. You didn't see him take Christopher from behind?"

"No."

"What makes you think that he surprised him?"

"Look him over," said Farman. "Is he within twenty pounds of Christopher?"

"No," said Enright, "I judge that he is not."

"Does a gent give away twenty pounds to Christopher and put him on his back in the dirt?"

"I think not," said Enright. "No, I think not, unless he is a pugilist or a wrestler."

"He ain't," said Farman. "He's a greaser, as you can see for yourself!"

The glance of Blas left the face of Enright for the first time and shifted to that of Farman.

Then said Mr. Enright: "You took the guns from those holsters?"

"No," said Farman, "there wasn't no guns in 'em."

"I think that's all I'll need you for, for the moment. Will you wait in the next room, Farman?"

And Farman stepped through the door and closed it behind him.

"Will you tell me your name?" said Enright.

But Blas was silent and thoughtful.

"It will be better for you to speak," said Enright. "I know the sheriff fairly well. I know the judge, also, before whom this case will come. And I think that my recommendation might carry some weight with them. Will you tell me your name?"

"My name is John Smith."

Enright's gaze sharpened a little.

"You speak good English," he said. "What is your name? Really John Smith?"

"For the time being," said Blas, "it is John Smith."

"John Smith, will you tell me, then, what became of your guns?"

"In the grass beside the road where I met Christopher, if that's his name."

"You didn't know his name?"

"No."

"But you took him from behind—for amusement, Smith?"

"I did not take him from behind."

"I think you know our reasons for suspecting that you did?"

"Look at the left side of my jaw," replied Blas. "Is there a lump there?"

"Something that looks like a red bruise."

"That's where the right fist of Christopher struck me, Mr. Enright."

"Where did you go to school, Smith?"

"South," said Blas, and he smiled faintly as he thought of the solemn-faced old man who had put him through his paces. Indeed, there had been much school for him. For the other sons of Forseno, little, or none—but school he had insisted upon for Blas. It had been his only labor from the first.

"Christopher struck you with his fist. And that is your proof that he stood up to you and had a fair chance to fight you?"

"Yes."

"But," said Enright, "in a fair fight, in this country, men do not use strangleholds, Smith."

"Will you look at my throat?"

"Well?"

"You'll see the red mark of his hand, Mr. Enright."

"You mean that Christopher forgot himself enough to do that to you?"

"That's what I mean."

The older man leaned back in his chair, frowning slightly.

"That is hard for me to believe."

"What's Christopher to you," said Blas with a sudden light beginning to dawn in his mind.

"My son," said Enright. "And you didn't know, I suppose?"

His faint sarcastic smile did not affect Blas. But he set his teeth in silence. If he had known that— why, it would have been a very great temptation to have made that fight with something more deadly than fists.

"Now," said Enright, "I confess that I'm half inclined to believe what you've been telling me. If you'll only explain—"

There was a rattle of hoofs in the street, and then a deep, strong voice that Blas remembered.

"He is here now," said Enright. "You'll have the pleasure of hearing what he has to say—"

"Thank you," said Blas. "I'd like to be in the room."

"You shall be," said the other, "because that's a peculiarity of the American law, Smith. The accuser has to face the accused. And we'll see what face he puts on it—"

They had not long to wait.

Through the door came big Christopher and at sight of Blas he started and flushed. He hesitated only an instant. Then he stepped up with outstretched hand—

"I'm going to apologize—" began Christopher, when he saw that the hands of the other were tied.

He flushed a deeper crimson than ever.

"Your men have made a fool of me again, Father!" he exclaimed. "They've taken up a fellow who was having a friendly tussle with me—"

"A friendly tussle with you—choking you to death in the middle of the road?" said Mr. Enright slowly.

"He was asking me if I had enough," said Christopher, his red face turning to purple with emotion and shame. "And as for choking me—why, damn it, sir, I think that I had made a reach for his *own* throat!"

Blas, in the meantime, steadied himself with great effort, but the shock had almost unnerved him. This was not the way with the men among whom he had been raised. They gave away no tricks to an enemy over whom they had established the slightest advantage. And this frank and free confession from Christopher Enright broke down a great wall of preconceptions. A new sort of personal conduct was revealed to him. It was no wonder that he gaped at Christopher.

"You'd better start at the beginning," said Enright. "I want to know the facts, Christopher."

"When I get his hands freed!" said Christopher, busying himself with that work.

He threw the rope to the floor and handed Blas two revolvers from which he had already carefully wiped the dust. Two guns and the long sheath knife. They were dropped methodically into their appropriate holsters.

"I'll start at the beginning," said Christopher, "though it's not any pleasure to me to tell the yarn. I rode up after this man—"

"Smith is his name," said Mr. Enright.

"Smith, I'm very glad to have your name."

"Thank you," said Blas, and he found his hand taken in a gigantic grip.

"I rode up to him, sir, and looked over his mare. I think I made a rather slighting remark about her as I started to go back—and—he picked me up a little sharply. I rode back to him. I—damn it, Smith, weren't we talking something about proverbs?"

"Yes, I think that we were."

"And, the first thing that you know, we were down in the dust of the road, and having it out. Smith threw his guns into the grass—I'm glad that your name is Smith. Confound it, I thought that you were a Mexican—"

"Smith may be an international name, Christopher."

"Gad, sir, so it may. I beg your pardon, Smith, if I've hurt you again. At any rate, it was a fine go, Father. And I found—er—that Smith was a great deal too fast for me. I was hitting air, most of the time, and he was hitting—me! Which makes a difference, as you may imagine!"

"I can imagine that it might," said Mr. Enright dryly.

"And in the end, I got a crusher along the head. The minute before I thought that I had him. He slipped away and hit me harder than I've ever been hit before. I went down and pulled him with me, and I'm afraid that I began to maul him while he was down with me—I'm sorry for that, Smith!"

"It was nothing," said Blas.

"And, in the end, there I was, as I've said before, flat in the dust, with Smith asking me if I'd had enough, when your men came tearing in and jerked him away and treated him like a murderer. Smith, I'm dreadfully sorry!"

"Is that the whole story?" said Mr. Enright, his face as unmoved as before.

"Yes, sir. That's every word of it."

"Very well, then," replied Enright. "I think that you'd better try to learn how Mr.—er—Smith managed to turn the trick, before you let him get away!"

Chapter Nineteen

It had all been serious enough with Blas. He knew that the weight of the Dial rancherio would have told mightily against him. He knew, furthermore, that if word came to Sheriff Gregory, that stern man would throw in the weight of his authority against him. And for an attack with intent to slay—what would be the result? Some long years in the penitentiary, no doubt, and all that he could have said in his defense would have gone for nothing. For that matter, his record in San Pablo was not in his favor at all.

But now everything was brought to another conclusion. He had come here prepared with nothing but hatred for everyone on the rancherio. But now he could not help revising his opinion, a little. The coldness of Guy Enright, he had to admit, covered a great sense of justice, and as for

Don Christopher, the manly fashion in which that youth had made his admissions warmed the very heart of Blas. If he himself had been driven to a need of confessing that another and a smaller man had beaten him in a fair fight, would he have come out of it so honorably? He felt that he would not.

"The very thing that I want," said Christopher. "Come up to the house with me—Smith. We'll have a talk."

"I am a vaquero, senor," said Blas. "I came here to find work—"

"We'll arrange that, too," said Christopher.

And he fairly dragged Blas away.

Outside, they found Farman waiting, with a few others, a look of bewilderment on their faces as they saw the rescued man come out, arm in arm, with his "murderer." Christopher paused for a careless word of explanation.

"Smith and I," said he, "have found that we made a mutual mistake—a bigger mistake on my side than on his. If you had waited until I got back my wits, fairly, Farman, I would have told you that it was a fair fight from first to last. Matter of fact, Farman, you owe Smith, here, an apology, you know—"

Apologies did not flow freely from the set mouth of Farman. He merely bobbed his head a little at Blas.

"If it was a mistake," said he, "it was a mistake. But it looked like a pretty good picture of a strangling to me and the rest. All that a man has to go by is his eyes!"

And he glanced Blas over in barely disguised dislike.

"Tough old curmudgeon, that Farman," said Christopher, as they went on together. "He's honest, and he has pretty much his own way around here. He taught me to ride and shoot; taught me to hunt, too. So you see why I couldn't be too hard on him for the way that he treated you—"

"It is nothing," said Blas in his gentlest tone. "It is nothing at all!"

But as he spoke, a side glance passed from him back to the tanned face of Farman, and rested there long enough to make the other start and stiffen. He knew the meaning of that glance as plainly as the rooster knows the sailing shadow of the hawk which sweeps the henyard. He would not have to be twice-warned!

But Christopher had already forgotten; so it seemed that there could be no further trouble between Farman and his new companion. He had transferred his interest to the gray mare, La Blanca.

"She has stuff in her, well enough," said he. "I like those black points all around. That should mean something. But I think that she might have a little more in the leg—when it comes to speed, you know!"

Blas looked calmly at the mare and still more blandly at Christopher.

"I am fairly well contented with her," said he.

"Are you?" said the other, with a little challenging inflection of his voice.

"Yes."

"Now, I might point out to you, Smith, that there's a good road from here to the house. It's a half-mile, straightaway. Or, when we get over the hill, there's a fine road all the way around the lake. That makes a mile and a half. With a smaller horse, like that, I suppose that you'd want the shorter road, in case you agreed to a race?"

Blas, remembering the burning leagues of the desert over which he had ridden the mare, could hardly keep from smiling.

"I would trust her to the long way," said he.

"You would?" exclaimed Christopher. "That's a real contest. Up hill and down. And I think before it's over that you'll know what Salamanca, here, and his long legs, are good for!"

He was in his saddle before he had finished speaking, and Blas followed suit, but a little more slowly. There were a good many miles behind the mare already, on this day, and now he looked her over critically. Her ears were as ready to prick as ever. Her head was as high, and her eyes were watching him as brightly.

So he swung into the saddle.

"Are you ready?" cried Christopher.

And he seemed to Blas like a great child, keen with enthusiasm for the contest, and quite forgetting the humiliation of the last encounter. There was a touch of open-mindedness about him that amazed Blas. He knew that he himself did not possess the quality. He admired it from a somewhat dim distance.

However, he was by no means eager for this race. Those long legs of Salamanca, he feared. Besides, was not La Blanca meant rather for work in the long leagues rather than the short furlongs? However, it was through the cultivation of Christopher that there spread before him a keen hope of entering the house of Dial. And how much that was beyond his expectations such a little time before! Grimly and vaguely, almost sooner than it had begun, he saw before him a chance of ending his quest for vengeance.

So he called back: "Ready, Enright!"

"I count three—then we're off. No—Farman, shoot off a gun to start us, will you?"

Farman obediently drew his revolver. The news had spread like oil upon water. Scores were hurrying out to the edge of the long, tree-shaded avenue. And Farman balanced the long Colt in his hand.

"Are you ready?"

"Ready!"

Salamanca was dancing with eagerness, and tossing his head to get more rein, but a single whisper had set the mare on edge. Blas could feel La Blanca grow tense with a quiver, but she merely thrust out her head a little.

Crash! went the gun and Blas loosed his rein and touched her flank. She was off like the bullet from the revolver. Before long-legged Salamanca was fairly under way, La Blanca had gained half a dozen lengths, and Blas felt that the race was ended before it had begun.

However, he would let Christopher Enright learn what a desert horse could be! With the cool wind whistling about his ears, he settled forward in his stirrups and let La Blanca fly—

And then, unbelievably, he heard the approaching sound of hoofs from behind!

In San Pablo, where her speed was famous, men would not have believed this thing. And even with the fact coming up behind him, it still seemed impossible to Blas.

They rushed from the edge of the town with a tingling roar of shouts behind them, and as they straightened away for the gradual hill, the head of Salamanca came up on the flank of the mare!

From his straightened body it was easy to see that he was doing his best. But Blas would never have guessed it from the long, bounding gallop with which the horse went by.

"You have a fast mare!" shouted Christopher. "But legs and blood will tell, Smith!"

"Legs and blood!" said Blas fiercely to himself. "We'll see before the race is over!"

But his heart sank rapidly when he saw the fashion in which the horse went up the hill, widening the distance between him and the mare with every rolling stride.

They topped the hill, and as they went down the incline beyond, the advantage of long legs was more manifest than ever. Salamanca drew rapidly away. But Blas had something else to think about than the race. Before him there was a silver-faced sheet of water, long and irregular in outline, surrounded with beautiful willows and with young poplar groves nearby. It was that lake which Guido Forseno had planned. And the thin, tormented face and the sunken eyes of Lavera rose before the memory of Blas and seemed to speak to him with words.

They ended the incline. They stretched away on the broad, beautifully kept road surface which edged the lake, following all its windings. And to their right, across the water, Blas looked up towards the tree-fringed plateau where the house of Dial stood, looking down at them from its deep, narrow windows.

La Blanca was doing her best without faltering, but she was well away to the rear now—so far away that Blas could not make sure whether she was losing or gaining ground.

Now they flew past the farther corner of the lake, and a steeper hill rose before them. It seemed to Blas that as the big bay struck it, his gallop faltered a little. He had burned up the road for the first mile, but from that effort something was gone from his first strength.

"Now, La Blanca, for the honor of the desert!" called Blas.

And she rose to the hill like a bird on the wing. Those days of steady campaigning in the mountains had their effect now. To her this gradual slope was a mere nothing, and with every stroke of her legs the bay came back to them.

She shot over the crest with Salamanca not three lengths in front, and though the level going helped him again, still she gained a little with every stride.

They had a straight shot at the Dial house now, the road at the end only rising gently and disappearing among a gentle curve of trees. By the time they reached the edge of the trees, the nose of the mare was at the saddle of Salamanca. And then the final bit of slope told against the horse again. He wavered and, with that wavering, La Blanca shot ahead as though flung forward by a mysterious hand from beneath. Blas saw the strained, eager face of Christopher. And then, with a great rattling of pebbles, struck up by the sliding hoofs of the mare, he went by and drew up in front of the patio of the house.

Chapter Twenty

A white-haired man stood at the arched entrance to the patio—a tall, thin-faced aristocrat, and at his side a woman with a young face, but with hair silver-white, also—paler by contrast with the net of black lace mantilla which veiled her head.

They looked in some alarm at Blas. And then they waved their hands at Christopher.

Blas knew them before a word was spoken by his companion. It was Don Teofilo, the arch-fiend of his fancies. And this was Maruja, beautiful, unfaithful Maruja, who had broken the heart of Guido Forseno as surely as Don Teofilo had wrecked the spirit and the body of his father!

But how would Christopher Enright take this second defeat in a single day?

He drew up the bay horse, full of exclamations.

"By the Lord, Smith, it couldn't have happened!

I can't believe it! The little mare was done—we walked by her like nothing at all. And then she came again. God bless me, how she was streaking it at the finish. Tell me, man, were you holding her in at all during the middle of the race?"

"Not a bit," said Blas. "It was the weight that tolled. Salamanca has twenty pounds more on his back. And besides—the mare is desert bred, you know!"

"Desert bred!" breathed the youngster. "Well, I'd like to have another like her. Come here, Smith!"

He was out of the saddle, standing beside Blas, who had already dismounted, and now he led him forward to the others.

"Mother, I want you to know a new friend of mine. John Smith is his name. He's given me two lessons in one day. How to box, and how to ride a horse—and how to buy one as well. Grandfather, shake hands with the hardest hitter I've ever met— at any weight. It is Senor Dial, Smith!"

The gentle eyes of Maruja smiled upon Blas. And then, for a single instant, he had the cold, thin hand of Dial in his. A trembling desire came over him to crush that hand in his grip and then drive a bullet through the aristocratic head of the tyrant.

But he heard Christopher saying: "A desert man with a desert horse, grandfather. How confoundedly she can run. But you saw her beating Salamanca. She passed him so fast at the end that I thought he was quitting like a dog under me."

"Legs, my lad," said the old man quietly. "You must not go in for such a stretch of legs. They don't run horses on level racetracks out here, you know. Mr. Smith, we are always glad to welcome the friends of my son, and the men who come out of the desert!"

The speech rang dimly in the ears of Blas and in his memory they struck up another echo.

In almost these words Guido Forseno, coming like a starved man to the house of Dial, had been welcomed:

"The desert has brought me much bad fortune, senor. But I still welcome what it sends me. You have come out of the desert, and I am glad to have you with me. She has beaten you, and she has beaten me. Let us both rest together!"

Such were the gracious words which Don Teofilo had spoken into the ears of Guido Forseno, and filled him with such a joy that from that moment he had vowed a deathless gratitude to Dial. How well that debt had been paid the blossoming valley portrayed.

Blas murmured some sort of thanks. A mozo had appeared to take the horses.

"You are staying with me tonight," said Christopher. "You have to teach me a lot of things, Smith. Where I can find a horse like that one, among the rest. Just come in with me. Your pack will be brought along—"

"Senor," protested Blas, a little awkwardly, "my clothes—"

"Are dusty, and so are mine. We'll have them brushed. Now, come along. Mother, Mr. Smith is with me as long as he'll stay. That room next to mine, eh?"

"Yes, Christopher. I will send word—"

"Come in, Smith. Now, may I say that this house is big, not for the sake of formality, but big to make the people who come to it comfortable."

"Thank you," murmured Blas, as he stepped reluctantly across the archway of the patio.

It seemed to him the most important act of his life; for, now the straight course of revenge, which had been so simple, so justified by duty, now became dreadfully involved. He would sleep under the roof of Dial. And he would eat the bread of Dial's providing. And having taken on his shoulders the great obligations of hospitality, he was to repay those obligations by inflicting some dreadful form of death—as yet not even conceived—upon Don Teofilo!

So thought Blas, and hardened himself as he stepped into the cool of the patio. They were walking across a flagging of great green stones, joined with the exquisite delicacy of Mexican masons. On all sides, the flowers flashed against the wall, and the climbing vines rose in a green tangle.

They passed through the patio. The fountain waters rose through the evening shadows and flashed at the top in the slanting ray of the setting sun. The coolness of its whispers lay behind them. They came into a great hallway with the ceiling arched above them. The heat of the day was banished from this place. Young palms stood glimmering in the corners; and birds sang from a little aviary beyond.

They turned through a side hall and climbed a sweeping staircase.

"And here you are—your room, Smith. And there's your bath, beyond. Everything exactly as in my room. You see, this is the room that was to have been for my lost brother. My elder brother,

Smith. Kidnapped, my poor mother thinks. And the rest of us humor her, though we all know that he was carried off, down the river. It was flood time, that spring. However, this room is always kept like this, and never used, except when I bring a friend home. And—er—but I'll explain that, later. I want a bath. And I suppose that you do, too!"

A bath he wanted, to be sure, but he had never had one like this before! A dip in the San Pablo river was the usual way. Or else a scrub in a tin tub at home. But here there was a blue-tinted pool of water drawing into a great basin of white stone. It all seemed too ethereally pure for human ablutions.

But when he had bathed, he found his clothes laid out for him, all ready, with the surface layers of desert dust brushed away from them. He dressed soberly, without pleasure. He was beginning to feel that revenge, after all, would not be altogether an unmixed pleasure. . . .

"You've beaten me with your fists," said Christopher, as they drifted on the lake in a canoe the next afternoon, "and you've beaten me with your horse. What the devil else can you do, John?"

"I was raised with horses," said Blas gently.

"And raised to fight, eh?"

"Yes, perhaps."

"Now, will you beat this?"

He picked a broad lily pad from the surface of the warm water and sailed it through the air. Before it fell, his revolver was out and barked. The lily pad twitched to the side, and fell with a splash.

A few strokes of the paddles brought them up to

it. It had not done settling under the surface, and they could see the little round hole, not far to the side of the center.

"That's a good trick," nodded Blas.

He followed suit with another lily pad. Out of his slim fingers, it sailed to twice the height and distance of the other. It hung a twinkling instant and began to shoot down towards the water, but not before bullets were streaming from the gun of Blas. Once, again, and again, the weapon spoke; and Christopher was shouting with amazement.

"By Gad, that's fast. But *could* you hit it, when you fire so fast. You couldn't, John. Not in human nature—"

He was digging at the water with a nervous paddle in the meantime. Then he backed water with a long stroke. The canoe staggered under the might of his paddle, and stood still. The foam and ripples cleared, and there was the lily pad, but in a crumpled heap.

So Christopher reached down the blade of his paddle and raised the pad to the surface.

They were grouped neatly together, close to the center of the pad—three holes punched cleanly through the big green leaf.

Christopher, with a little murmur, drew it back into the canoe. He studied it with a frown and then he looked up sharply at Blas.

"Who are you, John?" said he. "You're somebody. Will you tell me who?"

But Blas merely smiled.

"It came down slowly," said Blas. "I had more time than you—"

He was beginning to see that it would pay him

to do some things less perfectly if he wished to keep from arousing suspicion.

"Ah, well," sighed Christopher. "They had to jam me into a university. A mess I made of it, at that! I wanted to be out here. The sort of life that you've had, John. The stuff that's made your skin as brown as a berry, you know! And that open-air life has steadied your nerves and toughened you. When we were fighting, it was like hitting into India rubber. I might knock you out of shape for an instant. But I could only bend you. I couldn't break you, you know. Well—I'll let Don Teofilo have a look at this. He smiles when I tell him such things about myself or my friends!"

Blas bit his lip. He would a great deal rather that this thing should remain untold, of course. But it was too late!

"By the way," broke in Christopher, "I wanted to explain last night, but it comes a bit queer and hard. Yet I always have to! My mother was so depressed, you know. So sad, John—you understand? Of course those eyes of yours don't miss anything."

"I hope that I have not offended her," said Blas.

"That's the point. Whenever she sees a chap about my age, especially if he's a shade older, she begins to wish and hope and sorrow. She never forgets, you see. That dead brother of mine is just as living to her as I am!"

Chapter Twenty-one

It was a tantalizing method, this in which young Christopher chose to exploit the story that evening. They sat in the patio, with its silences deepening around them. Don Teofilo did most of the talking. Guy Enright spoke not at all, and his wife but seldom. So that usually there was the steady bass of Senor Dial, still unshaken by the tremor of age, and accompanying him, the murmuring of the fountain. The rich fragrance of Don Teofilo's cigar drowned the scents of the flowers, just as the voice of Dial, and his strong personality, overshadowed all other things which were near.

But when Christopher found his chance, he spoke. "I was out with a party of Indian hunters when I got my first bear," Don Teofilo had been saying. "Would you like to face a bear with a revolver, Christopher?"

"I wouldn't mind," said Christopher, "if I could shoot always as straight as I've shot today."

"Ah?" said Dial.

"Threw a lily pad twenty feet away and knocked a hole near the center of it with a revolver shot as it was falling, sir."

"Well, Christopher. But who saw you do it?"

"John saw me."

"Senor Smith?" said the old man, and he leaned a little and fixed his keen eyes on those of Blas.

Here in the patio, listening to the voice of Dial, to his tales of hunting exploits, to his deeds with men and horses, Blas almost forgot that he was other than a youngster, like himself. And there was nothing about the aristocrat so young as his eyes.

"Yes," said Blas, "I saw it. It was very close to the center."

"A neat shot, then," said Senor Dial. "I wish that I had been there. I wish that I had seen it!"

"However," said Christopher, "it shows that all the good shooting was not done in your day, sir!"

"It does, indeed. The nerves of the younger generation are steady as rocks—when they shoot at dead targets! But living targets—ah, that is the test, my lad. That is the test of a man—when you see the teeth of the bear glisten and feel the ground quiver under you as he charges—!"

"Perhaps," said Christopher. "But when I can hit the leaf, I can hit the heart of the bear, eh?"

"One shot—who can tell. It is a rare thing to stop a grizzly with a single shot."

"Then you have to look to John, grandfather, because he threw a lily pad twice as high and as far as mine, and he put three bullets through it before it hit the water!"

"Eh?" cried the old man.

"I've said the truth, though."

"Christopher, Christopher—dear!" said his mother gently.

"Why, lad," said Don Teofilo, "there would hardly be time to shoot three times, let alone aim the shots."

He added: "But you were the witness, eh, Christopher?"

"Yes!"

For the first time Enright spoke:

"They give testimony in behalf of one another, sir. Which reminds me of the rhyme of the Oxford students in the old days. You may have heard it—

" 'Both ladling butter from adjacent tubs—
Stubbs praises Freeman, Freeman praises Stubbs!' "

"I thought that it might puzzle you a little," said Christopher with an air of carelessness which, it was plain, he did not feel. "So I brought in this bit of proof—"

He held up the lily pad, withered and faded now, but with the three holes plainly visible in the center of it.

Don Teofilo half rose from his chair, and then he settled back in it.

"Young man," he said to Blas, "that is a beautiful piece of work. I would rather have that to hang on

my walls and keep as a memorial than an oil paint-
ing, eh, Guy?"

But Guy Enright said nothing. Only his keen,
steady eyes were fixed upon Blas, and the latter
knew that Christopher's friendship had been far
too eloquent.

He had further need to believe this when, a little
later, Enright found a chance to draw him to one
side of the patio—to see the moon, horned and
slender in the east, as it rose above the patio wall.

"Smith," said he, pitching his voice under the
tone of Don Teofilo, who was again the narrator,
"you have heard my wife's father say, of course,
that we welcome the desert men who come this
way. But, as you will understand, we have to look
into them, now and again, and especially I make
it a point of trying to learn something about the
friends of Christopher."

"And you have been finding out about me,
then?" said Blas coldly.

"You see, I am talking frankly with you, my
friend. I have made inquiries through a number
of channels. The telephone is a great servant. We
have electric hands, in these days, to dip into the
pockets of information, many miles distant. Shall
I tell you, then, what we have learned about you?"

"Thank you," said Blas, more on his guard than
ever. "You will do as you please."

"You must not mistake me," said the older man.
"I have one son. My wife lives in him. He means a
great deal to me, also. Consequently, his friends
are important to both of us. I am not hostile, but
very curious; because, my friend, though Christopher has brought home a good many compan-

ions at different times, they have usually been fellows who had to look up to him, so far as horses and guns and such matters were concerned. But with you, sir, it is different. You add a new page to his life. He has formed an enthusiasm. And since I saw that at once, I made an effort to learn what I could. In a word—where shall I begin?"

"With my horse, if you please," said Blas, for he knew that if the identity of La Blanca was discovered all was known.

"We begin with the horse, then," said Guy Enright, not a whit abashed by this singular request. "That horse is a mare which was wild, caught in the mountains, and came into the hands of a great horse-trainer in the town of San Pablo, on the San Pablo river. Now, one night, close to the time of morning, a young man came to the house of Guadalupe Pissano—shall I go on?"

"Yes," said Blas.

"The young man offered the high price at which Pissano held the mare. She would, in fact, have been priceless to Pissano, except for her wicked temper. But five hundred dollars was not enough for the horse trader. He guessed that he had a man in earnest to deal with. And therefore he asked a thousand. Are you interested?"

"Yes."

"The matter of importance, it seems to me, is that the thousand dollars was paid on the nail, so to speak, and by a youth who had never done a stroke of work to make money in his entire life. Does that irritate you, Blas Lavera?"

"No," said Blas.

"This Blas Lavera had fled from San Pablo, his

home, because he had gone a good deal out of his way to rub the fur of the great Vega the wrong way. Now, Lavera, I know Vega. I have had dealings with that most illegal and most clever devil. Will you tell me what possessed you to make an enemy of him at the very beginning of your life?"

"Certainly. He was beginning to think himself a king in San Pablo. We do not like kings—we Americans, senor!"

He said it in Spanish, with a faintly sneering smile, and Guy Enright smiled also—but rather grimly.

"Very well," said he. "Blas Lavera rode away on the fastest horse in that district. There was a good deal of betting here and there among the people of San Pablo as to the number of days which would elapse before they heard that Blas Lavera had been found dead. The bets were generally odds on that he would not live out the space of three days. And yet he *did* live them out. He shifted out of the sight of Vega and all of Vega's men. And suddenly he turned up with a new name and the same white mare at the house of Teofilo Dial— back in the very territory of that same Vega! A very daring stroke, my young friend!"

"When one hides from a clever man," said Blas, "it is best to be where one is not expected to be found."

"Ah!" said Enright. "There is something in that—and yet I cannot help wondering. You are no fool, Lavera. But the sheriff says that there is apparently no girl to bring you back to this district. You were never a very great home-lover. And we cannot help being surprised that you should have come back instead of preferring to find new lands and new fortunes for yourself—say, in the northland."

"You have heard a good deal from the sheriff, then?"

"Nearly everything that I know about you. It seems that he takes an interest in you, Lavera. I think that I may go a little further. The sheriff, whom I respect as a rare good fellow and a wise man, tells me that you are apt to be dangerous, and that you are apt to be valuable, also. And he is inclined to think that you are even able to beat the great Vega, and put a period to that clever rascal's long career. I hope that you may. But, in the meantime, you do not mind hearing me say that I am watching you—with a great deal of interest?"

"I understand," said Blas. "I shall disappear to-night—"

"No!" exclaimed the other. "Do not misunderstand me. I am not hostile, I say again. I am simply frank. Though young men are not apt to like frankness. But I take you to be above the flight of the average of young men that we meet in this world. If you disappear, that wild-headed son of mine is apt to start out to trail you, and that might bring him into more than a little mischief, so I want you here. I very much want you here! Only—I prefer a game in which the number of the cards is known. I have shown you frankly what I know, Lavera!"

There was such a ring of honesty in his speech that it stirred the very heart of Blas, and what an-

swer he would have made could never be known,
for at that moment Mrs. Enright spoke.

"My wife is asking for you," said Guy Enright.
"We'll have to talk another time."

Chapter Twenty-two

"My husband," said Maruja, "is such a serious man that you may begin to think that he was never a boy. But he was, John—a very grave boy but with a good deal of fun in him. But once on a time a thing happened which for a good many years almost made us forget to smile. And now what has he been talking about to you so seriously?"

"He was talking about my home and my family," said Blas.

"Ah, then, I wish that I had been there to listen. But father had been talking so steadily that I could not overhear. We have to be patient with older people, don't we? We, with my dear father; and you, with us, John. Oh, I know you young fellows! All fire and strength, and interested in great things like work and death. But we older folks grow simpler—and very curious. So, I wish that you would tell me some of the things that you were beginning to tell him. About your home, I mean."

"It is in a little town at the edge of a river, with cypresses along the bank."

"Not in Mexico?"

"No, in this country. But they are mostly Mexicans in the town. It is a very quiet village. You would think that the people did nothing but sleep in the day and sing by night."

"I know such places," said Maruja. And she nodded and smiled at him. "I think that you must have disturbed the slumber a very great deal, John!"

"A little," admitted Blas.

"Was your father a landowner, then?"

"He had only a little patch. He raised vegetables and enough food to live on—beans and such things. We did not need much. There was hardly more than one room in the house. Do you know such places?"

"Yes," said she with a curious glance at him. "I know such places! Your father is a jolly person, with guitar in his hands—"

"No, he never sings. He is crippled—"

"Ah?"

"I mean, his heart is crippled."

"He had some great sorrow, then?"

"Yes. Once he used to work for some great people. He was a vaquero."

"That is a good, bold life! Do you hear, father? John Smith's father used to work for a rich rancher. He was a vaquero!"

"I hear!" said the old man through the grey swirl of his cigar smoke.

"But they were not kind to him."

"That was a pity," said Don Teofilo, and yawned.

"How were they cruel, John?"

"It was a matter of a woman, I believe," said Blas, "though I never understood it perfectly. My father was only a peon from old Mexico, you must understand!"

"Ah?" said Maruja in a tone of kindest interest.

"Ah?" said Don Teofilo, as though the light had been cast in a flood upon his guest.

"He found this rancher very proud and grand, but poor."

"Well?"

"My father knew the ways of cattle. What made them thrive and what made them fail. He used all of this knowledge. The senor watched and saw that my father understood. So he gave the management of things into his hands."

"And the ranch prospered?" said Maruja gently.

"Oh, yes, in a wonderful way. There was much land, but it needed the right care of the cows. And there was not enough water—"

"Ah?" cut in Don Teofilo.

"So my father bought a good water-right, and he had the water pumped to make tanks in different places. Then the cows no longer had to travel a great distance to get their drink. In the old days, you must understand, they had had to go a whole day without water. Sometimes they only drank once in two days. And the traveling back and forth from the water to the pasture in the hot sun—that kept them small and thin and they did not have the strength, then, to live through the bad winters."

"Mountain winters, John?"

"Yes, mountain winters. They were very severe. A great deal of snow, and hard, sharp winds that made the cows drop their heads and turn their backs to it and give up."

"I have seen the poor things do that! Poor, stupid creatures."

"But the coming of the water changed matters. The ground would keep many more cows, after that. The calf harvest was better and bigger. My father kept improving the stock. He had all the care of the marketing, too. And as he knew just when to buy and just when to sell, he always made the greatest possible profit for the senor. In that way, the ranch prospered amazingly.

"It prospered so much that in the first five years it was said that the value of the property doubled, and in the next ten years it doubled twice again!"

"What a wonderful thing!" cried Maruja.

"And who was this rancher?" said old Don Teofilo sharply.

"He lived in Chihuahua," said Blas calmly. "Perhaps you have heard of him, because he is so rich. His name is Estaban."

"No," said Dial. "I have never heard of him."

"Perhaps he is dead, then," said Blas. "After all, this all happened so many years ago!"

"But after your father made him rich?"

"It was a great work that my father had done. And it was for the sake, you understand, of a girl. He was in love with the daughter of Senor Estaban—"

There was a muffled cry from Maruja.

"That is enough!" snapped Don Teofilo. "Young man—"

"No, no!" said Maruja, in pain, but still eager. "I wish to hear it, father. I *must* hear it!"

"Very well," said Don Teofilo, "but—continue then!"

He sat back, and under their bent brows his eyes burned at Blas.

But the latter continued mildly and blandly, as though all unaware.

"I cannot tell just what arrangement was made between them. But I believe that when everything was prospering so much, Senor Estaban must have promised his daughter to my father—at such and such a time."

There was another faint cry from Maruja, but she said: "It is strange! But continue, John!"

"But just when that time came, a great grandee arrived from Spain, and he turned the head of the senor's daughter. And therefore my father was slighted."

"Was it wrong of Senor Estaban?" asked Don Teofilo in a harsh voice. "Or should he have married his daughter to a—peon?"

The hand of Blas clenched to a fist; but he sat in a shadow and therefore the gesture could not be seen. He was smiling genially as he answered: "I do not know about these things, Senor Dial. I should think that like should go to like. Do not you?"

"There is some good sense in you, lad," said Senor Dial. "Do you hear, Maruja?"

"I hear!" she breathed. "And then your father—it cut him very deep, did it not?"

"He was foolish about it, madam. He went back to the little town where I was born. He could

have done other things. There were other great se-
nors who knew of the clever things which he had
done for Senor Estaban. They would have been
willing to employ him and give him much money
and make him a happy place. But he would not
talk with them."

"Only fools sulk after they are beaten!" said
Senor Dial.

And there was a little glint of hatred in the eyes
of Blas. He had to look down suddenly to the
ground.

"My father was not wise, perhaps," said Blas.
"But he had poured so much of his life into the
making of that ranch that he could not take his
thoughts away from it. He could only sit and think
and dream and grow sadder and thinner every
year."

"He married, however," said Don Teofilo.

"He married my mother. I am his eldest son. He
is still sitting in the sun with the shadow in his
eyes, no doubt, just as he was when I left him."

"And he has never forgotten!" sighed Maruja
gently.

"Maruja," commanded her father, "I forbid you
to maunder like this! It will give you a bad night!"

She did not seem to hear him.

"And the girl?" said she.

"Ah? Oh, the lady went to Spain with her husband, I believe, and they live at the king's court
and are very great. And I suppose that she has forgotten that the money that put her there came
from cows!"

Blas laughed, but Maruja was pensive and sad.
And old Don Teofilo stared angrily at the youth.

"What is gold but dirt?" said he. "Many a fool with luck has dug it out of the dirt!"

"Aye," said Blas, "and has been made a duke for having been a lucky fool. And the duke's sons forget that their father was a fool. They only see the gold, do they not? That is so bright that they never dream of looking around the corner of their coat of arms to see what may be there! They would be in a great rage if anyone should say that there was only luck!"

"I see," said Don Teofilo in a tone colder than ice, "that you are one of those who have taken up with the new democratic ideas. The seeds of the ruin of this country are planted in them. However, it is a fever that burns away the grander and the older society. Well, there is nothing to be done, Maruja!"

He spoke the last word sharply, and Blas, watching her, saw that her head was bent.

"And was it a great wrong that was done to my father? Or, was my father only a fool?" said Blas.

"It was a wrong!" said she suddenly, raising her head. "It was a crime and a sin that was done against him!"

And she stood up and left them, overcome with emotion.

"What is wrong?" asked Christopher, coming up in haste.

"Your young friend has been telling a little fairy story," said Don Teofilo. "However, it is nothing!"

Chapter Twenty-three

Whatever Blas felt about the others, he began to think that he could forgive Maruja.

He went up to his room that night, listening with only half an ear to the talk of Christopher. A mountain lion had killed a calf the night before. And Christopher was suggesting a hunt the next day, with horses and dogs, to find the great cat in its lair in the mountains. So Blas agreed automatically and turned into his room.

When he snapped on the electric light, he saw none other than Poco, whose squat form was filling a chair in the far corner, a gleam in his eyes, and the polished barrel of a Colt leveled at Blas.

"Hands up!" said Poco.

And Blas drew his hands slowly, haltingly, past his hips, and shoulder high; and then, with a struggle, he raised them level with his head, still glaring at Poco.

"It is no good!" said he. "You dare not shoot, Poco. The noise would raise the house, and they would tear you to bits. You know that!"

"Do I know that?" grinned Poco. "I know that the window is wide open. That I can be on the ground in two seconds after I shoot, and there I find my horse saddled and waiting for me. A fast horse, Blas. Then, what have I to fear?"

"I cannot tell," said Blas. "If you are foolish enough to make the try. Only, I know that in the very next room to mine there is a man who can shoot the heart out of a lily pad at twenty paces, while it's on the fly, and he has a horse that is within a shade of La Blanca in speed."

"Would he fight for you, and follow me through the night?" asked Poco curiously.

"Yes, I think that he would."

"So," said Poco, "you make friends, too!"

As though it were a matter of surprise that this young man could do anything other than make enemies!

"I think he is a friend," said Blas. "If you pull that trigger, you'll find out."

"Do you think that fearing him will stop me?" asked Poco.

"I don't," said Blas, after a moment of thought. "Matter of fact, I don't think that you're quite up to a murder tonight, Poco."

The Mexican grunted.

"What makes you think that?" said he.

"Murders," explained Blas, "have to be done from behind—or quickly, while a man's heart is up."

And Poco shrugged his thick, powerful shoulders.

"Well," said he, "I can kill quickly, and I can kill after a time, also. Are you pale, Blas?"

"You may see for yourself," said Blas. And he stepped forward a little so that the light shone more fully upon him.

"You are a calm devil," said the Mexican, filled with a quick admiration. "No, I have not come to murder you. Put down your hands, Blas!"

Blas lowered his arms.

"There is no fear in you," grinned Poco. "*Madre de Dios*, Blas, if you and I were together, I would forget all about Vega. I would snap my fingers at such a man as Vega! We would steal nothing but diamonds. Gold would be too cheap for us. We would be rich in a year, if you would let me show you the way!"

"Someday, perhaps, I shall," said Blas.

"But now?"

"I am busy."

"Humph!" grunted Poco. "You will never rest easily until you have killed Vega. And I don't blame you for that. However, he is playing fairer than usual. He is not troubling your father and your brothers. They are left alone in San Pablo."

"That is a good thing," said Blas. "Besides, it goes to show that Vega has sense. He knows that there is no telling how this fight between him and me may turn out. He does not wish to give me *too* many reasons for killing him. Is not that true?"

"Perhaps it is," nodded Poco. "Give me something to smoke."

"Here. And talk softly. There are sharp ears behind that wall."

"I know just its thickness," said the Mexican. "I know everything about this house. I learned, of course, before I came into it."

"Are you as clever as that?"

"I look like a fool," said Poco. "But that is because I have a fat face. Behind that fat face there are good wits working. You may trust that!"

"I shall trust it, then."

"Ah, Blas," said the outlaw, "I have had some strange hours behind me since I last saw you. I have told myself that I am alive by the grace of the devil. But no, the devil does not love me well enough to waste time over me. He would take me when he could. Is it by the grace of God, then? And if by the grace of God, is there something good in me? Is there something worth saving?"

"Shall I tell you?"

"Tell me, Blas, in the name of God!"

"I'll tell you, then. God wants to keep you alive a little longer, because you are the most impudent man that he ever made. He is curious about you. Even God does not know what you will do or say next!"

Poco leaned back in his chair, at ease. He puffed at his cigarette, and when he smiled, his eyes were lost behind wrinkles of fat. He looked to Blas like a pig—but a very powerful and active pig, at that. A wild pig, with tusks—a match for a bear!

"Tell me what you do here?" said Poco.

"I am here to rest."

"That Vega has found you, Blas."

"Still, I am here to rest. What is Vega? Is he a

king? Am I one of his slaves?"

"The next time that you turn on the light, one of his slaves will send a bullet through your head, Blas."

"Well, you have taught me a lesson, Poco, and I shall not forget it! I shall be on my watch."

The other shook his head.

"How can you tell?" said he. "The hand of Vega is everywhere. And in this great house—who is there that knows how many mozos and mozas work here? Every day they hire new ones. Every day old ones are sent away or leave. And one of the new mozos, as he walks behind your chair, will drive a knife into your back—eh?"

"I shall sit with my chair against the wall."

"Then when he fills your glass at the table, one little drop falls into it—and you are dead, Blas. You die before the drink is halfway down your throat. And that is the end of Blas Lavera! Does that thicken your blood?"

"Not a whit," said Blas. "A man dies only once. It is as easy to die now as later. It is just as easy! Why should I care? Later, I may have more things to leave—a wife—children—but now I am a free man!"

Poco drew a long breath.

"Ah, God," said he, "you were made to be my brother. I love you, Blas, and all the words that you speak. But why did you not cut my throat, quietly, when you had me at your mercy the other day?"

"I cannot tell," said Blas. "It was not because I guessed that you could be honest towards me. It was not because I guessed that!"

Poco set his teeth; but then he laughed.

"I am not impudent. I am only polite. I was made first, so that God could improve on me and make a true bold man and liar in you, Blas. However, I have come to find out something. From such a friend as me, you will not keep it hidden!"

"Keep what?" said Blas.

"I ask you in a word: What have you done with her?"

"With whom?"

"With the girl."

Blas was silent.

"It will be worth your while to talk. I can tell you that from Vega."

"From Vega?"

"You know that his word is good?"

"Yes, his promise is an honest promise."

"Then I tell you from him—that when you give up the girl, Vega becomes your friend."

"He is kind."

"He means it. He is your friend in truth. He will make you rich. He will make all his people serve you. And his people are more than you would guess. You would be surprised to know where his men are and what they are doing, amigo! With the hand of Vega behind you, you will be like a king, Blas. Do you hear me?"

"So?" said Blas, and smiled.

"And as for the girl," said Poco, "Vega thinks that you did not take her because you love her. But only to spite him. Be wise, Blas. This is a cheap bargain which you can make with a very bad man, my friend!"

"Poco," said Blas, "let me tell you that I have no

idea where Liseta may be."

Poco shrugged his shoulders.

"Is that all that you say?"

"That is all."

There was a faint whistle outside the house, pitched low and rising gently up the scale, no louder than the song of a distant bird.

Poco canted his head and then rose.

"I leave you, Blas. You have told me your whole determination, then? You will not give her up?"

Blas waved his hand. There was no use, he knew, in making further denials.

"However," said Poco, "we all know that you have her, somewhere. She would not leave him for nothing. And who else has she ever looked at except you and Vega?"

"She has sung and danced for the whole of San Pablo."

"Danced for them, but not with them," said Poco, "and that is the difference. Adios, Blas!"

And he was gone through the window.

Chapter Twenty-four

It left Blas with something more in his mind than he could go to sleep on. He sat by the window, watching the brightness of the stars, with the room black behind him.

He thought of the whistle, and the suggestion of confederates waiting outside the house, for the help of Poco. He thought of the strange request which had been sent to him by Vega.

The girl had disappeared, then!

It filled his heart with a strange, light happiness to know this. For she had always seemed to him worthy of a somewhat gentler fate than to become the bride of Porfirio Vega. But why should they come to him with so much assurance that she is with him? Why should they ask him to give her back? Why should they do that?

But, as he closed his eyes over the problem, he

remembered more clearly that other night—how far distant it seemed—that night when he had danced with the girl, while the gunmen of Vega surrounded the hall and guarded the windows. There had been a fire, a sort of wild joy in her eyes as he recalled it.

Yes, perhaps that had made it more difficult to face life as the bride of Vega. He prayed to the just God that it might have had that influence.

And then a little swirl of madness passed through the brain of Blas, and he was on the verge of breaking into loud laughter. He wondered at himself, and at the very joy which had him by the throat.

However, the sleep of Blas was very light, on this night. And when the heavy hand of Christopher beat on his door the next morning, he sat up with a groan of weariness.

There was nothing for it but to join the hunt, however.

They worked with the patient dogs all through the morning, losing the trail over and over again, but when all the rest of the hounds were at fault, a little yellow mongrel cur was the one always to solve the trail problem.

So, finally, they worked their way into the hills, and Blas saw the pack close on the tawny monster, and saw it break through them, leaving a trail of mangled dogs behind, and get into the dark recesses of a cave among the rocks.

Then Christopher crawled with his rifle pushed before him into the blackness of that cave; and Blas, sick at heart over such work as he had never seen before, followed as closely as he could force himself to creep. Finally, two glimmering balls of phosphorescent light showed dreadfully close to them as they rounded the elbow of a rock.

The rifle of Christopher exploded with a mighty roar in the cave, but with a snarl, the beast flung itself towards them—straight at Christopher, and straight into the stream of bullets which Blas was pumping from his Colt.

At that distance, the big .45 caliber slugs would have smashed their way through steel plate. The mountain-lion struck Christopher, indeed, but struck him as an inert mass, unable to endanger him with even a dying kick.

When they dragged the body to the open air, they found that the rifle ball of Christopher had gone straight to its mark. It had glanced down from the head of the puma, and ranged back through its entire body, before it issued near the right hip.

Certainly it was wound enough to take the life of half a dozen cats, but dreadful though the hurt had been, there was still enough energy left in the big cat to make a dying struggle. And the dying struggle of those mighty jaws and those heavy forepaws could have ripped Christopher into shreds.

However, there was a very clear explanation for the absence of harm to Christopher.

Blas had managed to put in four shots, as fast as his trigger finger could work; and, in the half-light, he had found the target with each one.

The face of the puma was literally blown to pieces; its brain was shattered to shreds, and only a dead body landed from the air on the son of Guy Enright.

So they wiped the blood from Christopher; but, it was Blas who received the compliments. As for Christopher, himself, he was too moved to talk a great deal. He did not have a chance to attempt much before his companion said:

"Chris, listen to this, will you? When I crawled down that dark hole with you, I was shaking. I'd never done that sort of work before, and I never want to do it again. When you spotted the cat, I wanted to yell, I was so scared. You brought me back to life by shooting it. And after that, I acted automatically. And I'll tell you this on my honor. I didn't stop to think where it was heading. I thought of only one thing—that it was aiming at *me*, and that I had to stop it or be clawed to bits. Well, Chris, I've seen a cat make away with a rat. I thought of that ripped and tattered rat, and you can bet that was why I shot fast and straight, I *had* to. But get this rooted pretty firmly in your mind. It was for myself that I was shooting. And you hand your thanks on to the next man, who deserves them."

It made Christopher smile; but, apparently, it did not change his mind, though he said no more about it.

Neither did he talk about it during the lunch they ate when they got back to the house that afternoon. But afterwards, he must have talked eloquently enough, for while Blas lay stretched on a couch in his room, using that siesta hour to daydream, with his hands folded behind his head, there was a tap at his door and Maruja Enright came in to him.

She sat down in a chair beside the couch and looked gravely at him.

She would not let him sit up. She pressed him back, smiling.

"My own boy is resting," said she, "or trying to rest, if he can get the picture of that dreadful thing out of his mind. Ah, John, he has told me everything—!"

Blas would have made a little disclaiming speech, but she lifted her hand.

"Don't you understand?" said she. "We've lived in daily terror. If there's white water in a river, he has to swim it. If there's a desperate chance to be taken in climbing a cliff, Christopher has to take it. If there's a wild horse to be ridden, it's the neck of my Christopher that has to be risked. And if we won't let him do what he wants while he's at home, why, he would leave us and go where he could be wilder and freer still!

"Do you understand me, John?"

"Yes," said Blas.

"There is something in him that lives for the sake of the dangers that he can find out. And he is constantly at work doing his best to make trouble for himself. That is his way of amusing himself, John. He knows that it breaks my heart, though I try to keep from showing it. He tries to control those impulses, but when the time comes, and when he sees the black mouth of the mountain-lion's cave—he can't remember his mother. He can only remember that the thing he loves most in the world is calling to him—danger, danger!

Oh, John, he would give a fortune to be able to rub elbows with death for five seconds running!"

It was true enough. Blas, thinking back to all he knew of the youngster, could see that it was correct. And that was the thing which set Christopher apart from other men. It was the pale fire that was so often in his eyes. It was the glaring light which had challenged Blas on the first day, and driven them into a desperate fight for no reason whatever.

"Other men will not stay with Christopher," said the mother. "He shames them. Sooner or later, their nerve begins to give way, under the dreadful series of strains that Christopher puts upon them. They have to leave him or lose their self-respect—and his! Besides, everything is a contest with him. He wishes to excel everyone. We only thank heaven that, so far, he has never gone on a man trail. God help him and us when that time comes! Because sometimes it seems to me that come it must!

"And now, John, do you know what I mean when I say that I begin to thank the kind God that sent you to us? For Christopher is beginning to lose all hope of excelling you. You are simply the perfect man to him—not to be rivaled, but to be imitated from a great distance, if he can. And if you are contented to be quiet, he is more contented, too. Because what you do, must be right! So, for our sakes, you are going to give up your own roving for a while and live here quietly with us?"

"I wish to make you happy," said Blas.

He sat up and looked straight into her troubled eyes.

"I believe you," said Maruja. "And as long as you are with him, our hearts are easier. I know that when he goes out by himself he has only, say, one chance in three of coming back, unharmed. John, John, already nearly every bone in his body has been broken in one way or another! But now when he goes out, I know that there is another great chance of safety added—because you are with him!"

She was too deeply moved to remain much longer with him. He saw the tears in her eyes and followed her helplessly to the door. Then he sat down with a strange sense of not unpleasant melancholy in his heart.

For it was very strange, it seemed to Blas.

Those many long years ago, his father had come to this house and had begun the building of the great fortune of Dial.

Now he himself rode on the same trail to take revenge for the crime against Guido Forseno. But instead, he found himself taken into the machine of the household, and used there as an important cog—for the service of the family—for the service of the heir of that same Dial!

It looked to Blas as though a peculiar and ironical fate was in the thing. He smiled half sadly, half happily. He was beginning to feel that it was useless for him to plan and think; but that a current was setting beneath him, and carrying him along, he hardly knew where. He could trust himself to it. No matter where it bore him, he had the surety that it would carry him into adventures wild and strange enough to satisfy the heart of even a Christopher!

Chapter Twenty-five

Light of a new kind fell upon the figure of old Senor Dial on the evening of the next day.

They had walked out from the patio to take a stroll beside the walk—Maruja and Don Teofilo leading, and Blas with Enright and his son behind. But as they passed through the arch of the patio entrance a shotgun roared, and a load of heavy slug whistled past the head of Dial and raked the wall.

A revolver flicked instinctively into the hand of Blas, but he had no chance to use it. Dial, with a lightning stroke of his walking stick, cut the would-be assassin across the arms. The shotgun dropped to the ground, where the remaining barrel exploded and blew a wide furrow through the grass. He who had carried the weapon shrank away as though to flee, but then, as though he knew that he could not escape from the fleet feet of Blas and Christopher, he drew himself up and remained standing, rubbing his bruised arms and staring blankly at the group.

He was a grey-headed Mexican of the lowest class, round-faced and dressed in ragged white clothes; his Indian blood told in the impassive face with which he watched the others. Christopher had him by one shoulder, now, and Blas by the other.

But Dial said quietly: "Let him be, for a moment. Take your hands from him. Do I know you, my friend?"

"I am Pedro Onate. I keep a flock of your sheep in the hills," said the other.

"You came down here to kill me, Pedro."

"It is true, senor."

"For this, you will be shut up in a prison."

"It is true, senor."

"However, there was a reason for this murder, was there not?"

"Yes, senor."

"Tell me everything."

The shepherd looked to the ground, and then to the sky, to find his words.

"I had a son, Mateo," said he at last. "He came down to be a vaquero and ride herd on your cattle, senor."

"I remember him," said Guy Enright. "He stole a wallet from one of the cowpunchers and was sent to jail for it. Six months he got. He should have had two years for such a sneaking trick."

"Is that true?" asked Don Teofilo.

"It is true that he was sent to prison. But it was not true that he stole."

"The wallet was found on him," said Enright.

"It was put there by the other man," said the shepherd.

"Stuff!" said Enright.

"Let him alone," commanded Dial. "Tell me your own story, Pedro."

"My son had won a little money—a few pesos—at dice, from Ignacio. That was the name of the other vaquero. And Ignacio was angry and so, he put his wallet in the pocket of my boy and called him a thief."

"Where is this Ignacio?" asked Dial of Enright.

"Discharged."

"Continue," said Dial, to the shepherd.

"When my son came from the prison, he tried to find work. But men knew that he had been called a thief. They would not have him. His wife was sick. He had no money. I had given him all that I could get. And so, Mateo went out to find more money. He could not get work. So this time he stole. He was taken again. His sick wife heard what had happened and it broke her heart also. She died. My boy was sent to prison again. His children are beggars in the streets and are starving. I saw that all this ruin had been done by Senor Dial's wish. So I took that gun and came here. I was ready to die also."

Don Teofilo leaned upon his walking stick.

"What shall we do with him, Guy? Is this a true story?"

"The lamest thing that I've heard of," said Enright. "Let the law take its course with him. The law is a little wiser than we are, sir."

But Dial shook his head.

"What he says is true. You forget the thing which I have always known and which Forseno always knew in the old days. That these people are children and have to be treated as such. Pedro," he added to the old man, "I believe that you have told the truth to me. Much harm has been done. As for your life and mine, we are old men and do not matter. But a woman has died and children are suffering. Take this money. Go find your grandchildren and take them to your house. As for your son, we shall see if he can be pardoned if his debts are paid. Then he shall come back to work for me. I believe that he may be a good man. We shall see! Come, Maruja. The pleasantest time of the evening is still before us!"

He paused only to drop a little sheaf of bills into the hand of the stunned peon, and then he moved on, and Maruja walked at his side.

The world of Blas was falling about his ears. This was not a side of the nature of Dial that had ever been turned to his notice. And the world was falling about the ears of old Pedro, also. He gaped after the party as one who has seen a miracle and still cannot believe his eyes, though he clutched the treasure with both his hands.

But here was the voice of Christopher saying: "That's the Dial way, father!"

And Guy Enright said quietly: "Perhaps it's the right way, too. To the last day of my life, I shall be a stranger in this land! But Maruja understands these things. Listen to your mother, Christopher!"

They listened, and they heard her saying—no,

not a word concerning the sudden death which had looked her father in the face and which he had escaped by chance and the speed of his strong old arm—but she was murmuring happily:

"When that cloud in the west turns red, then there will be a lovely light over the lake, Father. Shall we take a canoe?"

Christopher and Guy Enright looked at each other and shook their heads, but Blas understood. She had seemed a foolishly sensitive creature before this moment. But now he could see that there was the strength of steel in her, as well.

Guido Forseno, in those old days, had not chosen wisely, perhaps, but too well! And the first doubt entered the mind of Blas. If this woman had ever loved Forseno and had promised herself to him, was it not strange that even the authority of her father could have induced her to change to Enright at the last moment?

So, full of thought, Blas came back from that walk. They were sitting in the patio when Dial turned to his daughter, with a faint tremor in his voice: "We must have some music. Will you sing, Maruja?"

"There is something better for you," said his daughter, smiling. "There is a new house moza, hired yesterday, I believe, and she knows how to sing. You like the old Mexican songs, Father, and she can sing them, I think."

Blas, listening, regarded the words only vaguely. And then, a moment later, his glance fixed on the flagging, he saw only the feet of the moza as she walked out. But it was such a free and light and graceful step that the heart of Blas lifted a little and he looked up.

He could not see her face. She had taken her stand against one of the thick pillars at the farther side of the patio. On the ground beside her crouched an old fellow whose coppery skin told of his blood. He struck the strings of the guitar, and the voice of the girl floated softly through the evening quiet and melted and lost itself in pause, and trailed almost drowsily through the old wailing chant.

Blas lifted his head, with his nostrils quivering. He had heard that song many a time before. It carried to him the sudden sights and the sounds of San Pablo, the evening at this very hour, when the coming beauty of the night kept the tired workers from their beds, and when even the dogs forgot to snarl and quarrel over their bones; and when the voices of the children, as they played in the dust, threw up the only discordant notes. In such a time, the men and the young girls of San Pablo sang. And such a song as this was sure to rise and go pulsing softly through the shadows and fill the heart with an ache of joy and of longing.

Don Teofilo, lying back in his chair, let his cigarette burn to a long ash that dropped over, unregarded; and still he smiled with closed eyes, and listened.

When the last note had died, he said:

"Maruja, that girl can dance, also. She has the beat and the swing of the dance in her throat. But tonight we will have the singing only. You have found a treasure for me. *Madre de Dios*! *Madre de*

Dios! It carries me back how far—! How far! I see the face of your mother as it was on the first day that I saw her. Well, the world is kind! There is no real sorrow, even in old age. Let her sing again."

The word was given, and the guitar clanged with a sudden stroke of power. Out above its jangle and snarl leaped the voice of the girl. It thrust like a sword flash in the eyes of Blas.

And he stiffened in his chair. A hand of a fierce happiness gripped his heart. There was something that he remembered—either the song, or the singer.

No, not the song. It was a song of the trail and of fighting. It launched forth like the flight of an eagle. It carried one's heart to the central heavens, like a great beating of wings.

And it ended on a rising note, with the same savage abruptness with which it had begun.

"Did you understand, Guy?" asked Don Teofilo, his eyes still closed.

"Not a word!" said Enright. "What was it all about?"

Senor Dial looked slowly up to the sky and smiled. He made no answer. But Blas had risen and had stepped through the shadows until he could see her face.

It was Liseta!

Chapter Twenty-six

It was not that Liseta with whom he had danced the other day in San Pablo. Her finery was gone, now. The mantilla flowed over her head and fell in a delicate fretwork across her shoulders. The dainty slippers were gone, and now her sun-browned feet were in huarachos—huarachos ridiculously small. The jewels were gone from her throat, too. But a pendant of cheap red glass glowed faintly beneath either ear.

Her face was as though cut in stone. Even her eyes seemed dead, as she looked straight down to the ground before her and waited for further commands.

Blas drew back, softly as a cat slinks through the shadows. And now, in the black, safe darkness of another pillar, nearby, he could watch her by the demi-light, with no fear of being seen. No one must see his face; and she, least of all. There was too much to be read in his eyes, and he knew it!

Maruja had asked for another song. There was a slight sign of the hand from the singer to the accompanist, and Blas saw the old musician raise his ugly face and look up to the girl with an expression of savage worship and delight.

She did not leave her place against the pillar, ghostly dim, when the guitar began. But she raised her right arm slowly. It shone glimmering. So still was it held that the highlight did not tremble on her skin.

It is a song of the distant southland. The mist rises like a frosted breath across the green face of the forest. The ancient temple crumbles against the face of the cliff. What do the pictured stones say? It is love that they speak of. It is love that rises like a mist from the earth and links man with God.

And here in the patio of the house of Dial is Liseta, like a priestess of a vanished race!

Blas Lavera listened and closed his eyes. He went back to his place and, by a gigantic effort, made his face calm.

"She should be on the stage, that girl," Guy Enright was saying in his deliberate, authoritative manner. "There is money in that voice of hers! Let's have another song from her, Maruja!"

But old Dial lifted his age-thinned hand.

"There has been enough to hear and remember. Do not drain the cup at the first taste, Guy."

And again Blas knew the mind of the old man and sympathized with it with all his heart.

Dial and Maruja went into the house with Enright. Christopher, stretching out his mighty arms, yawned. "Singing, talk, singing—rot!" said he. "What a life! My God, John, you and I would die in this place. We must find something to do. I'm going to sleep on it. I'll have an idea for us in the morning!"

He was gone, with the others. How little of the blood of Dial had come down to this descendant! No, Christopher was truly the son of his father! It seemed to Blas that he could understand why the death of her first son had left in the heart of Maruja such a void, never to be filled!

The guitar and its player were gone, and the girl with them. But Blas himself remained in his chair and watched the burning of the stars with a sad, unquenchable delight. Or he closed his eyes, and the stealthy wind of the night wafted to him the unknown fragrances from the flowers that slept beside the wall, or lifted the slender shadows of their heads, higher up, against the stars themselves.

Then he became conscious of something stirring behind him—something softer than the sound of any drawn breath, something fainter than the beating of a heart. But since his last experience with Poco, his nerves had been drawn more taut than the string of a bow.

He left his chair with the leap of a panther, springing into the shadows, gun in hand. But there was the shadowy form of a woman!

He brushed the mantilla from her face. "Liseta!" he exclaimed joyously.

"Hush!" said the girl, and she laid her finger on her lips.

A footfall sounded within the house, and then a heavy heel gritted on the flagstones of the patio.

"John!" called the deep voice of Christopher.

He had his idea, his plan for action, and he had come to reveal it to his newfound foster brother. But Blas made no answer.

"John!" called Christopher again, louder, this time.

Another instant of silence, and then: "He's gone off into the night, the wildcat!"

And Christopher laughed softly, to himself, and went striding farther out into the darkness.

"You are not smiling, Liseta?"

Even then the face of the girl remained as stone, and she shook her head.

"I understand, then," said Blas. "You are sorry that you came?"

She made no answer.

"Vega still wants you and waits for you," said Blas. "It is not too late for you to go back to him—"

At that, she raised her wide, dark eyes, and looked him in the face. And Blas caught his breath.

"But it is too late for Vega," said he. "I have you now!"

He took her in his arm, and so he brought her face close to his, but still it was a face of stone.

"And the things that I take, I keep, Liseta. Do you hear me? Are you dreaming?"

"No, but I'm thinking."

"Well, of what?"

"Of you, Blas."

He leaned in a sudden tremor of delight, but she

shook her head, and somehow, he could not kiss her.

"Now tell me why you are like ice?"

"Because I see that I was a fool."

"In coming here to me?"

"Yes."

"I don't care much for your thinkings, Liseta. Now that I have you, I shall keep you no matter what you think. Do you know that?"

"Yes, I know that—"

He would have kissed her again, but her dark quiet eyes were so busily reading his face that he could not touch her lips.

"Then tell me why you are a fool."

"That wise young Don Cristobal. He knows!"

"He knows nothing about me, or about anything else."

"He knows a great deal about you."

"Tell me how you are so sure."

"He called you by your name."

"Is my name John?"

"He called you a wildcat, Blas. That is what you are! When you sprang at me out of the chair, a moment ago—that was what you were! How close were you to putting a bullet through my heart?"

"A tenth part of a second."

She nodded, still watching him gravely.

"How long will it be, then, before they kill you?"

"Never, Liseta!"

"No, it will not be very long."

"Why do you say that?"

"A wildcat dies young, when he begins to kill sheep. They go out with dogs and rifles. They find it and they kill it, and they bring back its skin and make a little rug out of it!"

"Will they tan my skin, Liseta?"

"They will keep the memory of you, however, which is the same thing. There will be a dozen men, all famous because they took part in the killing of you! You will be famous, too. But what good is your fame to me when you are dead?"

"Shall I tell you what I shall do?"

"Yes, tell me."

"I shall go to the far, far south, where people have never heard of the name Vega. I shall go to that land of which you were singing in the last song."

"Well?"

"There I shall become a farmer. Everything shall be quiet—"

"A farmer? Bah!" said she.

"I shall, however."

"What do you know of farming?"

"Well. I shall do something else."

"What can that be?"

"I can hunt and trap."

"Yes, you could do that. But very soon you would stop hunting for fur, and begin hunting men. I know you!"

"I am no devil!"

"Do you think that I would have followed you here, if you were not?"

"Then, if I am a devil, I shall be glad of it!"

"But do you mean that you will go away with me, Blas?"

"Yes. If you kiss me, Liseta. I shall go, then."

"I shall not kiss you. Not until you promise to start away with me the next moment."

"And leave this place?"

"Why not? Is it your house? No, no, it is only a trap where Vega will catch you!"

"Listen to me. There is only one little thing that I have to do. When that is done, I shall go with you. Do you believe that?"

"Perhaps I do. I think you mean it, now. Who is the man you must kill?"

He started.

"I have not said it was to kill."

"But I know!"

"*Por Dios*, Liseta, you are so beautiful! Who taught you to wear that red flower in your hair?"

"The same devil that taught you how to kill men!"

"That red flower—it is burning and blossoming in my brain, Liseta. And—"

He pressed her suddenly to him and bowed his head above her.

There was a sudden chattering of guns, through the distant night, and then a tingling scream of pain.

Chapter Twenty-seven

The shots and the scream brought Blas quickly enough to the patio entrance, and there he heard a man come screaming through the dark towards him. He passed Blas, yelling with terror and woe. And the iron hand of Blas gripped him and held him, helpless.

"What has happened?"

"Don Cristobal! He is dead! He is murdered! God deliver us all—"

When Blas heard those words a mist of darkness blew across his brain. He flung the peon from him and sprang off into the night.

He had never realized, before, that Christopher was so dear to him. But now he felt as though his blood-brother lay dead, yonder in the darkness.

He could find the spot as easily as though a light were shining on it, there was such a clamor from it. A cluster of peons must have been close at hand when the shooting took place, for now they were scurrying, everywhere.

And lights, in fact, were being lighted as he approached. And, above the shouting, he heard a sudden stentorian voice ringing: "Stop this damned noise! You'll kill him with yelling!"

The sound of that voice was a sweet thing to the ear of Blas, for he knew that it was Christopher who had spoken, and it was not the voice of a man on the point of death!

Christopher dead? No, by the time that Blas came up, he found Christopher on his knees beside a man who lay prone on the ground, with a great bandage, made of torn-up shirts, being wound around his breast, by Christopher himself.

And the man who lay there was that dark-faced Rafael, who had ridden out upon the long trail of Blas in company with Poco.

"Here you are, John!" cried Christopher. "Beg gar took a shot at me while I was lighting a cigarette. By luck I saw something glisten as I was standing there, match in hand. I jumped sidewise and I drew at the same time. By the grace of good luck—and some of the revolver practice that you've been putting me through lately—I managed to down him. Will he pull through?"

He was sweating with eagerness and work as he spoke, laboring as earnestly as though a dear friend and no murderer lay on the ground before him.

"I am done," said Rafael suddenly and calmly. "Your bandage only tortures me. Let me be in peace, senor!"

Blas, standing over the fallen man, noted the place of the wound and the way the blood kept pressing out through the layers of bandage and leaving the broad red spot upon the cloth.

"It is finished, Christopher," he said. "There is no use bothering him."

There was an exclamation from the man on the ground.

"Ah, there you are, amigo!" he called to Lavera.

"*I* am here," said Blas sternly, and he looked the doomed man in the eye.

"Give me a cigarette," said Rafael. "Somebody prop up my head. So, that is better. A cigarette!" And he snapped his fingers imperiously.

So a cigarette was rolled for him by the lightning fingers of Blas. It was placed in his lips and lighted, and he drew in a great breath of smoke and lay there for a moment.

Then he smiled.

"That is better!" said Rafael. "You, senor—I am rather glad that I did not kill you. It was meant for him!"

"For John?" asked Christopher with innocent excitement.

"Is that his name?" sneered Rafael, and he turned his dark, sardonic eyes upon Blas. "Is his name Juan, now?"

"What else?" demanded Christopher in anger. "You would have killed him, then? Now, by God, I'm glad that it was my chance to strike a blow for you, John—you've struck enough for me—and at me!"

He smiled quickly as he spoke, and looked across to Blas with shining eyes.

"Tell me," said Blas.

"Ah, you?" sneered Rafael. "What do you want of me?"

"I want to know only this. If Vega sent you after me why did you try to murder Don Cristobal Enright?"

"That is his name? He is the heir of the great Don Teofilo, then?"

"Yes."

The outlaw, with a great sigh, half closed his eyes.

"That would have been a way of making myself remembered—if I had killed him!" said the rascal. "Well, why should I tell you why I made that mistake?"

"Because it makes a good story, Rafael. And that *also* will be remembered. They will want to know all about it in San Pablo, eh?"

He considered this a moment this a moment then he spoke reflectively:

"Aye, they will want to know there. Then I'll tell you. Though if you have eyes, you can see for yourselves." Indicating Christopher he went on. "When the match flared inside of his hands and threw the cone of light upon his face, I thought that it was you, and I started to pull my gun—"

"You thought he was I? Then you were drunk, Rafael!"

"Was I drunk?"

"He is twice my size—and blue eyes—and light hair—"

"Who sees the color of eyes and hair at night?" snarled Rafael. "You talk like a fool! I saw his face, and that was the same as your face. If he was bigger—I hadn't the time to make measurements. You've always looked big enough to me—and if my gun hadn't hung in the leather, I would have killed him. And when you ran down through the dark to find him, I would have killed you, too, like a pig at the slaughter season!"

He nodded his head, a little, and grinned up to them in a ghastly fashion.

"As a matter of fact," said Blas, "I would have been a fat prize for you, Rafael. And it has been a long trail, eh?"

"I have ridden more than two thousand miles for you," said Rafael calmly. "I have worked myself and my horse like a dog, and this night I should have had you—except that a gun hung in the leather for the first time in my life. The devil helped your friend. He knew that it was not the right target, and that was what killed me! But you, Senor Enright, where did you learn to shoot from the hip, like that?"

He looked curiously at Christopher.

"My friend John," said Christopher, and pointed with a faint smile to Blas.

The brow of Rafael turned darker.

"And then I owe this to you, after all?" said he. "I thank you for that, Blas! Well, I shall not go to hell long before you—"

A stream of noisy voices headed towards them, through the night.

"God let me die before they come to stare!" said Rafael, and he set his teeth in rage and hatred of the whole human species.

Christopher dropped on his knees beside that dying man.

203

"Consider, Rafael," said he gently, "that you have not long. Speak to me as if I were a good friend. I shall be better than perhaps you expect. Tell me what you wish from me. Messages—or someone who is dear to you, Rafael, that I may—"

"Bah!" sneered Rafael. "Do you think that I'll weaken, now, and begin to pray and call for a priest? No, I've bought my medicine, and now that the time comes to swallow it, down goes the dose. I want no messages. I have no friends—except the horse. And I know who will get him!"

He looked, wild askance, at Blas.

"If Poco had stood by me to the end," said he, "his gun would have brought this great hulk down, even if mine failed to do the good work. And now Poco will have my horse besides his own cream. The devil damn him black! I hope that he meets you. Blas, I hope that you have a fair chance, gun to gun, with Poco. Because I know how that would end. Only live long enough to send him before you to see me. And then come after—yourself—and you'll find me waiting—at—the—door, Blas!"

His voice choked away. His livid face was convulsed, but he recovered for a single instant more.

"Blas!"

He leaned at that whisper close to the dying man.

"Two are easier to catch than one. You will lose her because you have found her!"

He stiffened, threw out his arms, and suddenly his empty eyes, devoid of life, were staring at the stars.

Guy Enright, with a dozen of the servants of the

house behind him, and all heavily armed, rushed up to the group. No doubt he had heard the same wild alarm which had been given to Blas in the patio. And Blas saw the father lay his hand on the shoulder of his son, as though to make sure, against his hopes, that Christopher, in very deed, was still alive.

Half a dozen words were enough to explain what had happened. And while Enright was giving quick directions for the disposal of the body and the warning of the sheriff of what had happened, Blas found himself drawn apart by Christopher.

"Is that your real name, John?" asked the heir of Dial.

"My real name, yes," said Blas.

"Is there anything else that you wish to tell me?"

"Is there anything else that you want to know?"

"A thousand things. Beginning with the reason why he should have taken a shot at you—at me, I mean, because he thought that I was you?"

"He's one of Vega's men. That's the simple reason, and Vega is after my scalp. I killed one of Vega's men. I'll tell you that story later on, if you want to know it."

"And the woman that you've found—and who will make it easier for you to be caught?"

"He was dying fast, then, when he said that." Blas made a deprecatory gesture, indicating that the subject was of no interest to him. "I don't know what was in his mind," he supplemented.

"Make you easier to be caught," repeated Christopher. "Caught by whom? By Vega, then?"

"I suppose that he meant that."

"Gad!" laughed Christopher suddenly, "And

here I was wondering what we would do for action—and this thing waiting all the time! However, I don't want you to tell me anything, except voluntarily!"

He drew the arm of Blas inside his own, and they walked up the hill together.

Chapter Twenty-eight

Guido Forseno, coming through the night of another day toward the house of Dial, rode in a sort of happy torment. For every time he clutched the reins of the burro, the stiffness of his crippled hands sent a pang not through his flesh, but through his soul. And he looked up towards the lighted windows of Dial with a burning heart.

But when he turned his head away, even by starlight, the beauty of the valley stole upon his senses, and a great joy filled him, mingling with his sadness. For all this was the work of his mind. Yes, and the vital part of it was the work of his hands, as well. How little—how very little they had ventured to alter his original conceptions! All was as he had first dreamed it and then had laid out the plans. Nothing was vitally redrawn. No, they were merely so many hands employed on the task which he had in the first place set; and set for them so well that they could not help but succeed.

He felt like some exiled king, returning by night through the streets of the city which his power and skill had planned and partly built. This was as he had wished the valley to become. And the great blunt face of the dam, glistening in the distance— that was the proof that his labors should outlast centuries. That was the promise that this arm of the desert should be perpetually reclaimed to sweet verdure!

Close under the shadow of the house, upon the hill, he paused to recast his thoughts.

He was grateful, then, that time and a plentiful water supply had reared the grove that he planted about the house to such a seasonable height. Twenty-five years of prosperous maturing had made the little forest seem as though it had been rooted there from eternity. It made a close shadow, in which he could brood, at peace—quite free from the danger of any spying eye.

Only, glimmering dimly through the trunks at the edge of the world, he could see the distant lights of the house—big as he had made it in those other happy days of planning and of striving and of the steady realization of dreams.

But the fact that he had done these things did not make them seem less marvelous to him now. For twenty-five years, he had been shrinking in the little town of San Pablo, eating his heart out with bitterness, whenever he thought of the past. And how dwarfed he had become by comparison by that which he had once been!

It almost seemed to poor Guido that in those

other years there had been a different spirit inhabiting his flesh. As though in one thing Dial had had his way—and he had racked the tormented soul of Forseno out of the flesh that had sustained it—racked it out, and left behind only the trembling weak thing—*Lavera!*

How should he approach, now, the great house and the people within it?

They had been strong and fierce even in times of poverty. They were stronger and fiercer, now, and over a hundred eyes kept watch and a hundred hands were ready to strike in their defense.

He left the burro here, tethered to a sapling on the edge of the copse. And he went softly forward. A dozen times he paused and trembled, as he heard the voices from the house.

Then a girl's voice began to sing a rhythmic, pulsing song of Mexico. That gave him heart. When men listened to music such as this, their ears were opened and their eyes were closed.

Near the gate of the patio, as he drew nearer, the stalwart forms of two men were stationed.

It was as he had expected. After the strange incidents which, as all the world knew, had been happening in the valley of Dial, it would have been strange if Don Teofilo, or his keen-eyed son-in-law, Guy Enright, had not arranged some manner of watch.

But these fellows kept their guard in a perfunctorily formal manner. It was plain that they did not dream that danger would dare approach the house of their great and rich master. And so, as they sauntered back and forth, they paused to chat, a moment, each time their beats overlapped.

After Guido Forseno had observed this, he took advantage of the next moment of talk to slip into the shadow of the patio wall. There he was well screened, partly by the steep shadow from the stars, and partly, also, by the enveloping foliage of the climbing vines which mounted the wall.

On a day, in the early spring, he and Maruja, together, had set out these plants. Delicate, slender slips, their heads wavering in the hot breeze, and the crusted sand around them, seeming to promise a short life to them.

But they had grown into veritable trees! The hand of Forseno closed upon a trunk larger than he could enclose in his doubled span!

He waited for the next interval in the walking of the guards, and then he tried the climbing of the vine. That stout trunk was like a natural ladder, so often did it bend back and forth. And it held him up easily, easily! Ten times his weight, so it seemed, would not have caused it to creak beneath the pressure of his steps!

He gained the top of the wall and there he lay prone on his belly, with a great green cloud of slender branches closing about him. Some moths, roused by his coming, rose on soft wings and hung in a dim little white mist before they settled back again.

His heart fluttered with fear, for an instant, but no one's eye was attracted by the moths. And now he ventured to peep forth, through his screen, upon the patio.

The singing had ended. The guitar was strumming with a noisy jangle, keeping a swift rhythm, and through the patio spun and whirled the figure of a dancing girl. She seemed a miracle of grace to Guido Forseno. And in the beauty of her dancing he saw all that he might have been—all that had been stolen from him by the cruelty of Dial.

He, Forseno, might have been sitting in that little closed court, clad in white, like the others, drawing gently at his cigar, and smiling at the grace of this girl. Instead, he peered in at the peril of his life, an unwanted interloper!

The dance ended.

And a voice that he well knew sounded from the court. "Now one more song, eh?"

That was Blas, speaking like the very master of the house.

"She's tired," answered Guy Enright. "Have a bit of pity on her, Blas!"

Ah, did they know his name, then? And how much more had he confessed to them?

The teeth of Forseno closed and gritted hard, together.

"She's tired, surely."

That was the soft voice of Maruja. And that was unchanged. Time might have altered her face, but her voice held the sweet music which had once charmed him and maddened him with love for her!

"Tired?" echoed Blas, carelessly and confidently, like one who knew that he could presume much in this company. "Tell us the truth. Are you too tired to sing again?"

Behold, he stood before the girl and she looked up to him with a laugh.

"No, Don Blas. Not tired—if you wish to me to sing!"

Was there not a little falling cadence of caress in her voice, as she said this? Assuredly there was! And it was for Blas.

She turned back to the musician who squatted by the wall, and as she turned, Forseno recognized the face.

Liseta!

He almost felt like starting up and shouting: "Beware! Vega will pull the house down about your ears, if he knows that she is here! Does not the whole world know that he is mad for love of this truant?"

But he settled himself again and grinned in savage content.

That was one more danger gathering over the heads of the household, while they remained unaware!

Another song, not softly soothing like the first, but as gay and filled with dancing steps as the dance itself. And when it ended, Liseta and her companion were gone.

Another voice from out the shadow—another voice entering as there was the sound of a door closed heavily.

"Hello, Blas! Is the nonsense over?"

"Here's Christopher come back. You have no ear for music, Christopher, my dear!"

That was Maruja speaking to her son. Ah, if the father of that boy had been Forseno, perhaps he would not have been as broad of shoulder, but assuredly, he would have been as handsome, and there would have been a sense for music in him too!

There was Christopher standing by the side of

Blas, one arm thrown over his shoulders.

"I've cut a trifle more lead in the handle, Blas. Do you want to try it, now?"

And he laid a slender-bladed knife in the hand of Blas.

The latter weighted it for an instant, with his eyes closed, like a connoisseur. "I don't know," said he. "It might do. I'll see."

The knife left his hand. A streak of light crossed the patio, went out, and from the shadow of the wall there sounded an ominous humming like that of a monstrous hornet, enraged.

The knife had stuck in the stout trunk of one of those giant climbing vines, and at the first pull, Christopher failed to disengage it. He had to make a second effort before he brought it back, triumphant.

"Father," he cried, "did you ever see anything like it? Ever in your life? Why, gad, a man doesn't need to wear guns. He can depend upon a knife, if he can only acquire a skill like that. Blas, how long did it take you to learn to handle a knife like that?"

"I was fairly good at it when I was twelve. It's a knack, you understand. Nothing important. But—"

"You hear? A knack, like shooting, too. That's only a knack. Oh, sir," added Christopher, turning to his father, "I wish, that you'd given me a chance to learn some of the things that a man may need to use in his life in this part of the world—instead of a lot of college stuff that does you no good when you're in the saddle!"

Said Guy Enright slowly: "Is Blas the right type for you, Chris?"

"And why not?" asked Christopher bluntly.

"And why not?" said Guy Enright, and his seriousness sent a throb of wonder through the heart of Forseno.

Chapter Twenty-nine

"I'm going out to say good night to La Blanca," said Blas. "Will you come along, Chris?"

"Of course. And—Blas, do you think you could teach me that knack of the knife, as you call it?"

"Yes—"

"Christopher," said Maruja, "I want to speak with you a moment. You don't mind, Blas, my dear?"

"Oh, no," said Blas, and went away, whistling, in the direction of the stables, saluted with a respectful word on either hand from the two mozos who were supposed to be guarding the patio.

"And now?" said Christopher, patiently, but with his head turned towards the disappearing form of Blas.

"Your father and I have been talking it over. We know that you would like to remain on the ranch.

But we think that it's a great deal better for you to go back to college."

"Good gad, no!" groaned Christopher.

"We do," said Maruja. "Three or four years seem a long time to you, now. But it won't when you look at it from the other end. No, Christopher dear—"

But poor Christopher made a gesture of despair.

"Are you set on it, sir?" said he to his father.

"I see no good reason against it," said Guy Enright.

"It's Blas," said the boy bitterly. "You want to get me away from Blas. Confess that that's it! Because he teaches me something about guns—and weapons in general, and how to use them—"

"Christopher," said his father, "we like Blas. You know that."

"But you think he's dangerous!"

"Now, frankly, don't you, yourself, Chris?"

"Yes, God knows that he is to some people. But not to us!"

"You're very set on that, of course. But still, there are various ways of doing harm. A man who is apt, at any moment, to put a gun to my head is not a great deal more dangerous to me, from my way of thinking, than a man who teaches me put a gun to the head of another man!"

"Has he taught me that?"

"While you're with him, you think and talk of nothing but a chance to live a wild life in the hills—to be free—to be on the back of a fast horse—to be able to laugh at the law—that seems to be your chief topic of conversation with your Blas. Am I wrong?"

And honest Christopher, bowing his head, replied: "No, I don't think that you're wrong, entirely. I don't think that! But—I've never in my life found a finer fellow than this same Blas. Perhaps he's a bit wild. But he's honest. And there's something good in him. There's an edge to him. Every minute that I'm with him, I'm closer to life. I feel as though I'm getting the taste of true living, you know!"

"Do you?" said the father. "But aren't you a bit young, Chris, old fellow, to know just what the real taste of life should be?"

There was a sudden voice from the shadows.

"Why is he too young? When I was his age, I knew what I wanted, and I went out to get it! Do you know what I wanted at his age?"

It was Dial. He had been slumbering, it appeared, or at least dozing, behind his fuming cigar, his old, bright eyes fixed upon the starry skies.

And now, all faces were drawn towards him. And it was always that way, so far as Forseno could remember. Whenever Dial had chosen to speak, there had always been auditors to listen. And all faces had always turned to him with respect.

"Well, sir," said Christopher, "I think that you'll be able to tell them what I want! You can explain my mind a lot better than I can. You always could, sir!"

He went and stood behind the chair of Dial, his hands resting on the shoulders of his grandfather, and the old man gave one upward smile to the face of the young giant.

"Perhaps I'll be a bad interpreter for you, my

lad. But I'll tell you something about the things that used to go on inside of this old head of mine! When I was your age, I mean!"

"We'll want to hear that," said Enright. "At the same time, sir, I shall have to use my own discretion in the matter—though, of course, I welcome your advice—"

"Would you cross me, Guy?" thundered the old man, suddenly.

Enright stiffened in his chair.

"I hope that it will not be a question—"

"Father!" cried Maruja.

"Be still!" shouted Dial. "Let him answer for himself!"

"My son," said Enright quietly, "is still too young to judge for himself. And until he has reached the proper age of discretion he will have to take final decisions from me."

"On what authority, Guy? On what authority? On pain of being disinherited by you?"

"Senor Dial," said Enright, leaning on his chair, "lower your voice when you speak to me, sir! I am not a peon in your service, and I wish to have you keep that fact constantly in mind when you address me!"

It seemed to Forseno, as he lay trembling upon the top of the wall, that he had arrived at the very moment when the household of Dial was about to be rent asunder by the subtle influence of Blas.

And it seemed a terrible and wonderful thing to the eavesdropper, when he heard a voice actually raised in challenge of the fierce old man, in his own patio.

But who could tell, ever, what would be the next

change in the manner of the dictator? Terrible thunder had been in his voice one instant. The next, he was leaning back in his chair and laughing softly, as if anger had never been in his mild mind.

"There is that same Guy Enright," he said. "The same fellow who rode into my life these many years ago and began to shape matters as he would have them, beginning with Maruja, yonder!"

He paused, and laughed again:

"You hear, Christopher?" said he. "I'm to have no voice in your upbringing. The scoundrel is going to have you entirely in his own hands!"

This jovial tone brought an instant response from Enright. "I did not mean to be so extreme," said he quietly. "I am sorry if I lost my temper a bit."

"No," said the old tiger. "You're not to be sorry. I know that most of the people around me are shadows. And I'm glad to know that there is one *man*. But we'll forget this for a moment. You'll permit me to give you a little advice, Guy. Not as a dictator, but as a very old man, a grandfather, in fact?"

"Certainly, sir," said Enright.

And Maruja settled back in her chair, with a sigh. Matters had not gone so far that her active intervention had been required. But still Forseno hardly heard the speech that followed, for he had been witness while the lion was bearded in its den, and that scene appeared to him almost too wonderful for credence.

"I was about to tell you, in brief, something of what I was when I was the age of your son, Guy.

I don't wish to stand as a model. I've never been a model. And I never expect to be one. But the point is that I've made a tolerable success of this life—from a practical viewpoint, at least. And in addition, from the side of character, I have not turned out to be a weakling—even though you occasionally are a bit sharp with me, Guy!"

He chuckled as he spoke. Yes, it was very clear to the listener on the wall that Dial had altered somewhat from the old days. Or, had this always been the right way with him—stern and ringing defiance in the time of need?

He listened, breathless.

"Of course, our minds are open, and wonderfully interested, senor," said Guy Enright.

"Very well, then. Ambition is the divine spark that sets a man on fire, eh? Well, when I was the age of your son, my dear Guy, my ambition was perfectly clear and definite. On the one hand, I liked all the good things in life. I loved power. I wished to be surrounded by obedience. I loved money for its own sake as well as for the things that it can buy. But the other side of the picture was that I also loved to lie half in shadow and half in sun and dream life away.

"And how, Guy, was I to do the two things? A fool's ambition, you will say?"

"A very odd combination, I admit," said Guy Enright.

"And, as a matter of fact, most people could not have accomplished it. But I'll tell you, Guy, how it was done. You ought to know, but perhaps you've forgotten. And besides, when you arrived, the work was so far under way that you did not have any real conception of how it had started. But onto this burning desert—for that was all it was at the time of which I speak—there came a young man who had no desire, as I had, for lying in the sun and shadow. He was a maker, a builder, a doer; he was everything but a gentleman. And so, I laid in the sun, and I let him work for me; and I paid him just enough in power to keep him contented. It was not money that he wanted, Maruja. It was power—you remember?"

Maruja leaned her face upon her hand and made no reply.

"Tush, tush!" said the old man gently. "Is that still such a keen subject with you? Why, child, I thought that you had almost forgotten that there had ever been such a man! At any rate, I want to tell you that I was able to realize my absurd ambition. I realized it because it was a great and burning thing within me. And things come to people who really burn for them. Oh, yes, if the fire is hungry enough, God will find a fuel for it!"

"Including revenge!" whispered the eavesdropper, inaudibly.

"And the miracle was finally performed for me, simply because I had such a wild desire for it! Now here is the case of your boy, Christopher. He wants to go out in the mountains, live by his gun, catch wild horses and ride 'em. Follow a man trail or two, if he can come across a little trouble. And he particularly wants, as his companion, this same Blas. Now, sir, my earnest advice to you is to say to Christopher: 'Young man, the thing that you desire to do is apt to send you to the devil. But if you wish to try it, here is my hand! There is no money in the palm of it. I give you an outfit of clothes, a good horse, and a rifle. Now make your way. Take three years of wilderness instead of three years of college. Good-bye!' That is the manner in which I should talk with him!"

Chapter Thirty

He spoke with so much sincerity and conviction that it made a pause in the mind of the eavesdropper, and brought a silence through the patio.

"God bless you, sir!" whispered Christopher.

Dial patted one of the big hands which rested on his shoulders.

"As a matter of fact," said he, more quietly than ever, "I am turning our Christopher over to a fellow who really, for the first time in my life, is the cause of frightening me!"

"Ah?" said Guy Enright.

"Do you mean that Blas has frightened you?" asked Christopher.

"I mean exactly that. There was a time when I was much too proud to admit that any man in the world could ever have frightened me. And indeed, except for an occasion when Guy, yonder, grew ruffled, no one person has ever disturbed me a great deal. But I have to make an exception in favor of that boy. Once or twice, I have found his eyes fixed on me with such a light in them that it gave me bad dreams all through the next night!"

"I know what you mean!" cried Christopher. "Sometimes, when he begins to think of something, his face grows set and his eyes really wild. You've noticed him when he looked like that. But, sir, he never could mean any harm to you!"

"And could he not?" said Dial, raising his thinly-arched brows. "Could he not? Well, I suppose that it was all a fancy of mine. But that Blas—ah, well, every man that is not a fool can see that he is a tiger!"

"But you do consent to what my grandfather says?" cried Christopher, turning to his father.

"My boy," said his father, "I think that Senor Dial has spoken a great deal more wisely than I. And I've decided on the spur of the moment that you can take your leave of us tomorrow—if you are willing to accept his terms!"

"Accept them? Yes, if they were a thousand times harder. Wait till I find Blas and let him know that—"

"One minute. I want to talk to you about a few of the conditions before you go. And then—"

Forseno heard no more of the matter. He had worked his way back over the crest of the wall and down to the ground, stealthily using the twisting trunk of the stout vine, as before, to aid him in his descent. Then, in the bottom shadow of the vine, he waited for his chance to slip into the woods once more. He had heard far more than he had dared to expect. He had heard enough, in fact, to make him half pleased and half anxious. One thing, at least, was certain: And that was that Blas had been taken into the family as completely as though he were a member of it by blood.

And something in this thought made Forseno throw back his head and break into soft, ghoulish laughter.

He rounded the house towards the stable, walking stealthily, always. And when he came to the stable he had no trouble in finding what he wanted. The glimmering form of La Blanca showed from afar in the little pasture where she was kept, with only one other horse for company.

There, standing in the shadow by the rails, Forseno called, and Blas was instantly before him.

He caught his father by either arm.

"What in the name of all the wonderful saints—father? How have you come here?"

"I got out the old grey burro," said Forseno. "He brought me here. Slow work, but steady work."

"And why?"

"What was there to keep me at home?"

"Mother will go mad with worry!"

"She worries about nothing except how the alfalfa is growing on the ground that you bought for them—"

"For them? For you!"

"Ah, well, what good is land to me? I have no hands to work it, and I have no hands to enjoy it, my son! What good is land to me?"

"There is nothing that will make you happy," sighed Blas. "But I thought that you might have been more contented—"

"More contented knowing that you are searching for Dial. More contented for that. But as for the rest of the family—your mother and your brothers—why, they are living only to wait for the irrigation season. They talk nothing but water, grass, and cows. They are not selling the hay. They are feeding it to cows. They have put up a shed. Then they make butter and send it down the river. In that way—why, they make three times as much money. They begin to get fat. There is not enough to keep them busy. Next year they are going to borrow money from the bank and buy some more land. They will soon be rich. Yes!"

"Did you come here to tell me that?" said Blas.

"I thought," said the other, "that you might want to go back to see them, and perhaps to help them till the ground!"

"Bah!" said Blas. "Would that content me?"

"And yet you expect that it should be enough for me?"

"I am sorry—"

"For me? And yet, I have had my hands so filled that I have made this valley and all that is in it! You smell the pines in the wind. My hands planted them. You see the shining of the lights from the house—my hands placed them there—! All that you see except the immortal stars that shine in heaven—all was made by me. The stars, and the back of the mountains that rolls against them, God made those things. But I made all the rest, and then you speak to me of an alfalfa patch? God forgive you!"

"I was a fool!" said Blas humbly. "I knew that

you could not have come to ask me home to the farm, however!"

"Why not?" said the other. "Why should I not ask you home? I heard that you had settled down. I sent you out to revenge the wrongs of your father. But it seems that you changed your mind. You found that Don Teofilo was wise enough and rich enough—aye, and old enough!—to be worthwhile as friend. And so you used him for that instead of as a target. Is it not true?"

"Not true!" said Blas heartily. "Indeed, it is not true, at all!"

"You are not living in the bosom of their family?"

"I only—"

"They do not call you by your first name?"

"Father—"

"You have told them everything, however, and you have given yourself a new life. It is well."

"No, no!"

"You have turned your back upon me. Why, I should have expected that! All things that I have given to the world have been used by Dial. All things! It is fate! And now you—"

"Will you hear me?"

"No, I do not reproach you! I only came—"

"Father, I swear that I still intend—"

"No, do not touch him. Do him no harm, Blas. As for the tortures which he has worked upon me—"

"Ah, I have not forgotten."

"You must teach yourself to forget, however. It is not well that you should remember, I tell you. It is really not well, my boy. Remember only that

Dial is rich—immensely rich—"

"A rich devil!"

"Cannot a devil be used? Assuredly he can! And so can Dial, I trust! Yes, yes, so can Dial! Why, my lad, has he not millions?"

"What are they to me?"

"Millions made from the blood of your father— But that is nothing—"

"Damnation! I shall tear him to bits!"

"No, no, Blas, you must not dream of that. I tell you that he already loves you!"

"He? I care not for that!"

"But you must learn to care! I tell you, Blas, that that love of his can be made to produce rich gold!"

"May his gold be cursed, and Dial with it!"

"Tush, Blas! Will you not listen to sense? As for us yonder in San Pablo, we will not trouble you. We will only listen to the stories of your greatness and wonder at you! Make yourself useful to Christopher. Make yourself necessary to him. Teach him all that you know, and someday he may—kick you out of your place, as his father did with me—"

"I shall find Dial now and break his back!"

"No, no! What could be more fitting, my dear son, than that after I have been the slave of the father, you should be the slave of the grandson! What could be better? It is like a pretty story from the Bible, is it not?"

"You have said enough. I admit that I have been wrong. But I shall not fall asleep again. You will drive me mad if you say any more!"

"No, Blas, I am serious when I tell you that you must not harm Dial! In a few years more he will die—unless he proves to be very tough. And how easy it will be to pretend, for those few years longer, that all is well—that you are his friend—that you love him—it may mean millions—"

"Millions of poison, I say!"

"What! Is it possible that you are actually my son, then?"

"Have you doubted that?"

"How could I help doubting it?" said Forseno, through his teeth. "I lay on the wall like a whipped dog, cowering in the dark. I looked down into the bright court, and there was Blas Lavera, the son of Forseno, laughing and talking with Dial and the blood of Dial—and the cursed witch, Maruja—she was there—"

"Senor!"

"Ah?"

"Listen to me carefully. I believe that you have right to say what you have just said to me. But now I assure you that you have said enough. I cannot stand any more. And while you may say what you please about Dial and Enright—you will leave Christopher and Maruja out of your talk."

"They are sacred, then?" sneered the older man.

"Not that. I mean that they've been wonderfully kind to me."

"They could afford to be kind," said the other. "It's an easy thing to be kind when somebody else has paid the cost of the kindness. And it was that way with them. But Dial—why's he to be kept safe, too? He's given them the cash to be kind to you—"

"I'll go back to the house now!" groaned the youngster, as he turned on his heel and made at a half-run towards the dimly lighted mansion.

Chapter Thirty-one

The stumbling feet of Forseno carried him hastily after Blas, through the darkness. He seized the boy's shoulder and cried: "Blas, Blas! D'you hear me? Are you mad? Have you lost your wits?"

Blas pressed the hand of Forseno away from him.

"I've owed a bullet to him, and now I'll pay it—"

"Blas, there's no saddle on your horse. What are you aiming to do? Run in and shoot him? They'll blow you to bits. Blas, will you listen?"

He brought the other back to reason for the moment, at least, and he watched Blas saddle La Blanca, while the moon, rising late, climbing through a bank of eastern clouds and filling the sky with a dim radiance, so that the trees and the mountains, half-seen, looked more tremendous and more distant than ever.

"We'll need another horse," said Blas, "because when they go over the place afterwards to find me—they might find you! I suppose that you walked? No, you rode a burro."

"Yes."

"Can you sit in the saddle on a long-striding horse, father?"

"I am no child, Blas."

The latter made no reply. But, in silence, he led the way to the closed paddock, where the tall silhouette of Larribee showed beyond the bars.

"Can you ride that?" he asked.

It seemed to Forseno that he was peering through vast wasted years, back to the days of his youth, when he had dared to sit on the back of anything that called itself horse. Many a wild mustang he had backed, and many a wild tumble he had had on account of it. Half a dozen times he had barely escaped from being "savaged" by some wicked brute. But in those days he had been Guido Forseno, maker of men. And now he was the beaten cripple, Lavera!

He stared at the tall outline of the horse.

Then he called to it softly and held out his hand.

Larribee tossed his head and sprang back half the distance across the enclosure.

"I'll try him!" said Forseno. "But isn't there another gentler horse—that's just as fast?"

"Nothing except La Blanca. And you know that she's a tiger, except to me. If we don't take Larribee, then he'll be ridden after us, and when he's ridden after us, he'll catch anything except La Blanca. Do you think that you can sit him out?"

"I shall try."

"Then I'll saddle him. Take his head. He may get a little used to you!"

Forseno saw Blas slip between the bars and enter the paddock. The gelding had no intention of submitting readily to capture. He spun about and drove his heels at the head of the youth. But Blas merely laughed at a peril which turned Forseno cold. In an instant, he was standing at the head of Larribee, and then led him across to Forseno.

"Here he is. Hold him steady! Keep talking. He likes that!"

It seemed very wonderful to the older man. For here was Blas on the verge of breaking to bits all the bonds which had linked him through so many cheerful, happy days with the family of Dial, in the great house. And yet, the youngster went about it with a sort of assured calm, as though he were doing nothing which injured his spirits. He even made a small joke, as he adjusted the saddle on the back of Larribee. And he commented on the fact that after the great bulk of Christopher, the gelding ought to carry Forseno like a mere feather.

This, while he was saddling for a theft the prized horse of his dearest friend!

They took the pair to an agreed place—the lee of the woods, beneath the house. There were closer places to the Casa Dial, but there was none which would give them a chance to bolt downhill all the way from the mansion. Also, they were on the side of the river and the lake.

So Blas pointed it out, a dimly silvered face under the veiled moon, and showed the narrow streak of shadows, where the bridge was drawn across it.

There were always men armed and ready to mount on fast horses near that bridge. For that was the key point to the valley. No one could ride towards the mountains, across the valley, by any short route except this. And, in a similar fashion, no one could cross the valley from the mountains, except by a broad detour, unless he pointed his course across this bridge.

They themselves would be sadly handicapped unless they could cross by the bridge, and Blas declared that he intended to attempt it.

"They know La Blanca," said he, "and I think that they won't question me when they see me coming, and shouting, on a white horse. They'll recognize me and let me through. Then we'll have to shake them loose and get on towards the mountains. We have to cross the bridge if we want half a chance to get away, and the mountains are our only real chance. Do you understand that?"

"Yes."

"Then, after the thing is done, we'll ride straight down the slope, towards the bridge. I'm telling you beforehand, so that you won't be alarmed when you see a dozen riders boil up around the place. I'll simply shout to them and try to scatter them. Is that clear?"

"Yes, that's all very clear."

"And you'll keep your nerve. You won't be frightened by the thing?"

"No," said Forseno faintly.

"There's one other way," persisted Blas in the same calm voice. "You can stay behind me, here.

233

In that way, while I've drawn all attention after me, you might get away, later in the night. But I doubt it a good deal. The whole valley will be buzzing for days, after Dial is dead."

"Are you so confident that you'll kill him, Blas?"

"Yes, I know that I shall. Nothing can call me off—except you, father."

"If I forgave him, then?"

"Yes."

"Do you think that I should forgive him, Blas?"

"God knows what you should, mio! If I were you, I don't think that I could ever forgive!"

"It is going to be hard with you, though?"

"Yes, hard—a little."

"You cannot hate him?"

"He is an old man, you understand."

"I understand that. He was a good deal younger when he did this to me!"

He extended his hands, and Blas suddenly bowed his head.

"That's enough," said he. "You don't have to spur me on. I know what my duty is, and I'll do it!"

"Duty, Blas? They'll hang you for doing this duty!"

"They'll never catch me. Never until I've had my fling!"

"And that will be what?"

"I don't know. Fun enough to make me happy. But I want you to think over the thing again. If you intend to wait until after I've gone, and then to slip down the valley, we'd better take the gelding back and let you ride on the burro, because speed is not what you'll want, but secrecy. Isn't that true?"

"That is true. But let me stay with you, Blas! I think that all the heart would run out of me if I were alone."

"That's as you please."

"Ah, Blas, there's little love for me in your heart. It's cold duty and a sense of justice that makes you do this!"

Blas was silent, and the older man continued in a trembling voice: "I'm no nearer to you than that marble-heart—Guy Enright!"

And still, from the bowed head of Blas, there was no disclaimer.

"They've stolen my place with you!" sighed Forseno. "Ah, Blas, is that true?"

He stepped closer, and Blas Lavera lifted his head suddenly.

"Senor," said he softly, "I think that we have talked enough. It is time to act, now. Wait here. Hold the reins of the horses. I don't think that it shall take me long. Only—pray God that his hand is steady when he stands up to fight!"

"You are going to give him a chance against you, Blas?"

And the son turned on the father with a suddenly wolfish snarl: "You cruel coward!" gasped Blas. "You want me to murder him from behind? That is not my sort of work!"

He turned his back.

"Wait, Blas. How will you go to his room?"

"By the stairs, of course."

"Ha? Like a fool, lad! By the stairs, so that everyone may know what you've done?"

"Yes—there's no other way. The window, do you mean? There's a sheer wall beneath it—"

"I know his room. Did not I plan it? Yes, and I know other things—it seems that you have not heard of the secret way to his chamber, Blas?"

"Secret way?"

"In case of need, a narrow corridor winding all through the house. An old Mexican tradition to have such things. And there is plenty of wall space, you know. But perhaps the entrance to it has been walled up, in the meantime?"

"Perhaps."

"Where does the bed stand in Dial's room? Can you tell me?"

"At the side, with its head against the east wall—"

"About ten feet from the edge of the fireplace?"

"Yes."

"That is the same. If the bed still stands there, then the passage should still be beside it. I'll show you the way—there is no reason why you should ever be so much as suspected, for this deed of justice. Follow me!"

He stepped to the side of Blas through the trees, and into the spacious garden of the Casa Dial. There was no need to fear the men who kept guard. They sang softly to themselves as they paced lazily on their rounds. The air was too delightfully cool and sweet on this night. How could a man give over his time and his mind to the thinking of unpleasant thoughts?

Chapter Thirty-two

So Blas and Forseno merely waited until the first watchman strolled idly by. Then they were through the shrubs and under the lofty wall of the Casa Dial.

Here Blas paused.

"Wait here among the brush," he whispered to Forseno. "I have one thing to do first—wait here. In two minutes, I shall be back!"

Between the rear of the Casa Dial and the quarters of the servants, which stretched in little, low-built houses, there was a broad lawn, interspersed with shrubs; and among these Blas stepped until he came to a wing of the servants' quarters.

There he paused.

The Casa Dial was silent enough, but here there was still noise, though all was covert. It was as though the servants knew that their laughter might easily wind its way through the dark to the ears of the master.

Even the lights were veiled, to a certain extent, by placing them away from the windows.

And then Blas, first practicing the notes softly to himself, uttered the low and mournful note of the screech-owl as it drops off the top of the stump and sails across the face of the ground, with soundless wings.

After that he shifted his position until he was directly beneath the largest of the nearby pines, under which the grass had thinned out until the spot was almost bare.

There was presently the drift of a shadow past the white wall of the out-building. And then, turning straight towards the pine, the shadow came to a pause.

"Blas?"

"Yes, Liseta."

"What has happened?"

"I am going away."

"Ah? And where?"

"I don't know. When I know, I shall write the word back to you?"

"Has there been trouble?"

"Nothing that I can tell you. But there may be trouble before morning. I don't know. When I send word to you—"

"I'll go wherever you wish. Yes!"

"Brave Liseta! I am waited for. Good-bye!"

"Good-bye, Blas," said the girl, and raised her face to him.

"Why, Liseta, you are true steel, and I knew that

you could act like a man if the need came for it. Good-bye again!"

He kissed her and turned back through the trees. At the verge of the deeper shadows, he whirled about and waved to her. She stood where a broken shaft of moonshine—for the moon had reached the clear heavens—fell upon her face, and by that light he saw her laugh and wave towards him.

Then he was gone, and when the rustle of his step had died out, she slipped down against the rough face of the pine trunk and leaned there, weeping. It was the end of her happiness, felt Liseta, and the pain in her heart was so great that she almost knew that she would be dead before the morning.

So she went back to the house, and Blas went on to the Casa Dial, and the older man who waited for him, there.

"She let you leave her soon," commented Forseno.

"Did you follow me?" asked Blas coldly.

"No need for that. Nothing but a woman could have turned a man aside at a time like this. Are you ready now?"

"Yes, all ready."

"Then follow me. We go to the rear of the house and try the back door, to the cellar. Is that usually locked?"

"Yes, I think so."

"There is no matter, because I think that I shall be able to find another way, then. Now that my time has come, Blas, nothing can keep him from me!"

He spoke in a voice of absolute confidence and rejoicing. And Blas followed gloomily at his heels.

He loathed the work that was before him, but according to his standards, there was only one thing for him to do, and that was to obey the voice of Forseno, in this matter of honor.

They reached the back of the house, went down the steep pitch of steps to a double door, and found it securely locked. The shoulder of Blas made it groan, but did not budge it.

"Try the windows!" said Forseno.

They were tried rapidly, and the third one yielded and went up with a little screech. At the same moment, the crippled hand of Forseno closed upon the shoulder of his son.

Blas, turning, saw the older man pointing, and, the next moment, he heard the rapid fall of feet as two men turned the farther corner of the building.

It was Guy Enright, by the grace of misfortune, bringing with him a new watchman, to be made to walk the rounds of the house. And at this corner Enright paused and turned his back on the two figures who crouched in the shadow of the building, not ten feet away.

They could hear the manager of the Dial estate giving curt, matter-of-fact directions. They had ample reason to believe, he declared, that the celebrated Vega and Vega's men were continually near to the house, and therefore they would be most happy if a single sign of that bandit or his crew could be reported.

For this work of guard the pay was ample, as stated. But for bullets turned into scores, in the shapes of wounded or dead outlaws, the rewards would be almost infinitely greater. Thus spoke Enright, and sent the other about his business.

The Mexican went off at a brisk step, and Enright, standing listening, shook his head and sighed, as presently he heard that briskness of gait change to a slow and dragging step. However, apparently, he had resigned himself to such things.

He was turning to go back by the way he had come, when his eye caught something at the side and he stopped abruptly.

It was well-nigh enough to have made another man take to his heels—that glimpse, by surprise, of two men crouched in the shadow, to all intents hostile. But Enright was no coward. He steadied himself for half a breathing space, and then he reached for his gun.

Perhaps there would have been bloodshed very quickly on this night of nights had not that weapon hung in the holster; for Blas had not chosen to draw his own Colt and fire in answer to the threat. He merely leaped in, covering the distance between them with a long, light bound, and as he came to the end of it he struck.

The ground was jerked from beneath the feet of Enright. He fell heavily on his side.

And Blas caught him up and carried him swiftly back into the shadow of the house.

"Is he dead?" gasped Forseno.

"And would you care?" growled Blas savagely. "It's blood that you want. Would you care if he were dead?"

"God forgive you!" whispered Forseno. "If you've done that, Blas—you are damned! Quick, then. Listen to his heart—"

He himself was on his knees and his head pressed against the breast of Enright, who stirred now, and groaned faintly.

"He is safe!" gasped Forseno. "Praise God for that! He is safe. And now—where shall we fly, Blas?"

"Fly?"

"Quick! Quick! The watch will be back here—"

"Would you run away now?"

"Oh, Blas, will you stay here and throw yourself away?"

"I am not thrown away. Climb through that window first! Hurry!"

Senor Forseno leaned for an instant against the wall, dizzied with fear. Then he threw himself forward in a frenzy and scrambled through the window and dropped softly into the darkness within. His head and shoulders reappeared faintly, from within.

"Enright!" said Blas through his teeth. "Do you hear me?"

The other stiffened with a groan and then partially came back to his wits.

"Blas, is it you, lad? Thank the Lord that you've come. Some scoundrel struck me down—two of them—they are waiting to—"

"Steady," interrupted Blas. "My fist knocked you down. I'm the scoundrel!"

Enright, straightening to his full height, now looked down to the gun which was naked in the hand of the other, and he seemed to understand.

"It is you, after all!" said he.

"Yes."

"What is it that you wish, Blas?"

"Not to harm you, if you keep quiet. Will you believe that?"

"Yes. There's logic in you, and I know that you wouldn't wish to injure me, because I haven't injured you. Only, lad, if you have loot in mind, believe me when I say that you are throwing away a comfortable fortune! Will you trust me when I say that? Dial is mightily fond of you!"

"Senor Dial is kind," said Blas curtly. "I cannot talk any longer. You will climb through that window—"

Enright, watching the window, hesitated; then he shivered, as though from the deep blackness of the interior he guessed the worst. But, finally, he raised himself and swung his legs through the opening, with Blas following close behind him, a revolver ever pressed against Enright's body.

So they slipped into the blackness of the cellar, one after the other, and while they stood there they heard the lounging step of the new watchman go slowly past them, outside the house.

"I have rope here," said Blas. "I know how to make a gag that will keep you from making a sound. But it won't stifle you. I am going to tie you and gag you, Mr. Enright."

"Very well," said the other. "Do what you must!"

And he submitted himself quietly, without further argument, almost as though he knew the thing which had to be done, and knew also that it was vain to protest.

But when he was tied and the gag fitted, Blas lighted a match to make sure that all was well. The very first spurt of the light sent a start through the body of Enright as though a bullet had gone into his flesh.

And Blas found that his prisoner was staring with wild eyes into the face of Lavera.

Chapter Thirty-three

It seemed to Blas that he could see fear, wonder, and a sort of great horror in the expression of Enright, but there was no time to ask what. The gag was firm. Only a faint bubbling sound came from the throat of Enright, and then, seeing that the bonds were fast enough, Blas and Guido Forseno turned away through the darkness of the cellar.

The older man had become the leader. He moved through these shadows with as much assurance as though there were a bright light to guide him. So they passed through another pair of doors and came to an angle of the wall, where Forseno paused again, fumbled, and finally drew a stone out from the face of the masonry. Reaching into the little cavity which was left there, he appeared to pull and twist at something, and finally, on soundless hinges, a heavy door opened in the face of the wall.

"And they have been using it, too!" said Forseno. "You can be sure of that. The door moves too easily. And see how fresh the air is in the passage! Light another match!"

Blas lighted a match, obediently, and, looking up the stairway, he observed that a narrow flight of steps wound steeply up and out of view in a quick circle, light steps cut in the wall of some ponderous medieval watch tower.

He hesitated about them entrusting themselves to that place.

"Where does it lead?" he asked.

"It winds around and has its first opening beside the dining-room, between the two west windows—"

"The two west windows! There's nothing beyond—"

"No, the thickness of the wall is enough. You forget how thick that wall is! The passage runs straight through it and then at the end of the dining-room turns up again. I shall show you!"

All of this was delivered in a whisper. And as they closed the door behind and beneath them, Blas felt that he was committed to a wilder adventure than any which he had ever entered upon before. Because it was such a perfect trap for rats. Once they were known to be inside, it would be a simple matter to plug the holes—and then let them die!

He ventured that suggestion to Forseno, but the latter shook his head.

"Luck does not come in little glimpses," said he. "It comes or it does not come. And luck has come to me and to you, now. It will not leave us again until we have had a chance to bring this thing to an end. You may be sure of that. Are you nervous, Blas?"

It seemed a strange thing, to Blas, that he should have his courage questioned with so much sympathy by this broken hulk of a man. He shook his head, and they pressed on, up the stairway, with Forseno still leading.

He said: "I could go up and down it with my eyes closed!"

"Then why was it made?"

"Dial always has had enemies. I never thought that I could be one of them! But the idea was that this passageway would run from one important part of the house to another, and in case of some surprise attack, we could slip out from under the danger and get clear in a twinkling. That was the plan!"

"Then, when you became the enemy of Dial, why did he not change the passage?" asked Blas, for it seemed to him that the rancher was placing himself terribly at the mercy of even a weak foe, as long as he left this secret passage open to an enemy.

"There are two reasons," said Forseno. "One is that, after the last interview he had with me, I seemed so thoroughly broken that Dial thought I would never dare to lift a hand against any man— far less against him. The other reason is that he is shiftless. He is a lazy man. Half a dozen times, or half a hundred times, he may have had the thought that he would have to have the secret passage filled in. But every time that the idea came to him, he remembered that it would cause a great deal of noise and confusion. He decided that he would put it off to some more convenient time. But the more convenient time never came, and so he has not done the thing. And that is why we are here tonight; and that is why Dial has come to the last of his life, because God has kept him at our mercy, Blas, my dear son!"

He reached back a trembling hand and laid it upon the shoulder of the youth, and Blas felt an instinctive desire to shake off the touch; but he restrained himself, and they climbed on up the winding stair until it turned suddenly into a level footing.

"Here is the dining room," whispered the older man. "You see that bar in the floor? You take hold of that and raise it. That opens the door in the wall. Coming back into the passage, you step on it, and the door closes quickly and softly behind you."

"Yes," said Blas, "I understand. Is that the arrangement in every doorway from the passage?"

"In every one. There are not many more, unless Dial has added new openings. But I don't think that he has. You see that he has not dared to alter my plans here in the valley. It is not his house that he is living in. It is mine. It is mine, Blas! And the very flowers that are planted in the patio are the flowers that I selected for the place! Do you understand that?"

"Yes," said Blas, much moved.

"And the whole valley is as I planned it and made it—"

"I know that," said Blas. "Because when I came into the valley I recognized the features which you had described to me, one by one. Except that the trees were big—and the dam was even huger than I had expected to find it. It was like riding into the middle of a dream that I had half seen before."

"And so nothing will be changed—not even the little secret passage through the wall, my boy. You can depend upon that! And you are not worried, Blas?"

"No. Only—God keep Enright from breaking loose and giving the alarm!"

"Enright? There was only one way to have disposed of him."

"And how?"

"A few inches of knife sent through his back would have done the trick for him. We need not have feared him then!"

Blas bowed his head, for calm and cold-nerved as he was, that suggestion shot a chill of horror through him.

"But he is tied hand and foot, and it will not take us long in here. Dial goes to bed early!"

"Must we take him in his bed, then?"

"Yes, or be waiting in his room when he enters it!"

"That is better, by far. Hurry on. We'll do that! I don't like the idea of stealing in the dark on a sleeping man."

"Dark or sunlight," said the other gloomily, "there is never a time when Dial is not fit for the devil and ripe to go to him. Have no fear of that."

"I have no fear, I tell you. Only, I want it to be ended and over with, quickly. I'm sick of it already! Hurry on!"

Old Forseno, lighting a match, by that flickering

light stared into the face of the youth and saw there something which made him pale and anxious.

However, he followed the order, and turning about, he hurried on up the passage. They climbed the stairway, again, but they had not taken more than the first quick winding of the stairs when Forseno came to a stop so abruptly that Blas, from beneath, struck against him.

A trembling, cold hand reached back and gripped the youngster.

And then he knew that somewhere in the darkness before them there was a danger—that Forseno had seen it—and that now he was waiting there, shuddering with dread, waiting for the other thing to move again.

The gun of Blas was instantly in his hand.

But when that danger came upon them, it came in such a form as no bullet could meet. There was a light sound as of a switch clicked home, and then a broad ray of light showered radiance down upon them. Blas, twitching up the muzzle of his revolver, thought of a snapshot at the eye of light, but now he heard a wild, thin voice shrieking above them: "Guido! Guido! God protect me!"

The light fell and rattled down the steps into the hands of Blas; and he saw a woman's form fall headlong on the stairs.

"It's Maruja!" groaned Blas. "If there is any harm to her, the devil will make us both rot through eternity. Get out of my way!"

He thrust Forseno rudely aside and in an instant he had the fallen body in his arms.

"Take the light!" he snapped at the other. "Show

me the way to the first door. Quick, quick!"

Forseno, himself, seemed to have forgotten the bloodthirsty gloating which had possessed him since he came into the passageway.

He took the electric torch from Blas, but as he squeezed past him to lead the way, he paused an instant and stared wildly into the face of Maruja, as her head lay back upon the shoulder of Blas.

"It is not death. Her eyes are closed, Blas. It cannot be death!" he quavered.

And he hurried on, muttering: "What could have brought *her* into the passage?"

Blas, striding behind, barely heard him. He was too busy, anxiously listening for the beat of the heart of the woman he carried. He thought that he had detected a faint pulsation once; but again it was lost.

And then it was certainly only the raging of his own heart which he heard and which confused him.

Then a door gaped suddenly, just before him.

He followed old Forseno and carried his burden out into a big chamber where the first thing that greeted his eye was a pair of old-fashioned, long-barreled rifles crossed upon the wall, with a big ammunition belt at the crossing.

And along the walls there were hunting trophies—they had come out in the chamber of Dial himself!

He laid Maruja upon the bed.

Her face was utterly white, so that her temples were covered with a distinctly blue shadow. There was no stir in her body. He could see no movement of her breast.

"Father, Father," groaned Blas, "she is dead!"

"She is dead? No, but I almost wish that it had killed her. Has she deserved anything else? But hurry, lad. Go back with me. The house is up. Do you hear?"

He held up a hand in token that there was enough to hear if Blas cared to mark it. And, indeed, clamors and shouts went helter-skelter through the old house, and it was patent that the cry of Maruja, from the passageway, had been heard, far and near.

Chapter Thirty-four

No matter what the danger might be, there was only one thing in the mind of Blas, and that was the white face of the woman who lay there before him. He loosened her dress at the throat, told Forseno, sharply, to bring water. And then he found that Forseno was standing wringing his hands at the entrance to the secret passage and calling on Blas in a pleading voice to follow him away from danger.

But Blas was adamant. He himself brought the water. It caused Maruja to stir suddenly and to murmur without opening her eyes: "It is Guido—come back from hell to haunt me!"

"She is wakening," said Blas faintly. "Are you ready, then?"

"Yes, in God's name!" breathed Forseno. "They are coming now. Hurry!"

He pushed Blas before him, towards the gaping entrance to the passage, and indeed, now they could hear footsteps hurrying up the hallway beyond.

So Blas, with a final glance backwards at the woman on the bed, sprang into the dark doorway which yawned in the middle of the wall—sprang with such carelessness that the descending feet landed on the bar which was placed in the bottom of the passage floor. Instantly the door swung shut, heavy released weights pulling it short on smooth hinges.

Behind, there was a frantic cry of anxiety from Forseno: "Blas! Help!"

And Blas, as the door whirred shut behind him, heard the thundering voice of old Dial, as he rushed into the room. Other voices roared and rushed in company with the master of the house, and Blas knew that it would be madness to attempt to re-enter the room by the same means which they had just used.

Yonder, in the room of Dial, that fierce old man, as he rushed in, saw his daughter fainting on the bed, and Forseno, with a pale, distraught face, crouched against the wall in the corner.

The only weapon in the hands of Dial was the long walking staff. Not that he really needed a stick to support him, but he felt that it gave him an air of more patriarchal dignity, and therefore he was rarely without it. With that raised in his hands he rushed at poor Forseno and struck him to the floor. Then with his own hand he caught the other by the nape of the neck, raised him from the floor, and dragged his half-senseless body towards the bed.

It was wonderful to see what strength remained in the nervous arms of the old man, while he shouted: "You see, Christopher? It is the peon who has come back! It is that damned insolent peon, Forseno, who has come back to murder your mother! Now God or the devil teach me how I shall burn him alive! Maruja!"

She was already in the arms of Christopher, and, waking, she clung to him and looked wildly about her.

"Father!" she gasped to Dial. "It is Guido!"

"He has stabbed you!" groaned Dial. "The wolfish devil has murdered you, child!"

"I am not hurt," said Maruja. "But I thought that I saw him suddenly—and my heart stopped. I thought that he had come back from death! You told me that he was dead! You told me that he was dead!"

"He should have been!" said the stern Dial. "If I had had a true man's sense, he should have been dead, a long time ago. But he is not dead. It is no ghost that you saw, child, but a murderous rat of a man. Stand up, you dog!"

And he jerked Forseno straighter on his failing feet.

As for Forseno, the blood was running in a slow trickle down the side of his face from a small cut which the cane had made along his head. And the blood seemed a deeper red, by reason of the extreme pallor of his face as he stared before him at Maruja, and at Dial himself, and at the stern face of young Christopher, like a terrible, man-slaying Achilles!

"And that's Forseno!" breathed Christopher. "My God, is that the man that I've always pitied so much—and blamed you so much about him, sir—"

He made a gesture to his grandfather, still cherishing and shielding his mother.

She, however, seemed to feel more fear than horror.

"Guido," she said suddenly, "speak to me."

"It is I, Maruja," said the cripple sadly.

She shook her head with a sudden breath of relief.

"It is not the voice of Guido!" said she. "It is not his voice, and now that I look more closely at his face—no, it cannot be his face, either!"

"It is not Forseno," said Dial, leaping instantly at this clue. "It is not Forseno. Only a damned lock-breaker and robber. Take him away from your mother, Christopher!"

"Gladly!" answered Christopher, and stretched his huge hand towards the shrinking form of Forseno. But his mother glided suddenly between.

"I must know for certain, before he goes. Can you give me any other token of what you are?"

"This!" said Forseno, and held out his distorted hands.

It turned the face of the woman sick and white. She leaned back against the broad breast of her son.

"What is it?" asked Christopher anxiously. "What have his queer-shaped claws got to do with the matter, mother? Were those the hands of Guido Forseno?"

Another voice came from the throat of the captive, a voice trembling with grief and shame and rage and bitterness gathered in a whole life of remembering.

"Ask this Senor Dial. He can tell you whether these are the hands of Guido Forseno!"

"Be quiet!" growled Dial, fingering the staff. "Here—you fellows here—some of you with strong arms—come and take charge of this—"

There was a lurching forward of half a dozen mozos, each savage, eager to signalize his zeal in the service of his master.

But the voice of Maruja stopped them again.

"Keep them back, Christopher! Don't let them touch him! Keep them away from him—he's suffered enough for one life—"

The big left arm of Christopher swung back like a beam of iron and stopped the advance of the mozos.

"What in the name of the devil!" exclaimed Don Teofilo. "Cannot I give orders in my own house?"

"Give orders when there is not such a thing as this!" said Maruja in great and trembling excitement. "Oh, my Father, we have done too much harm to him already! And what would the valley be, or the house we live in, if it had not been—"

"Peace!" said Dial, livid with emotion. "You speak too freely, Maruja. Here, you—stand outside the door. Do you hear. Stand there in calling distance!"

The mozos huddled from the room with many a backward glance. And Maruja was saying: "He has given us wealth and all the happiness that we have here in the valley. Father, you cannot forget that! And how has he been paid?"

"Tell me," said the old man sternly, "if he has not come to take a payment of his own choosing. Forseno, what are you doing in the Casa Dial?"

Forseno, raising his hand slowly, wiped the blood from his forehead and then looked down to the red stain upon his fingertips.

"I shall not talk," said Forseno.

"He will not talk!" said Dial. "Do you hear? Do you hear, Maruja?"

"Then what will be done with him?" asked the girl. "And with the man who was with him?"

Dial started.

"Was there another?"

"Yes—someone who picked me up when I fell—"

"And where did you see him?"

"In the secret passage."

"The passage! The passage!" groaned Dial. "Oh, what a vast fool I have been not to wall the passage up!"

"Mother, Mother!" exclaimed Christopher, who had been listening wild-eyed while this talk progressed, "what were you doing there and what—?"

"Hush!" said Dial. "Listen!"

He did not need to warn them to be quiet. The heavy sounds came booming through the house, like explosions from the heart of the earth, and so tremendous was the noise, that they seemed to feel the building quake with it.

"Where is it?" asked Christopher his nostrils quivering like those of a horse when it hears the battle far off. "What is it and where is it?"

He sprang to the window and threw it up.

There was another booming of guns from beneath, and much closer, but the noise did not roll in through the window.

"The cellar!" called Dial. "It's from the cellar, Christopher. Do you hear me? From the cellar! Call the men!"

"Mozos!" thundered Christopher. "We'll go down and smoke the trouble out. Where's my father? The devil can tell what's happening in this house tonight!"

"Then there stands the devil!" said Dial, and he pointed with a stiff arm, at the face of Forseno.

The latter seemed to have forgotten his fear.

He stood straight, with his head thrown back a little, and on his face there was a smile of triumph.

"My son, Senor Dial!" said he. "And the guns mean that Don Guy is dead—and others—because when my son shoots he does not miss, and he has shot many times! You, too, will see him soon!"

"He means it," said Dial. "The fool has lost his wits. They were never very sound! Christopher, watch him. He means some deviltry. And he's capable of blowing himself to atoms, if he could blow us along with him! Watch—"

"Watch!" cried Forseno, throwing out his arms in an ecstasy. "Watch, but you cannot save yourselves from him!"

Chapter Thirty-five

Now when Blas had heard the sound of voices in the room of Dial with the swinging door shutting him back from the side of Forseno, he knew at once that it would be inviting sure death without the chance of performing any good to his father if he re-opened the door and burst back into the chamber, to the rescue.

So, instead, he hurried on down the passage, past the level, beside the dining-room, and so down towards the damp coolness of the cellar.

He was in haste, and therefore he did not pause to listen, even if he had been able to hear through the thick masonry of the door. But he raised the lever, and the door sagged suddenly open. And that instant half a dozen guns blazed straight at his face, and as the torrent of lead crashed against the steps of the passage, he heard the voice of Guy

Enright calling: "Keep him back from the door—don't try to enter! Keep them bottled up, and then we can smoke them out—"

There was no doubt that smoke would turn the trick, at that. But Blas had still another desperate card to play.

He turned and raced up the steps of the passage to the dining-room exit. No doubt that door was long unused; for, when he raised the lever, it opened with a heavy groaning.

But the men of Enright were already at the exit and the blare of their weapons and the crashing of their bullets drove him back for the second time.

He felt that if he wasted time he was utterly ruined. In some manner to take these wary people by surprise was all that remained for him to do. And, therefore, he raced on, back towards the upper door by which he had before entered the room of Dial.

In that room, there was a swirl of hopeless confusion.

The mozos, called back by Dial, filled the room with a dozen anxious, excited figures, no one knowing what to expect next, but all presuming that something wonderful was about to take place. For Forseno was in an ecstasy, with his arms thrown wide, swaying with a fierce enthusiasm as he cried out:

"Do you hear me, Dial? When he comes, he will go through you like a wolf through sheep—"

"Take him away, Christopher!" commanded Dial. "This devil knows something of a real danger to us. Guard him like your life!"

"Get most of these fellows out of my way, then," directed Christopher, making towards Forseno. "I'll make him safe for you, but not with this litter around him—"

The "litter" had packed around Forseno. Half a dozen sets of hands were fastened upon him. And by the sheer weight of their anxious efforts to make him secure, they had pressed him directly back against the wall where the hidden door was situated.

Now fortune struck on behalf of Blas.

For at that very moment he had raised the lever and started to open the door, hastening the pull of the heavy weights, by throwing his own strong shoulders into the scale.

The door swept open with great force. It bowled over two of the Mexican servants instantly and flung them headlong into the other servants, so that two or three crashed into Christopher and brought him cursing to the floor. His wrist struck the wood, and, by the impact the revolver was snapped from his hand.

A dozen wild shouts tore the air. Dial was bellowing commands. The poor mozos, in a wild panic as though they feared that this falling wall was a token that the entire house was collapsing, rushed here and there, and just as the confusion began, imagine a wild tiger thrown into such a heap of humanity!

So it was with the coming of Blas.

At the sight of him, even the strong nerves of Dial seemed to give way.

"It is Blas! It is Blas Lavera!" cried Dial. "Mercy of God, this is the end of my life!"

And yet, for all his fear, there was enough sense in him to make him jerk up the muzzle of the rifle which he was holding, and drive a bullet at the head of Blas.

The bullet missed by a vital inch, for though the hand of Dial was quick and his eye was sure, yet to fire at Blas at that moment was like firing at a dancing will-o'-the-wisp. He dodged through the crowd of tangled mozos; one shout had brought Forseno out of the heap and following at his back; and now a snapshot, from his balanced Colt, grazed the head of Dial and flung him backwards to the floor.

Christopher heaved himself to his feet, hurling the confusion of mozos away from him. He had the scream of his mother tingling in his ears. He saw Blas rushing for the door, and pausing there only long enough to allow Forseno to precede him to safety.

But the hands of Christopher were empty!

He tore a gun from one of the servants and fired, half-blinded with rage and excitement. The bullet flew wild.

And as he leaped forward, firing again, he saw Blas glide through the entrance, swinging the door shut behind him. The lock clanked softly as Christopher hurled himself against the strong oaken paneling. He was thrown back, and he could hear the beat of rapidly receding feet down the hall.

Twice and again he fired through the lock. Then the sway of his shoulder cast the door open.

Glancing back, he saw the blood-stained head of his grandfather, as the old man raised himself to his feet. Then, leaping into the hallway, he found it empty, and he raced for the stairs.

But Blas and Forseno were already vital seconds, in advance. They were far down the stairs before Christopher was free from the room of his grandfather.

They gained the side door from the Casa Dial and now they stood in the garden for a single instant, listening to the sound of shouts from the big house behind them.

After that instant of pause, they ran on again. And fast though Blas went, Enrique Lavera was not far behind him. For victory seemed to have given strength and lightness to his feet.

They passed rapidly through the woods.

Now, as they gained the edge of the covert, they could hear the turmoil of many shouting voices issuing from the house behind them, and scattering this way and that. It would not be long before horses were saddled and ready for the pursuit, but now they were already on the backs of the finest mounts in the valley.

Below and straight before them dipped the road towards the bridge, and they galloped for it. Blas, looking askance at the older man, saw him jostled uneasily in the saddle on Larribee. But still, he kept his place surprisingly well, and settled rapidly to the long, soft stride of the gelding.

So they came down like a storm, towards the bridge.

As he had expected, the guards at that vital point were already swinging onto their mounts. And giving La Blanca the rein, Blas flew on in the lead.

Some one at the near side of the bridge was shouting to him and waving a hand for him to stop. That was Farman—Farman the much trusted, the infallible servant.

"Steady!" shouted Blas. "Friends, Friends, Farman!"

Perhaps it was his voice. Or, more likely the familiar silver form of the mare that brought the message to Farman. And he reined suddenly out of the way to give them free passage.

And now Blas, as he rode past, with the thunder of Larribee's hoofs behind him, was shouting: "Ride for the house, Farman! It's Vega! Vega! We'll carry the warning to the men at the dam—"

"Vega, by God!" cried Farman.

The words were already half dim with distance behind Blas as he whirled along, down the road. The bridge rang hollow beneath the hoofs of La Blanca. Now Larribee crossed with thunder, to the farther side.

And looking back, Blas saw Farman streaking his horse towards the Casa Dial, with the rest of the bridge-guard riding as hard as they could in pursuit of their leader.

But here was Forseno beside him, and the long, smooth road stretched before them. It seemed, now that the difficulties were ended, that they had accomplished a miracle too wonderful for belief.

The rolling hills shut the Casa Dial from view, except for its broad roof. And so he drew La Blanca back to a hand-canter.

Forseno swung instantly up beside him. The courage and the old horsemanship of Forseno seemed to have come back to him. He sat at ease in the saddle, calling: "Blas, Blas, tell me that I saw the truth and not a lie! You sent a bullet through the head of Dial and now he lies dead in his house. Is it true?"

"It is true," answered Blas. "And God forgive me for it."

"Forgive you? An eye for an eye and a tooth for a tooth. But what has he paid back to me for the years that I have suffered? Nothing! There is still a long account which he will have to settle in hell! But ah, lad, that he could only have known the truth before he died!"

"What truth?" asked Blas.

But there was no answer from the other; and Forseno merely swayed in his saddle with a demoniacal laughter.

They rode on at a mere trot now. For the trail was long that lay before them. This thing which they had done would rouse every hand against them. The law would strain its long arm to the uttermost to seize them. It would be strange, indeed, if he could win away to the safety beyond the Rio Grande with such an encumbrance as Forseno along with him.

So he looked forward, to the time to come, without hope. He felt that he had come to the last trail of his young life. And as they climbed to the side of the first mountain slope, he reined La Blanca to a halt and looked back over the wide, moonlit hollow of the valley, and the dark eminence of Casa Dial in the center of it.

And it seemed to Blas that the bullet which had struck down Dial had destroyed the slayer in the same instant.

Chapter Thirty-six

They tore on in a wide semi-circle through the mountains and towards the south. In those days when Blas remained at the Casa Dial, he had printed every feature of the countryside in his memory. Against such a time as this was, he kept that knowledge in reserve, for he knew that there might be a sore need of it. Now he could sit quietly and chart the journey as though with a map before him.

So he split the trip into two long stages. He planned on the second evening, a little after dark, to cross the Slosson River, and once past it, he would be in a tangle of mountains from which a hundred little ravines pointed down towards the Rio Grande and ten thousand men could hardly prevent them from making a crossing.

This was the intention of Blas, and when he

communicated it to Forseno, the latter agreed with a smile and a nod.

Their labors in the flight did not seem to mean a great deal to the older man. One would have thought that Blas was riding to have his own life, but that that of Forseno was completed, so that it did not matter how the rest of it was spent. He was willing to be led; but where they arrived he hardly cared.

So the pair pushed steadily on, taking advantage of easy ground where they could, but pushing twice across high ridges to cut off much needed miles to shorten their trip.

It was a lonely ride. And it seemed to Blas that La Blanca alone had been more company to him than now his father was. During the day, there was never speech from the older man, and at night when they sat by the narrow hand of flame which was all that they dared allow themselves in lieu of a campfire, Forseno still did not talk beyond a monosyllable now and again.

But he would sit with his face tilted a little, smiling at the stars, as though they were able to comprehend the invisible content which possessed him. And, the value of life being ended for him, he awaited the end with a perfect calm.

And Blas could understand.

He could see clearly through all the last quarter of a century. He knew that Forseno had existed for one purpose only: to live until he had brought up this one son in whom the fire of manhood burned bright—to live until the time that such strength would come to that son that he might avenge the old injury done him, Forseno, by his arch-enemy, Teofilo Dial. That work, as they thought, was now accomplished. And what happened to Forseno now was less than nothing. There remained for him nothing more worth the pain and the trouble of living.

As for Blas, he was a tool which had performed the required service, and therefore he could be thrown aside.

Something very close to hatred began to grow up in Blas, as he more intimately understood the mind of his companion. He, too, had no desire for speech. He cared for the two horses during the marches, and at the end of them he shot the game for the one meal which they cooked, in the evening of the day, and then he was glad of the time to wrap himself in his blanket and sleep.

Only a great weariness could have made him sleep, for conscience which never had troubled Blas before, now kept him in the hell of a new torment.

And often it seemed to him that the lives of his two brothers, spent on the little alfalfa farm, adding dollar to dollar, planning little new acquisitions of property, from time to time, were so far happier than any fate which could lie before him, that they were much to be envied. But he had not been reared for such a purpose or for such a life. He was the thing which his father had made him by twenty-five years of labor and deliberate planning. He had been brought up to destroy. And now there were no talents in him for a peaceful existence.

It seemed to Blas, too, that the only happy days of his life had been spent in the house of Dial. For there, in that house, were people to whom he could open his mind safely and easily, for the first time since he was born. He dwelt in a sort of agony upon the gentle womanliness of Maruja, and upon the stern but manly soul of Dial now sent to the long account, as he thought, by a bullet from his revolver. And not least did he think of Guy Enright—calm, wise, sober; and, thinking of him, it seemed to Blas that he could understand a chapter in Forseno's history which his father had never made clear—and that was why there had been treason in Maruja.

But had it really been treason? Had not the favor which she had shown to Forseno been the mere kindness of her nature? And from the first she must have turned to Guy Enright as soon as he had entered her horizon. As for the peon, Forseno, he was interesting for the great things which he had planned in the valley, and he was pathetic before of all the longings which possessed him. But as a husband she could never have considered him.

Now that the deed, as Blas thought, was accomplished, he could understand all of this. And he felt that he had been mad not to have realized it before.

But Enright, Maruja, and Dial were all hardly a line, compared with the long chapter which Christopher filled in his thoughts. He had taken in Blas as one brother accepts another; he had opened his heart to him, brought him into the family; and now he, Blas, had repaid him by such treachery!

There was no hesitation in Blas to understand what the result must be. It would be a rage so consuming that nothing but blood could sate it. Christopher would be sure to labor on this trail of his, with enough passion to supply ten strong men. Blas was sure of that.

But a consuming thought—one that tortured, was that he had enjoyed the gentle, quiet life, the still evenings, the sense of strength and of growth, the eternal peace and that he had violated all of it, after he had accepted so much hospitality.

It was no wonder, then, that he yearned for longer, for harder, marches—for greater hardships to numb his body with fatigue and so make possible the merciful oblivion of sleep.

Well before sunset—so well had he timed the march—on the second day, they looked down from the height upon the narrow streak of silver and yellow which was the Slosson River. Blas unsaddled the horses and turned them out to graze; for, they were weary with the two forced marches, and they would perhaps have a need of strength before the night was over.

For two long hours he had waited, until the sun was low, when the brighter crimsons had died down, where there remained only a faint flush in the west, for the moment to start on.

Forseno, as always, was ready without a word. He was pathetically weary after the rigors of the last two days; but still, he did not complain; and, side by side, they rode down the last slope towards the river and towards the safety beyond it.

The horses again were in good fettle. They had lost some weight during the ride. But now they were hard and in the pink of condition. And they galloped down the slope, to the level bottom land, beneath.

It was deep darkness before they gained the level going. The dark moment lightened gradually, not with a moon, but with the clear brightness of the stars, filling the heavens with trembling, lambent points of fire. As their eyes grew more accustomed to the starlight, they could make out the distant silhouettes of the mountains towards which they were traveling; and, right behind them, the heights which they left seemed an almost equal distance to the rear.

There were two fords crossing the Slosson River, and Blas aimed at the upper one. It was three times as broad as the lower, but at this dry season of the year, the water in the broad ford hardly reached to the knees of a horse; whereas a horse ascended more than belly-high in the lower one, with better footing, too, as Blas had heard; and therefore, he was glad when they came down towards a sloping, gravel bank, with the blank, glistening face of the smooth water beyond it.

It was a famous place in history. And of those whitening bones which marked either side of the ford, as with clear strokes of chalk, not all were the skeletons of animals which had been slaughtered for food. There was more than one human frame, in this debris, that had been lost here, in death.

But he paid no heed to that; for, he was too close to the threshold of, what he hoped would be, a new life. Once in the mountains, beyond, and an army could not catch them, or keep them from crossing the Rio, on the farther side. And beyond

the Rio Grande lay the broad bosom of the southland, where they would be able, perhaps, to find
quiet and forgetfulness from the world. What had
been done by men in the northland did not matter
there!

So thought Blas, and with a sort of guilty haste
he sent La Blanca into the water. She tried it dain-
tily with hoof and nose. Then with a shake of her
head, she went in, found the footing beneath,
crouched a little as her hoofs entered the slushy
sands, and soon gained courage and confidence.
It was not the first ford which she had negotiated.
But she had learned enough to distrust all such
places because of the chance that deadly danger
might be met in them.

They drew on towards the farther shore when
Blas heard a faint call to the left, and down the
bank. He looked, and saw a moving streak which
seemed to him to be the head and shoulders of a
man, racing across the horizon stars at uncanny
speed—and an instant later, he heard the sound
of hoofs.

One man would not stop them, if a guard were
placed there for that purpose. And his heart
swelled with a fierce pride when he thought that
the task of halting Blas Forseno might have been
given to some single outrider!

He pushed La Blanca on. Another moment and
her forehoofs would begin to grate on the shelving
pebbles which underlined the other shore. And
then, almost straight ahead, he heard two voices
cry in chiming unison: "Who's there?"

He strained his eyes, and by the glimmer of the
stars, he saw two thin streaks of light.

Those were rifles, leveled upon him, he well knew.

"Friend!" said Blas.

"Name, friend!"

"Harper. Sid Harper."

"Ride on in towards us, Sid Harper. You might hike your hands up over your head, too, while you're about it. Come on in, anyway, and let's have a look at you—and your pal, too!"

For an instant, Blas thought of trying to rush those rifles and ducking away to one side or the other towards the mountains. But there had been something in the drawling quiet of that voice that made him know such an attempt would be suicide. Instead, he made La Blanca rear, whirled her on her hind legs, and rushed back for the bank which they had just left.

Chapter Thirty-seven

The sense of fair play was cultivated just a little too strongly in the minds of the watchers on the other shore. Twice, and again, a challenge and a command to halt rang after Blas, and Forseno who was now scudding in the lead for the same goal. And when a bullet did sing after them, it passed humming far above their heads.

For answer, Blas spun about in the saddle and dropped two shots at the enemy. A shrill curse rang clearly in answer. There was a burst of angry cursing, and then came the metallic clangor of three rifles that filled the air with lead.

But the two fine horses were already turning the water white as they crashed on towards the safe shore. Now they darted up the bank, gathering instant speed as the liquid no longer clung about their legs. There was only starlight for that shooting, and there were two rapidly fleeing targets, so that Blas was hardly surprised when they dipped down the little slope just beyond the bank, unhurt.

In answer to his excited call, the voice of For-seno instantly answered him.

"The gringo dogs have not touched me, my Son! Shall we try the other ford?"

"No!" Blas had had enough of that river for the night. If the enemy was out in such force at this ford, it meant that there would be a strong watch, all along. Besides, from behind them he could hear the snorts and the splashings, as the men of the law sent their horses into the water, in pursuit.

There was only one clear course for flight, where the long strides of big Larribee would tell clearly; and they might need every possible advantage to make the speed of their horses equal the rush of the fresh horses of the posse-men. So, straight up the shelving valley they rode, and turned in at the mouth of the first ravine.

Looking back as they entered, they could see nothing; but, out of the blackness of the night, they could hear distinctly the pounding of hoofs.

Through that ravine they wound onto the high-land, and there, for an hour along a slowly sloping crest of the water divide, they had fairly good going again. But, when they paused at this time to loosen the cinches and to allow their horses a breathing spell, a scant ten minutes brought the noise of riders out of night behind them, and they had to strike onwards, again.

Twice Blas turned aside down ravines—once to the right, and again to the left, so that the pursuers would not be able to track him by the general direction in which he was riding. And twice, when he and Forseno paused to listen, they heard the riders come slowly after them, through the darkness.

It was plain that some master tracker had this work in hand, and Blas, combing his thoughts for an explanation, instinctively struck upon the famous name of Sheriff Gregory.

It seemed long years ago that the great sheriff had ridden into San Pablo and delivered his warning at the door of the house of Enrique Lavera. But now, if it were indeed Gregory behind, there would be reason to remember what he had said.

They struggled on through the long night. When they came to steep slopes, Blas insisted that they climb down and run along on foot so as to rest the horses. Half a dozen times, when they crossed rivulets, he made brief halts to splash water over the hot animals. And so, when the grey of the dawn came, they still were safely distancing their pursuers.

There was no sound of riders behind them, but as Blas turned his strong field glass over the broken sea of country behind him, he saw a sudden stream of riders jogging their horses over the crest of a stony wave.

He focused the glass instantly on that procession, and so he was aware of a big man riding strangely on a roan horse at the head of the list. It was too great a distance for him to be sure of who it could be. The face beneath the shadow of the hat was only a blur. But there was something disquietingly familiar, to Blas, in the width of that brim, and in the careless manner in which it was jammed upon one side of the rider's head. There was something in the resolute shoulders of the man, that made his identity almost a certainty—and with that feeling of certainty, came the feeling, too, that his instinct of the night before had been correct. There, fleeing towards the southland, at the very door of safety he had run his head into the lion's mouth!

But even though Blas was conspicuously brave, his blood turned cold and he quaked as he stared, counting the riders who trailed along behind their master. He counted eleven of them, and as he watched them dip out of view, he again groaned and cursed.

The good sheriff was not apt to take eleven men with him except on a mission that was of the greatest importance. He had been known to set forth *single-handed* on a mission which had as its goal the arrest of two or three offenders. His generous willingness to risk his own head and use his own hand, in the cause of the law, had saved the county a pretty penny during his terms of office. Still, when he felt that the occasion demanded it, there was no one more prodigal in dispensing funds for the apprehension of criminals. The lawbreakers knew this well. They avoided the county of Sheriff Stefan Gregory as though it were covered with a poisoned air. . . .

Blas felt a thrill of pride that he had been considered worthy of pursuit by such a troop as this.

Blas, rubbing the sweat from the belly of the mare, and then pouring a swallow of water, from his canteen, down her throat, recognized the greatness of his danger; and he wondered if this news would have the effect of bringing his father from his heavy lethargy.

"It's Sheriff Gregory," he said, turning to the older man.

"Gregory?" repeated Forseno in mild interest. "Gregory? Will you let me look?"

"Yes. You know him, and you have a keen long-distance eye. Take a look at him and then tell me what you see."

A long moment followed, in which Blas worked frantically over the horses, while the glass in Forseno's hand was riveted upon the train of pursuers, coming closer towards them, crawling over another crest.

"It is Stefan Gregory," exclaimed Forseno, lowering the field glass and handing it back to the young man. "The trail is at an end, my son!"

"Tell me what you mean by that?" asked Blas.

"I mean only that it is time to stop foolish struggling. It is time to surrender, Blas. Are you willing to do that?"

"Because Gregory has started after me?"

"You cannot escape him! You see he knows all the twists and the turns of your mind!"

"What is your proof of that?" asked Blas, sharp with antagonism at the suggestion that another could look into his mind.

"There are are a thousand gates into the southland," said Forseno. "But Gregory knew that you would try this one. He knew how to follow you through the night, too!"

"By flashing an electric torch to find the trail—"

"What torch," said the older man, "did he flash

to find out that you would ride south to the Slosson River?"

"That is true," nodded Blas, turning a little sullen. "That devil has the eyes of a lynx to find the sign of a trail. He has the wits of a fox—"

"And the eye of a lynx," broke in Forseno. "Wait here, my son, and surrender to him. Do you not see that the farther you ride, the greater is the danger that you may commit other crimes and so harden the heart of the law against you?"

"Can I hang higher," asked Blas ruefully, "for two murders than they'll hang me for the killing of Dial?"

"You killed Dial when a rifle was in his hand. He fired the first shot, moreover."

"I have thought of that," said Blas. "But they hang a man in this state not for killing but for the way that he kills. And they'll prove that we sneaked into the house by a secret passage and that we went there intending to kill a white-headed old man—"

"Old devil!" hissed Forseno.

"I can hear the lawyer talking against me," said Blas, half closing his eyes. "Yes, they are sure to hang me if they take me, and hang me they never shall, so help me God! I intend to fight to the last drop!"

"And kill others?" asked Forseno calmly.

"Not if I can help it! I want to hurt no one. I only want to be free, Father. But for freedom, I'll fight like a devil if I have to."

"So says the wildcat," murmured the older man.

"What did you say?"

"Nothing. Your way is your own. And I shall ride

on with you, I suppose, but I am growing tired, Blas!"

"You will grow more tired when they have you behind steel bars! Think of that and it'll give you strength. Now the horses have rested enough. Let's get on!"

They mounted, once more, and toiled slowly up the slope. It was not excessively steep, and the horses easily could have taken it at a trot, or even at a forced canter. But Blas had a reason for letting them take their time.

For if the posse came in sight of their prey toiling so wearily, and so slowly, up the height, they would be sure to break forward with a yell, to ride down two criminals. And that straining up the hill would kill off the last strength in their mounts.

So Blas made the horses take it very leisurely in their going up the slope towards the crest of the rise. Beyond, as he well knew, extended a long, smooth, even slope down the valley, and that drooping ground would add a double power to the long legs of the gelding.

But it seemed that the sheriff would never come into view.

Then came a far-off yell, accompanied by the ringing, faint explosion of a gun, and, looking back, Blas saw the whole procession stream down the face of a hill, flogging and spurring and whooping.

Chapter Thirty-eight

Startled back to the menace of the time and place, Blas once again permitted La Blanca to break forward in a trot. Meanwhile, he glanced anxiously at Larribee. As for his mare, he had no doubts concerning her. There still was an unexhausted, an untapped well of courage and heart in her. But the thoroughbred, with all of his tough strength, was now feeling the effects of his three interminable marches. Blas observed that Larribee's belly was badly tucked up. But he saw, too, that the animal still carried his head well, and that his knees were firm. And Blas reflected that he would do for a lengthy run and he determined to let him have it. So, he put the pair down the slope of the valley at a long, easy canter judging that they would be able to maintain it clear to the farther end of that narrow valley, lost in dim blueness beyond them.

They already had put a comfortable distance behind them when the crest of the wave of the posse broke over the height. Blas, looking back, was not surprised to find that the sheriff was not among the first. He had saved his horse in that exhausting and foolish burst up to the hill. But, the other horses stormed across the ridge, their heads already bobbing with exhaustion.

Still, looking down the valley, the men of the law, by the crystal morning air of the mountains, could see their quarry in clearest view; and they whipped their staggering horses down the falling ground, in the hope that the slope would make up all the difference.

They did not need a quarter of a mile to tell them that they were well beaten. Blas, carefully rating the canter of La Blanca and Larribee did not draw away from the leaders. And, still, for another mile they kept on, until one of the mustangs dropped.

With that, the whole group came to halt, and Blas could see the horses standing with fallen heads, and the men stripping the saddles off them and walking them anxiously up and down lest they should cool off too rapidly.

But La Blanca and Larribee, in the face of all that had happened, still had an untapped store of strength. They kept on for two more miles, until the turn of the valley shut them out of the view of the sheriff's party, then pulled up their nags to a walk.

The honest sheriff might have other expedients in mind, but certainly he was far from any place where he could remount his men with fresh stock;

and, in the meantime, his ponies were thoroughly put through the mill.

It seemed to Blas that now, if ever, they had their chance of shifting their ground so that wise Stefan Gregory could half-break his heart before he picked up the wished-for trail again. And when he told his father his thoughts, the elder Forseno nodding, shrugged his shoulders.

"Every day is a long day," said he, "when a man rides on a blood trial. You must never forget."

"Tell me," said Blas suddenly, "what you know of blood-trails?"

"I see no reason why I should not tell you," answered Forseno. "There are not many days of life left to me, perhaps. And so—why, Blas, I have told you that I came to the house of Dial in rags, exhausted, and on foot?"

"Yes," said Blas, "you have told me all of that, of course. And do you mean to say that you were driven on that desert?"

"Driven within an inch of my life," said Forseno calmly. "For eleven days I thought that every morning would be the last in which I should see the sun, and yet by the time night came I was still marching. My horse dropped on the eighth day—"

"And, why? Was there an enemy on your trail?"

"I had killed the brother of a man. He had made certain ugly remarks about me. And so I came up to him and shot him down and saw him fall on his face—"

"What?" said Blas. "On his face?"

"He happened to be walking with his face turned from me," said Forseno calmly.

"You shot him through the back, then?"

"What matter? Yes. However, his brother hunted me—"

"If you were not my father," said Blas, breathing hard, "I should have something to say to you—but go on!"

"Yes," said Forseno, "you have always been one of those young fools who are called chivalrous. A pack of dead notions lining your silly head, eh? Well, that fellow gave me a hard hunt. He picked up some friends along the way. There were three of them, before the end. When my horse died, I thought that it was sure to be death for me. But still I struggled on, and when my feet began to bleed, I threw away my guns, to lighten me. And it takes a good horse, my lad, to catch a man who knows how to use his strength in walking!"

"It is true," said Blas, frowning at the ground. "But continue!"

"And so I came to the rancherio."

"Then Dial took you in?"

"Yes."

"And kept the three from taking you?"

"Yes. He went out with his rifle. They told him that they had a right to me.

" 'I do not protect him because he is a good man,' said Dial, 'but because he is a desperate and tired man. Leave him!' And they left me. They were better to have done so, too. When Dial in those days started a war, it was a dreadful affair, my lad!"

Blas listened as one struck dumb. Then, he said, at last:

"You never before told me that you owed your life to Dial!"

"No, I never told you before," replied Forseno calmly.

"And yet that would have put a different face on the whole story, senor!"

"Listen to me," said the elder man, explaining with much gravity. "I have procured the death of Dial at your hand, have I not?"

"And my heart begins to groan because of what I have done!"

"Let that be! Would I have accomplished that end if I had told you in the first place I had owed my life to him?"

"No, no!" groaned Blas. "And now God forgive you for what you have said to me!"

"God," said Forseno darkly, "knows my heart. If it is evil, I was damned long before the death of Dial. If it was good before, his death would not damn me. It was not my hand that brought him down!"

And he looked at Blas with blazing eyes—such a fire that for a moment Blas thought his father had lost his wits. For surely this was either the flare of a great hatred, or of a bitter mockery.

"What does it mean, then?" asked Blas faintly. "God tell me what you mean by the manner in which you have covered my eyes and led me like a fool!"

"God, perhaps, will explain to you on some other day," said Forseno coldly, "but for my part, I have said all that I care to say upon the matter."

"There is no care in you for my opinion?"

"Why should I care, Blas?" said the other with

stern abruptness. "Have I not told you that I very well understand that I have not long to live on this earth? And therefore, I shall use my thoughts for something else than the consideration of the opinions of—my son!"

And he laughed in such a fashion that he seemed to be consigning Blas to the nethermost limbo of indifference.

As for Blas, it seemed to him that their escape from the sheriff was as nothing compared with this conversation, in importance. They were free, for the moment at least, from the strong hands of Gregory and his men. But now Blas knew that he would never be free from the pangs of conscience.

He strove to close his eyes against the picture that was now built up in his mind of his father; but that picture would not down. Still he saw the bitter truth creeping in upon him—Guido Forseno—or Enrique Lavera—or whatever name might really belong to him, had committed certain unrevealed crimes in his past. Of these, the shooting of a man in the back had been one. And he had been saved from a just vengeance, there could be no doubt, by the careless and generous courage of Senor Dial. It is true that his father had repaid that generosity with great achievements in the valley. But it was equally true that the escaped murderer, the coward, and fugitive from a just retribution, had been bold enough to claim the hand of the daughter of his rescuer. . . . And after that, the wild nature of Dial had done the rest!

It was a poignant thought to Blas that the patience with which Forseno had worked at the rearing of a brave son, to revenge him, was just the type of talent which one would expect from a man who had shot another man through the back. Blas suppressed a groan as his father broke in on that thought.

"We are not out of danger, yet," said the quiet voice of the new-made fatalist who rode beside him. "There ride certain fellows who wish to speak to you, Blas. Do you wish to stop for them?"

And Blas, looking up, saw a stream of riders breaking out of the mouth of a shadowy ravine, not far, before them.

He stared, and thought that he recognized a cream-colored horse—a beautiful creature stretching across the ground at its full speed.

That was the cream-colored horse of Poco, he could swear. And if that were the case, those were the men of Vega, rushing in to head him off, and so to drive him back into the hands of the sheriff.

He sent La Blanca ahead with a shouting, unsheathing his rifle, while she broke into a gallop. Larribee, swinging on, in his fine gallop nearby, showed there was much running left in him, too. At least Blas need have no compunction about shooting to kill, so long as his gun was bearing upon such assorted scoundrels as Vega led to war!

He could see how that fox-minded leader had worked out the puzzle. Perhaps, from lofty ground, he had followed the whole movement of that day, and had crossed the mountains to throw himself on the fugitives, just as they left the exhausted horses of the sheriff, behind.

These were not quite fresh mounts that the men of the Mexican rode upon, but they were fresh enough to make much mischief. They pounced out upon the valley floor like a charge of their ancestral Indians, whooping and screaming with the surety of victory. Then the rapid clangor of the rifle, from the hands of Blas, put a stop to their triumph.

Chapter Thirty-nine

He shot, from the shoulder, with no attempt at careful aim, for who can aim with care with a rifle from a galloping horse? But the distance was too great for even snap shooting with a revolver; and so, he took chances with the more powerful weapon. After all, it was a game at which he had had much training by Forseno. Surely those long early lessons were bearing a rich reward, now! He had been used to cantering a horse rapidly up and down a field, emptying a rifle at a post or a tree; and, he had been kept at such work ever since he was a boy.

He fired once, and again, and the leaders of the horsemen merely rode the harder, filling the air with their screeches, all the while. He fired, once more, and dropped a horse and man. The horse lay still. But, the rider, after turning two or three somersaults in the dust, hobbled to his feet and ran for shelter behind the nearest rock.

The whole party scattered at the same moment. They were all willing to endure their share of danger; but, they wanted no more such shooting as this. They spread to the right and the left, and Blas could see a magnificent black horse which carried a broad-shouldered, rather stumpy-appearing fellow. It was Vega, himself, he knew; and he turned his rifle on that general.

Half a dozen times he fired. And each time he knew that he missed completely; for, La Blanca was laboring over rough ground. But at least he had shot near enough to make Vega forget his battle fury.

He reined his horse to the side and took refuge behind a clump of shrubbery. From that clump, bullets began to spit out at Blas and his father, but they, in the meantime, were turning every fraction of a second into most valuable ground.

And now, from behind them, they saw the rabble of Vega, once more start out and climb onto the backs of their horses.

The hunt up the valley began again. And Blas knew well enough that it was likely to be the last trail on which he could ever expect to ride. It was never an easy matter to shake off the pursuit of hardy mustangs, Mexican-ridden. And after the enormous labor which La Blanca had undergone, it was plain that she could never keep them away for long. As for Larribee, his head was bobbing with every stride, and he was nearly done. But there was still some strength left in them.

Not far ahead, there was the mouth of a ravine,

yawning shadowy onto the broad, white floor of the valley, and, on its steep slopes, he saw a welcome mist of pine trees. Perhaps in that tangle they might find a way of escape.

So, he urged on La Blanca. His father was furiously whipping Larribee. They drained the last strength of the horses to gain the canon mouth. But a cruel disappointment met them there. A narrow fringe of trees grew within, and all the rest was bare, sun-beaten rocks and sands; so that, as they turned up the ravine, the flood of the pursuit roared behind them.

The canon forked a quarter of a mile ahead, and because of that Blas said to Forseno: "You take the left side. They will never leave off following me, and I'll ride on the right hand. Head for that canon, and when you see that they are not following you, get off and walk Larribee. Otherwise, you'll have a dead horse under you inside of two miles. Good-bye!"

He waved his farewell as he spoke, while Forseno turned his indifferent face and studied the younger man.

"What will become of you, Blas?" he asked.

"I shall find a way to dodge them among the rocks, yonder, I think," said Blas. "This is not my day for dying! Good-bye again. And remember—when you are safe from them, think of your horse!"

The other nodded. He spoke no touching farewell, but turned the big horse straight for the lefthand ravine. They had separated, to a little distance, when Blas saw Forseno turn his head and look back at him, and it seemed to Blas that there was a smile of mockery on the face of the older man.

Whatever the result of this wild day might prove to be, Blas felt that his father's home was closed to him from that moment. He could never go back and look upon Forseno with anything other than the deepest detestation. The veil had fallen from between them. It revealed to him that he was not the son of the older man, but a tool, to be used, for a purpose, and then thrown away.

He had been used, and now he was thrown away; for, looking up the valley, he knew that nothing but a miracle could save him. Beneath the saddle, La Blanca was failing at every stride, and the advance of the pursuit gained momentarily.

Once, and again, he turned in the saddle and with his rifle, drove the pursuers back to a safer distance. But that could not continue indefinitely. They were spreading out and working up from either hand, and all their forces were concentrated on him alone. A division, of half a dozen, had headed towards Forseno, up the left hand valley. But now they had turned back, recalled by Vega, apparently. For it seemed that that chief cared nothing about the older man—that he wished only to make his revenge doubly certain. There would be no stone unturned by him to accomplish his purpose. That was unmistakable!

The canon climb narrowed, every instant, and the ascent tolled cruelly on La Blanca. She had lasted well enough as long as she could stride on the level, or on a down slope, but the burden of climbing this valley floor was killing her.

They wound about an elbow turn, now, and

here in the center of the ravine, Blas saw the place where he felt that he was about to die.

A small spring gave out a silver thread of water that wove indifferently among the rocks for a little distance and then disappeared. And near the source of the spring stood a time-crushed shack. It might have been the lean-to of a prospector, working among these rocks in the search of—who could tell what? Or perhaps it was only the house of a sheep herder—perhaps sent to his long account in the days of the cattle wars, of the past.

At any rate, in that naked place, it was the one spot that was open to Blas for a shelter—if a shelter it could be called!

He rode to it, and leaning from the saddle, gave one glimpse at the interior.

It was a mere rag of a place. The cracks yawned wide on every wall. But, still, it would shelter him from the eyes of Vega's men. He dismounted. And, at that moment, around the bend of the valley, came the whole troop of the Mexicans, and he heard their ringing yell go up when they saw him halted there.

At any rate, he would be their only booty! Vega would not return to San Pablo riding beautiful La Blanca. With that decision made, he tore the saddle and bridle from the animal, letting her drink a single swallow from the rivulet. Then a stroke of his hand, upon her flank, sent her scampering away, up the valley. Relieved of her master's weight and the binding grip of the cinches; refreshed, too, by the taste of water, she swung buoyantly over the ground, with head lifted, and turned back towards him as though wondering what this game could be, and why, he did not come with her.

As for the Mexicans, they knew well enough what this meant. Their arms were waving. Their shouting came to him at the door of the shack, in a triumphant chorus.

He looked anxiously around him. There was no time for elaborate preparations. But, at least, he could secure the doorway. So he dragged a great flat rock across it, high enough to serve as a breastwork for one kneeling behind it. When his shelter was as complete as he could make it, he sprang back to the shack just in time to escape from the first rattling volley of Mexican musketry.

By the time he had raised his rifle to retaliate, every Mexican saddle had been emptied, the riders had taken refuge among the valley rocks, and there was nothing to be seen except the horses in the background—as though they knew well enough that he would not demean himself by dropping their animals. For the rest, there was only the clang of a rifle, from time to time, and then perhaps the trailing of a shadow between rock and rock. They surrounded him swiftly, methodically. They occupied every point of vantage with a skilled precision; and, presently, they opened fire, as carefully directed as all the rest of their movements.

Floor high, and breast high, the bullets combed through the shack, ripping through the rotten wood as though it were paper, filling the interior with a choking wood-dust and stinging his eyes with it until the tears ran unchecked. Those shots came with such a steady stream that he knew he could not last another minute, without a new shelter.

There was one wretched tool in the little house. It was a spade with a broken handle, but apparently strong, and undamaged in the blade. That spade he drove into the ground. But, at the first stroke it broke off.

He had only a stump of it left to labor with; but, fortunately, the floor of the cabin had a sandy bottom, and he was able to scrape his way into it, banking up the earth on all sides of him, until he had made a shallow trench.

He lay in the damp coolness of it, panting and gasping for a moment. But now he was safe from the shots that honeycombed the little building. It was only miraculous, to Blas, that such a mass of flying lead did not blow it from its posts and expose him to the eyes of the men outside.

But he could not remain long in this spot of safety. It seemed to him that the explosions of the rifles sounded louder and louder. So, he left his trench and stole to the wall. The instant that he looked through the first crack, he saw a spurt of smoke from a rock hardly ten steps away. He straightened, and he could see from this vantage, nothing but the tip of the rifle muzzle, and the heel of a foot, as the man fired again.

That heel was his target. He took careful aim, setting his teeth with grim pleasure, as he worked his bead as deep down to the edge of the rock, as far towards the center of the heel as he dared, without risking a ricochet. Then he pulled the trigger and a wild scream answered him. The victim curled in a knot, clasping his torn, ruined foot. And Blas saw that it was Vega, himself!

Chapter Forty

He raised his hand for a second shot. But, he was never to be able to tell what it was that stopped him—whether it was the wild yell of woe and astonishment that went up from the others—or a reluctance in his own heart of hearts to put to death a helpless man in agony. At any rate, he allowed Vega, the next moment, to twist away out of view among the rocks, groaning bitterly.

Still, he was far from help, and the wound must have been bleeding fast. For now, in a gap between the rocks not far away, he saw the head and shoulders of the wounded man come into view, and then as he dragged himself further into view—the rest of the body, with, finally, the wounded leg trailing behind it a miserable streak of blood.

It was too much for Blas. He shouted loudly: "Amigos, come to Vega. He bleeds to death! Do you hear me? I shall not shoot! Quickly, now!"

There was an incredulous murmur from every hand, as this proposal was heard. And then some one braver, or with a stronger love for his master, than the rest, stood up, and ran hastily towards the spot where Vega was struggling, over the face of the ground, among the rocks. Others followed, and soon Vega was carried away, towards a clump of trees.

Then, silence fell over the ravine. The last rifle had been fired. Among the rocks, the scurrying had died down. But still the shack was watched, despite their care for their wounded master. And, when he showed his hat on a stick outside the door, a little later, the old ruse drew an instant return of bullets.

They were still watching for him, then. And for that matter, unless their wits failed them, they had only to sit still and wait for hunger to drive him out of the shack. It would not take so very long. Besides, were not these people equipped with a marvelous and deadly patience?

That was the end that he expected. Or, perhaps, a surprise attack by night, or day, when he was drugged with weariness and could no longer keep his eyes open.

He watched the light of the day die down, wondering how long he could last, through the days to come before hunger tormented him into surrender. Or, would it be quicker, and just as manly, to end the struggle by putting a bullet through his head?

He turned that thought soberly in his mind.

The day died in saffron and rose. The valley

floor turned purple, and then blue, and the softness of the mountain twilight had begun, when Blas heard a wild outburst—shouting and wailing. It continued for a minute or two. And after that, there was a sudden crashing of guns.

"It is Sheriff Stefan Gregory!" said Blas to himself. "It is Gregory!"

And he set his teeth and gripped his gun, for he fully determined to sell his life as dearly as possible. And, if the terrible sheriff had come, it would mean a quick end to his problems. He knew that well!

So, listening breathlessly, striving to analyze the sounds which he heard, it seemed to Blas that he could make out a singular harsh jangling of voices. And then, after an interval, there came the noise of horses, galloping down the valley. Of that he could be sure.

He tried to tell himself that it was the party of Vega, retreating, but still he dared not show himself. He dared not leave the place, to investigate, even by starlight.

But, at length, a most welcome sound came to him from the night—the sound of Poco's voice, calling: "Hello, Blas! Ho, Blas!"

"I am here, Poco!"

"Oh, I knew that. But I thought that you might be asleep," Blas called back.

"Asleep, man, in a time like this?"

"Well, how can I tell what a devil like you will do? I do not walk up on your sleep any more than I would on a tiger's. Will you come out of that black shack, or must I come in there?"

"Is it safe for me to come out?"

"Would I ask you, otherwise?"

Blas stood out in the open coolness of the night and felt that his life was beginning again.

He could see Poco heaving through the starlight, mounted as ever on his cream-colored horse, although definite color was all lost in this light.

"Poco," broke from Blas, "what in the name of the devil has happened?"

"You and the devil are friends," said Poco. "Otherwise you could never have managed what you have done today. Tell me. Do you not know, really, what has happened, and why I am sitting this horse, here, and talking to you?"

"No," said Blas. "It is true that I cannot guess, unless by a miracle the men of Vega have gone away!"

Poco laughed softly.

"Now let me tell you, amigo," said he, "that the living things in this valley are four. There is Blas Lavera, and there is Poco, and there is my horse, and yonder among the rocks is La Blanca, breaking her heart to come back to you again, and coming, too, so soon as she's sure the cursed rifle noise has ended."

"*Madre, Madre de Dios*!" breathed Blas. "It is true, Poco?"

"I tell you the truth, Blas, of course. Why should I lie, then?"

"It *is* true," said Blas softly. "And now, by all that's wonderful, tell me what has happened!"

"I can show you," said Poco, yawning a little. "It will save time, and besides, the ear can never understand just what the eye can see! Come along with me!"

He led the way towards the little cluster of trees where Vega had been laid, earlier in the afternoon.

"I understand, though," said Blas. "When Vega found out that I was not a mere murderer—when I let him get safely away—why, his own heart relented a little! That was it, Poco?"

Poco laughed aloud.

"You are a great child, my friend. Let me tell you the truth. As he lay on his back, bleeding, between groans he begged his men to attack the shack."

"Ha?" said Blas. "That is very bad, then!"

"And who taught you that there was anything good in that Vega, except money? No, and he lay there, and when they would not go to get you and cut your throat, he cursed them for cowards, and then he showed us ten thousand dollars in paper money. He passed one of the notes around to let us make sure it was not counterfeit. And, after that, he said that he would give the ten thousand to the man who struck the first bullet or the first steel into the body of Blas Lavera! That was the way he forgave you, Blas!"

Poco paused and laughed, again.

"He is a swine," said Blas. "And the day shall come when I shall pay off this score against him!"

"Tush!" chuckled Poco. "You will have to wait a long time for that, now!"

"Well, I have patience. And I have a fast horse."

"Have you?"

"Yes, and here she comes glimmering to me through the night! God bless you, La Blanca, my beauty," he greeted her enthusiastically.

"Well, Blas, La Blanca is a fine mare, I know. But still, you will never catch Vega with her."

"Eh?"

"That is what I say."

"You will not bet your money on it, though?"

"Yes, but I will. A thousand—ten thousand pesos!"

"Very good!" said Blas. "Tell me what is the color of the horse that he is riding?"

"A great white horse," said Poco.

"A white horse? A white horse?" echoed Blas. "That is very strange! However, I suppose that I must believe you. But I thought that he never would ride a white horse—white was too easily seen!"

"This horse," said Poco, "he could hardly escape from riding, I suppose that you might say."

"Because he knew that I would come hunting him, the devil!"

"He knows that you will come after him, someday, for that matter. But he does not seem to care."

"He holds me lightly then, Poco?"

"Well, yes."

"So? Well, he will limp a while on account of me!"

"Do you think so? I tell you, Blas, that he feels not the least pain from his heel tonight."

"The devil take me!" groaned Blas. "This is too wonderful. And unless my gun lied to me, it sent a bullet smashing straight through the bone and the flesh of his heel, and it must have torn the foot all to pieces! And yet you say that he feels no pain?"

"Not a single twinge!"

"This gets more and more bewildering!" said Blas sullenly. "However, I wish very much to believe you. I wish to believe you, amigo. Only—it will take a great deal of proving, and I shall look forward to the time when I pit my grey mare against any white horse in the world! Why are you taking me here beneath these trees, though?"

"Look down, Blas, and you will see."

"Hello, who is asleep, here?"

"Look closer."

"It is Vega! Vega, by the heavens!"

"Yes, it is Vega. Why does that surprise you? Think, Blas, that his foot was spouting blood like a pump. His heart was driving his strength straight out of him through that great wound. He was as good as a dead man before I got to him and found the fools wringing their hands and shouting at each other. I clamped a tourniquet on that leg and stopped the bleeding, but had an idea that I was a good deal too late. Then he came to his senses a little and seemed to know that he was in a bad state. It made him angry, not afraid. He called for brandy. He lay all afternoon setting himself on fire with brandy, and then putting the fire out with water. And he shouted offers of money to the men who would kill you. He tempted some of the others, and he almost tempted me. If you shot just a little less straight, Blas, I would have tried to sneak up and take you from behind. But I know you, you murderer! So, finally, in the twilight, Vega stiffened and died, with a curse on his foul lips. There was a little fighting above him for the sake of his keys.

"I don't know who got them. But I know that he

lies dead under that rock, yonder."

"Ha?"

"Oh, it was a gay little circus! You would have been at home in it, but I got behind a rock and watched and wished them at the devil. And, finally, they pelted off down the valley, still chasing the next lucky man who had taken the keys, and so they will chase each other all the way to San Pablo, and when they try to use the keys, they will find nothing, because this friend of ours, this Vega, he would not keep his hands heavy with treasure, but he let the banks be his watch dogs. However, there will be plenty of work for the sheriff's posse, when it rides up this valley. Now, you and I should leave a little memorial here over Vega. We should make him a grave, or leave it to the sheriff?"

"Vega," said Blas, "the real Vega, is riding that great white horse. What does he care about graves? And yet for all the speed of that horse, I think, Poco, that he may still envy me riding below, here, on La Blanca!"

Chapter Forty-one

The way of Blas and Poco did not long coincide. The one rode north; the other rode east. And he who took the eastern trail towards the valley of Dial was Poco. He jogged the cream forward contentedly, taking his time, since a slow horse in the morning makes a fast horse in the afternoon. Poco knew that well.

So he rode in the evening to the back of the Casa Dial and found a group of house mozas there beneath the trees, gossiping in the cool of the breeze.

"Is Juanita there?" called Poco. For there was always a Juanita in so large a group.

"Here!" said a girl's voice, and she came out to him.

"Juanita," said Poco, without dismounting, "go quickly and bring the girl who sings."

"And who are you?"

"I am her brother."

"Her brother? Faugh! You are too short and fat to be her brother."

"Still, I am her brother. I have a letter here for her that will prove it. And here is proof for you." He tossed a coin to her.

She gripped the coin, caught her breath at the size and the weight of it, and instantly she was gone, in a scurry.

He waited a scant five minutes before another figure came, slowly and gracefully, towards him. The mozas had ceased their gossiping and were straining their ears to hear. Therefore he spoke very softly.

"Liseta?"

"Yes, it is I. And who are you?"

"I am a friend of Blas."

"God bless you if you have come to tell me that he is still safe!"

"Yes. For the time the whole mountains are buzzing with men to catch him, though I think, for my part, that they should give him a reward for killing Vega. That more than balances the killing of Dial."

"Killing of Dial? Do you not know, and does not he know, that Dial is not dead? For three days he has been in the saddle hunting for poor Blas. And the best of his men are with him."

Poco whistled.

"That is news!" said he. "But here is the letter."

He lighted a match to give her illumination for the reading, and incidentally so that he could read it himself. But she did not see that. She read eagerly, half aloud. And when she had finished, she took a pencil from Poco and wrote on the bottom of the letter, a single line. Then she folded it and gave the paper back to him.

"You will be there, then?" said Poco.

"Yes, I shall be there."

"Do not fail him. If he comes and does not find you there, ready, he cannot wait!"

"What could keep me from being there? And what is your name?"

"I am Poco, of course. Who else would risk his neck for the sake of Blas? Adios! My own time is short, if I am to get your message to him before he starts."

"But even without that message he will start?"

"Yes, I only wish to give him more surety."

"Adios, Poco! Tell him I shall not fail."

He reined his horse about and rode down the valley as slowly as he had come, pushing the cream on, until he was well among the western hills on the back trail. There he made his camp. A cold wind was blowing, and therefore—since all plump men love a little comfort—he risked making a fire, not a big one, but a slender hand of flame well fenced-in with shadowing rocks which would bar the light away from other eyes.

That warmth, when he was once wrapped in his blanket, was enough to induce quick sleep. But it was a sleep too sound for safety. Or else those who came were as silent as gliding snakes. It was only a whisper that finally alarmed him. He reached for his gun as he sat up.

The fire was dead. The wind was down. His body was cold and numb. And under the face of the broad, clear moon, he saw a giant form before him, and a rifle leveled at his head. . . . Other shadows stood in the distance.

"Very well," said Poco. "I am caught. What do you want with me?" he asked, straining his eyes at the face of the monstrous shadow above him.

It was Christopher Enright, as he made out, at once. The big hands of the other stripped away the guns and the knife from the belt of the Mexican. Poco stood up, his hands tied behind him. He looked around him on calm, stern faces, ranged in a circle—Enright himself, and that fighting cowpuncher, Farman; and yonder was the grim, lean form of Don Teofilo, himself.

It was Senor Dial who suggested a more careful search.

And that search brought, first of all, the folded letter into the hand of the searcher.

They read it aloud, rapidly, and then with a sudden understanding of its meaning, Don Teofilo snatched it and read again slowly, clearly:

"They hunt me, back and forth, like a dog. But still I manage to balk them. Poco has helped me. And La Blanca is a well of strength.

"I shall dodge through them again and ride where they least expect me. They think that I shall keep to the mountains, but I shall slip through and ride down the valley.

"You have heard, by this time, of the little shack where Vega cornered me, and where luck enabled me to kill Vega, and where his men butchered each other for the sake of his money?

"I shall be there the night after you read this letter. Do not fail to be there. If I have no word from you, I shall think that there has not been time to send a message first. But I shall wait for you, a little after dark, in that place.

"If you love me, do not fail me there. We shall ride south, together. Mexico waits for us—and a new life.

"Ten thousand ways, I love you. Be true to me, Liseta!"

That ended his letter. And beneath it was written in a trembling hand of haste:

"I shall be there, do not fear, and follow you wherever you would take me! LISETA."

"Forseno!" called the voice of Dial, after the reading.

And Poco saw faces turned towards a bowed, weary figure, whose hands were tied behind his back.

"Bring him nearer," said Dial.

And Forseno was dragged closer. His spirit seemed utterly broken. The calm which Blas had wondered at was gone now. And his eyes could not lift themselves from the ground. He seemed an old man at a single stroke. It was not strange, however, that, riding a horse so wearied as was Larribee, he had been taken in the busy dragnet of Dial.

"Forseno," said Don Teofila in his harsh, level voice, "this is the last act in our play, I think. The son who was to kill me is now about to fall into our hands. Christopher, do you hear? You will go to that place. Ride hard. Be sure that you are there in the middle of the afternoon. Then with four men—you may pick the best ones—hide yourself at the shack, and be sure that you hide well. And,

Christopher, there will be no nonsense like trying to take him alive, eh?"

"He is as slippery as an eel," said Christopher. "No, I shall try no nonsense like that. We want a dead man, sir. And dead he shall be, so help me God—the ingrate and traitor!"

He said it through his teeth, and Dial turned with a smile to Forseno.

And Forseno, suddenly lifting his head, stared at big Christopher with an eye of fire, but said not a word.

He had spoken not three words, indeed, since the moment when he had been seen and run down on the tired Larribee, and especially since he had seen the face of his old enemy living, and not dead, as he had so joyously and confidently dreamed.

Neither did he speak now. And Poco questioned him in vain.

One would have said that Forseno's heart was dead within him. Only, from time to time, during the rest of that night and the next morning, his eye turned with a fiery earnestness towards the direction in which Christopher and his four chosen men had ridden towards the valley.

Dial would permit no more to go.

"For we have a fox to deal with," said he, "and if we hunt him in too great a crowd, he is sure to suspect!"

And, after all, the thing was sure enough. For Blas, walking through the twilight into the shack, was sure to be riddled with bullets by the watchers. They would permit no chance to warn him first; for they looked upon him as upon a beast.

And Dial, with a cruel smile, said to Forseno as

the sun began to slope towards the western sky-line, that day:

"What is it, Forseno? Why do you watch that place on the horizon so carefully? Are you counting the last minutes of your son?"

At length, Forseno sighed and spoke, and if the smile of Dial had been cruel, there was a devil in that of the Mexican.

"Don Teofilo," he said coldly, "it is too late to send any rider to that valley and that hut before Christopher comes to it. Is it not much too late for that?"

"Yes," said Don Teofilo. "Do you smile, then, because your boy is lost, you incarnate devil?"

"Devil?" said Forseno, laughing aloud in a dreadful voice. "Yes, surely the devil must have taught me how to crush you in the end—even better than my plans, Dial! Listen to me! When the bullets tear Blas to pieces, they tear nothing of mine. It is yours, Senor Dial! It is all yours!"

Chapter Forty-two

Don Teofilo stared hopelessly at this old enemy.

"He is mad," he said at last. "There is no wit in him. Is there any possible sense in this? Does he call that Blas mine? Fool, is not Blas your own flesh and blood?"

The fire brightened in the eye of Forseno.

"Think again, Dial!" said he. "You should know. It has been shown to you before. Was it not that dying man of Vega's who mistook Don Christopher for Blas?"

That blow, if it were aimed at Dial, fell more heavily on another heart. For Enright spurred his horse suddenly between Forseno and old Dial.

"Speak out Forseno, you cunning dog!" he said through his teeth.

"Speak and be killed?" said Forseno. "Is that what you mean?"

"I shall not harm you," said Enright. "You have my word for that!"

"I do not care," replied Forseno. "There have been two parts to my life. One was to build a great work—the valley of Dial. The other, to undo the happiness which I made and which was snatched from me. Do you hear me?"

"I hear you," said Enright.

"Who is the heir to Don Guy and Senor Dial? A great bull, with no more wits than a brute. Don Christopher? Bah! Let him take the lands. They will run through his clumsy hands fast enough. But tell me, senor—was there not an older boy?"

"There was," said Enright, trembling. "What of that?"

"A boy with the eye of an eagle and the courage of a lion?"

"Yes," breathed Enright.

"Why, you blind fools!" snarled Forseno, "he is yonder in the valley, riding down now to meet his sweetheart, and finding only his brother and other armed men, all sworn to shoot to kill—and with rifles that cannot miss him! He, that elder son, is Blas! What fools you are not to have guessed before!"

Now, there is sometimes needed only a word to unlock the most startling truths in the mind. Green was never seen in the sky until a poet looked at the west some thousands of years after civilization and saw that color there. But all the rest, expecting blue above them, found there only blue.

So it was with Dial and his son-in-law. They heard the revelation of Forseno, and the same instant their minds turned back to the picture of

Blas—dark, burned brown by the sun, proud, gay, and free. They remembered his voice and every feature of his face, and suddenly they knew that it was true!

And suddenly, too, they wondered that they had not guessed before. Surely, now that their eyes were turned upon the fact, they could see how sharply he resembled the bigger Christopher. There was hardly more than a matter of complexion and a few pounds between them. And Maruja, surely, lived again in that youth!

And was it not, also, just such a manner of revenge as the tortured soul of Forseno would have conceived: to steal the son of his persecutor, and rear him for the act of vengeance?

In a breath, the truth was lodged in the hearts of the men. They gave no word to Forseno. Dial tore the revolver, from its holster, but he thrust it back again, unfired. Two remained, of the party, to guard Forseno; and all the rest spurred their horses westward towards the valley. Not in hope, but in wild despair.

They knew that they could not outdistance, now, the sun that was descending slowly towards the western horizon. But they rode on, in furious haste. No one dared to speak, except to damn his straining horse. Every cowpuncher in the group was doing his best. But Guy Enright passed them all. And yet even the father's heart in Enright could not urge him forward as swiftly as old Dial, who poured all the art of an almost forgotten horsemanship into this wild ride.

For now, as he settled his heart upon the work before him, he knew that only one true heir to Dial had been born in his family, and that was yonder boy who would die when the sun went down!

He dared not think. And if he hoped that Christopher would miss his aim, he remembered those other picked men who had been selected by Christopher for the execution. They could not fail, all of them! It was impossible!

The sun sank, and the head of Enright bowed, but old Dial, with the wind parting his beard, still rode erect, plunging far in the van.

Now, as he looked back into the past, he could see that he had been just such another youth as this Blas—not so handsome, perhaps, and not so wonderfully skilled with weapons, but with the same pride, the same lofty indolence, the same careless eye fixed on life.

And he wondered again, with a breaking heart, that he could have failed to see the truth.

For the first time in the life of the old man, he found himself breaking and bending and turning humble. It seemed to him like a divine punishment which had been stored up in the hand of God and reserved to strike him down in the very last moment of his life, at that moment when he added up his actions, one by one, and found that his days had been good, that happiness had been his!

Happiness? When there had been this glorious chance before him to live his young life over again in the person of Blas?

He struck a hand against his breast, and, looking up to the darkening sky, he vowed with swelling breast that even if the boy were indeed lost to him, he would find some way to perform one great and good action before the end of his own failing days.

Forseno, first, must be forgiven. Oh, with how clear an eye could he glance back to his earlier days and see the cruelty of the treatment he had given the Mexican! He saw the implacable indifference, and the proud scorn with which he had allowed the other to build up his fortunes and then had thrown him away like a broken tool! Upon what foundation was his wealth established, other than that of the labors of Forseno?

So, with a miserable cloud of sorrow before his soul, he rode his horse across the hills and descended swiftly into the valley beyond, still lifting his horse with him, while the rest of his men trailed on behind, Enright first, and all the rest tapering away into the darkness, out of which the rushing of their feet came up to him.

Had it not been for the work of Forseno, would he have been accompanied on this ride by attendants? Would he not rather have come to an old age of tatters?

He reached the valley floor, the swift miles rolling back under the tireless hoofs of his horse, and he blessed the impulse which had made him saddle for this journey the scion of a mustang race rather than a thoroughbred.

Now, heading by the moonlight towards the mouth of the ravine in which Vega had died—in which Blas, too, must be lying cold and white by this time—he saw a dark troop of riders pouring forth towards him.

Christopher, then, coming back with his men,

as from the satisfactory execution of a duty. Christopher—a fratricide?

He would send that boy away! His eyes must never cross the face of Christopher, after the truth should be revealed to him!

But no, this group was not made up of Christopher and his men! There were more than five men in that group! Another and another and another—eight! Yes, and now from the rear another cluster, riding close together—a dozen more!

Into the dark confusion of his thoughts a feeble ray of hope glimmered. Those men were calling to him, as he rushed his staggering horse upon them.

"Who's there? Draw up!" they shouted.

With desperate eagerness he scanned them as he drew nearer in the moonlight. Not one of them belonged to Christopher's group.

He would have ridden wildly through them, had not someone caught his bridle rein.

"It is Senor Dial!" cried another. "Let him be!"

"And in the name of God," groaned Dial, "who are you?"

"Posse of Sheriff Gregory—"

"Gregory? Gregory? And where is he?"

"Back with your grandson—"

"And the man—Blas Lavera—"

"Oh, him? Back yonder—him and the girl—by the sheriff—"

This brought a wild shout from the throat of Dial. He struck their hands away and burst ahead, through the cluster. And there he saw them riding side by side—Liseta between, and on either side, Blas and Christopher!

He drew up his foaming horse before them. Stefan Gregory was making up from the rear, calling angrily to continue the march—that it was already late.

"So he lives?" called Dial.

"Senor," said Christopher. "What could I do? I came here to have him murdered. But the sheriff came here, too. And he took the game into his own hands—and murder is not the sheriff's way. Besides, I thank God that we did not succeed! They have put irons on him, senor, but, by God, I'll stick with him till I have them off—"

And then, suddenly, he saw that his grandfather was laughing, and clutching the saddle horn to keep from swaying drunkenly about in it.

"Come to me, Christopher," said he. "And you, Liseta. Guards, stand back from Blas. Sheriff Gregory—"

"Senor Dial, are you giving orders to this posse?"

"Sheriff, this man who comes riding here has a special right to have ten minutes alone with Blas. I shall tell you this much—that the name of Blas is about to be changed. And as for you, Gregory, you rode out to arrest Blas Lavera, not my grandson, Richard—"

The sheriff was a dumb man. And the whisper ran suddenly through the circle and made all draw back, as Guy Enright rushed through the advance guard and came storming down towards Blas.

"And so," sighed the sheriff, "he is not a would-be murderer. There is no charge against him from Dial. No—he's to be turned at large, once more. Is that it? Ah, well, he'll give me trouble again before he's done! And even this time, Dial, we needed a woman to bait a trap for him!"

Who could say that happiness might return to Forseno again, after the life he had lived?

But when all was ended, he found a sudden wealth of fortune poured into his hands. Money, money, money, such as he had never dreamed of before! He could not stay in the northland. But south of the Rio Grande he went, with his wife and his two sons. There he found another great problem, and there he attacked it in the mountains. And at this day men watch the tens of thousands that he spends in damming a great valley and in smoothing the burning desert, and they shake their heads and point to their temples as a sign that he must be considered mad. But still, he continues with a deathless enthusiasm. He has found himself again. The dam grows, the waters will soon be backed into a great lake, and if the labor succeeds, other men will come to stare at another green spot in the desert and wonder that such a simple idea had not been executed long, long before. But his wife and his sons will be the last to believe in him and in his works.

There is only one ardent enthusiast who believes in him. He rides down out of the northland, brown-faced, eager-eyed. Twice his wife has ridden all the weary distance with him. They are Liseta and Blas. The young man doffs his new name when he is south of the Rio Grande. And when he and Liseta pay their visits to Forseno, together they hear his plans, and look into his half-mad eyes, and watch his crippled hands scratching plans, like a general, on a floor, or wall, or scraps of paper.

They look at him, and perhaps they would doubt, also, except that they remember the green Paradise which fills the valley of Dial.

There is a third member of the party. But then, he is to be taken for granted, since he lives like the shadow of Blas. And that, of course, is Christopher. For when one has been on the verge of casting away one's own flesh and blood—and when fate prevents it—one does not forget. It is a serious and sobered Christopher, and yet there are some who declare that trouble must still come from this union of two storm centers like Christopher and his elder brother.

The sheriff is the one who most persistently shakes his head, for as he says, "Who'll pour nitroglycerine into a red-hot furnace to make it burn brighter?"

But nothing has yet happened to indicate that the peace of Dial Valley will be broken. And when the restless fit comes, and Blas finds himself yearning for some wilder, fiercer action, he goes to seek out old, white-headed Dial, and he drinks in the smooth, wise current of his speech; then he learns what life can be.